A Northern Affair

A Northern Affair

She wants what you have

SUSAN WILLIS

THIS IS A REVISED VERSION OF, 'IS HE HAVING AN AFFAIR', WITH SOME NEW MATERIAL. THE NOVEL WAS FIRST PUBLISHED IN 2015 BY ACCENT PRESS.

Copyright c 2024 by Susan Willis All Rights reserved. No part of this novel may be reproduced in any form by any means, electronic or mechanical (including but not limited to the Internet, photocopying, recording), or stored in a database or retrieval system, without prior written permission from the author. This includes sharing any part of the work online.

Susan Willis assets her moral right as the author of this work in accordance with the Copyright, Designs and Patent Act 1988.

The characters, premises, and events in this book are fictitious. Names, characters, and plots are a product of the author's imagination. Any similarity to real persons, living or dead, is coincidental and not intended by the author.

Also By Susan Willis:

Payback at the Guest House
Confession is Good or the Soul
Intriguing Journeys at Christmas
Joseph is Missing
Death at the Caravan Park
The Curious Casefiles
Magazine Stories from the North East
Christmas Shambles in York
Clive's Christmas Crusades
The Christmas Tasters
The Guest for Christmas Lunch
The Man Who Loved Women
Dark Room Secrets
His Wife's Secret
The Bartlett Family Secrets
Northern Bake Off
You've Got Cake
A Business Affair
NO, CHEF, I Won't!

Chapter One

Phil Johnson gently moved his wife's hand away from his groin. 'Sorry, Laura,' he muttered, and turned onto his side, and rolled away from her. 'I'm absolutely whacked tonight.'

Laura fought back tears as she rescued her hand and placed it against her burning cheek. Being rejected was so humiliating. Laura heard his breathing change and a slight snore escape his nose. She squeezed her eyes tight shut, but couldn't stop a tear from leaking out of the corner of one. She rolled over, removed her glasses, and laid them next to the alarm clock on her bedside table.

Oh, why doesn't he want me any more, she agonised, burying her face into the pillow. Surely, this was the wrong way around? Wasn't it usually the wife who stated, 'not tonight, darling, I've got a headache'. She pulled the spaghetti strap of her silk nightdress back onto her shoulder and willed herself to sleep, but relentless thoughts tumbled around in her mind. They'd always had a good sex life up till a few months ago. Then, if she'd got into bed wearing something silky, he would have dragged it up around her waist before she'd had time to think.

Laura wiped her wet cheek and pressed her lips together. So why now and what had changed? At first, she'd wondered if it could be what people called the empty-nest scenario, as their son, Peter, had left home for university. Although there was definitely a shift in the atmosphere as the house was much quieter, and their daily routines had invariably changed, Laura was still surprised this had made a difference to their sex lives.

The week before Peter had moved into the halls of residence Laura had thought she'd be the one to miss him, but as he wasn't far away and often popped in for meals at the weekends, she felt as though she was coping well with his absence. Laura pulled the quilt over her shoulder and remembered how she'd asked Phil if he was missing Peter. All she'd received was a raise of an eyebrow and a derisory snort; therefore, she figured it had nothing to do with the problem.

Her closest friend, Jenny, had been full of reassurance and soothed, 'It'll just be a phase he's going through.' And, at the time, Laura had talked herself into believing this, but now, the longer the abstinence continued, the more she decided her initial thoughts were right – he was having an affair.

The next morning, Laura dragged herself out of bed and wandered downstairs into the kitchen. Phil was already showered, dressed in his grey suit, and making breakfast.

'Morning,' he chirped, and turned up the volume on the radio to listen to the news.

Laura nodded and slumped down onto a stool at the black granite breakfast bar. Her head felt thick and woozy after only a few hours of disturbed sleep. She watched Phil's light-hearted movements around the kitchen. This didn't seem fair, Laura frowned. Here she was, spending sleepless nights worrying about the growing distance between them and the lack of intimacy, but he appeared totally carefree and apparently was sleeping like a baby.

Why in God's name, was he behaving like this? And, whatever the reason was, why didn't he seem worried or concerned?

Phil poured coffee into her mug, and placed it in front of her. Laura looked up at him and grimaced.

He put his head onto one side. 'Didn't you sleep well?'

Laura looked into his dark brown eyes searching for something – anything that could tell her why he was creating this gap between them. But he simply looked indifferent. 'No, I didn't,' she grumbled. 'I lay awake for hours not being able to sleep.'

'Hmm,' he said, buttering a piece of toast. 'You're not worrying about the new fish lines at work, are you?'

She shook her head in disbelief and looked around the square kitchen with its brightly painted blue walls. How could he be so crass? It was almost as if he was in denial and they'd had rampant sex all night with her hanging from the chandelier. I wish, she thought miserably and sipped her coffee. 'No, I'm not worrying about work,' she sniped. 'I don't need to. I know my products are good.'

Phil nodded reassuringly and crunched into the toast. 'That's good, because we go through the same cranked-up pressure every year for Good Friday,' he said. 'But it always turns out OK in the end.'

Laura looked at him sitting astride the opposite stool. Just short of six foot, he was a good-looking man with dark brown hair, although it was receding slightly as he neared the age of thirty-nine. But it was his voice that was the sexiest thing about him. With age his voice had mellowed with deep throaty notes and had almost a singsong quality when he talked. When they were in meetings he commanded the floor with his articulation and Laura could tell that everyone, especially the women, hung upon his every word.

Swallowing the last mouthful of toast Phil smiled and jumped to his feet. 'Time I was out of here. I've got an early meeting with the commercial teams,' he said brightly. Grabbing his briefcase from the corner of the kitchen he hurried towards the back door. 'I'll see you later at work.'

As Laura stepped out of their semi-detached house she held her face up to a weak sun trying to break through the clouds. It was the first week of April, and unusually for the north east of the country, it looked as though spring had actually sprung. The fish company where they both worked was in a small town called Gosforth, on the outskirts of Newcastle-Upon-Tyne. It wasn't far, and what with the good weather Laura decided to leave her car at home and walk to work. She pushed the car keys back into her handbag and stared at a fat snail that was making its way up the garden fence. It looks as slow and sluggish as I feel this morning, she thought, closing the garden gate behind her.

She had chosen a brown trouser suit and cream blouse to wear and as she walked briskly the flared bottoms of her trousers flapped around her flat shoes – damn, she cursed, why didn't I wear heels with this outfit? The cul-de-sac was empty as she continued past Jenny's house on the corner. She looked up at the bedroom curtains which were still closed, and smiled. Obviously, Jenny wasn't rushing into work today.

When Jenny had divorced her husband, Steve, she'd bought his share of the semi-detached house, stating that she didn't want to live anywhere else, and Laura had been relieved. Although they would have remained great friends no matter where Jenny lived, it was a comfort to have her close by.

They'd all worked together for over ten years now, starting at junior levels and working their way up to management positions. Laura was the new product development manager, Phil was the company's marketing manager, and Jenny was head of Quality Assurance. It was a small company employing three to four hundred people, but in an area where other food companies were scarce, they all knew that without the fish factory the town might not survive.

Laura left the small housing estate and turned onto the high street, browsing in the shop windows as she walked.

And that was another change in Phil, she thought, gazing at clothes in a man's boutique. He'd recently bought a whole range of trendy clothes, from tight-fitting jeans to button-collared shirts. In the past, Phil hadn't been particularly interested in fashion and would dress more for comfort, but now ... Laura sighed, well, she wasn't sure what her husband was interested in any more. All she knew was that it certainly wasn't her.

She swallowed a lump in the back of her throat, pushed her hands into her jacket pockets, and quickened her pace. At the end of the high street Laura turned up the long treelined driveway towards the factory and kicked at a pebble with the toe of her brown shoe. Suddenly, she heard a toot from a car behind and swung around to see her father's Volkswagen slowing down.

He wound down the window and grinned. 'Hello, sweetheart,' he breezed. 'How's my favourite daughter this morning?'

Laura giggled and immediately felt her spirits lift at the sight of his familiar, reassuring face. 'Erm, I'm your only daughter, remember? Unless, of course, you've a hoard of secret love-children scattered around the country?'

David Stephenson was a psychiatrist and worked in the hospital which was situated across the road from the factory. Aged sixty-one he was ready to retire, but the health service didn't want to let him go, or so he told everyone. His twinkly blue eyes shone from under thick bushy eyebrows. 'Hop in, and we can chat for the last few minutes.'

Laura opened the car door and slid onto the passenger seat. The smell of old leather and musky pipe tobacco hung in the air, and she chided him. 'If our mam finds out you've been smoking that old pipe again you'll be in big trouble.'

He teased, 'Ah, you're not going to snitch on me, Laura. Are you?'

She shook her head slowly wanting to chastise him but couldn't help smiling at the little boy look on his craggy face. He had been, and still was, the steadying rock in life. She knew this position should have been given over to Phil on their wedding day, but it hadn't, and Laura couldn't imagine her life without him.

'OK, but just this once,' she giggled. 'And only if it's in exchange for lunch one day this week.'

St Nicholas psychiatric hospital cooked delicious meals in their canteen and Laura often popped across to have lunch with him when they could both fit it into their diaries.

After swinging the car into a parking space, David stared at her and frowned. 'I don't like those dark circles under my little girl's eyes,' he queried. 'We'd better get lunch squeezed in for tomorrow and then you can tell me what's wrong?'

Laura pouted. 'There's nothing wrong. I'm fine,' she said opening the car door. 'But, yes, lunch tomorrow will be great.'

Waving at her father she walked towards the reception door of the factory and through the swing doors.

The clocking-in machine tinkled eight o'clock as Laura looked through the glass door into the office area. Most of the desks were still empty apart from Phil's side office. She could see the back of his dark hair sitting opposite the commercial director and she sighed. As much as she wanted to talk about their marriage, she knew she wouldn't be able to tell her father about Phil. It just wouldn't be right.

Laura rummaged in the bottom of her bag, found her swipe badge, and pulled it through the machine on the wall. She headed down the staircase to her own office on the bottom level of the building. The long corridor which ran the length of the building had offices on the right hand side and her development section held the last two rooms next to Jenny's. On the other side of these office walls was instant access into what they called the low-risk area of the factory, where haddock, cod, salmon, and tuna were packed and supplied to the major retailers.

Laura stopped outside a wood-panelled door with a grey name plate which in black lettering, stated, Jenny Campbell, QA manager. She pushed open the door and smiled at the sight of Jenny's tidy desk as opposed to the usual chaotic mess that lay on her own. She pulled a post-it note from Jenny's pad and wrote; *I need to talk – please come and have a coffee asap. Love, Laura.*

Chapter Two

When Jenny Campbell opened her eyes that morning, the headache and hangover crashed between her eyebrows making her groan aloud. She felt her stomach contract and hurried along to the bathroom, sat on the toilet, and laid her head on the wall's cool blue tiles. She wanted to weep with misery. It was a ridiculous state to be in, she thought, and even though the rational side of her brain knew the damage she was doing to her body, she felt powerless to stop it.

There weren't many nights during the week that she went to bed without at least three glasses of wine. And, on weekends when she didn't have to get up for work, this amount escalated to a whole bottle. She padded back along to her bedroom and slumped down on the edge of the bed. She put her head in her hands. Don't cry, she willed herself, because she knew from experience that the act of crying would exacerbate her pounding head.

Hurriedly, she pulled on a beige pencil skirt and clean white shirt from the wardrobe. I wasn't always like this, she reasoned, but knew that over the last six months she'd become worse. And, if she was to tell anyone about the excessive drinking she wouldn't be able to give them an excuse or reason, because at the moment, her life was settled. If ever there'd been a time in the past to start drinking heavily it would have been when her husband, Steve, had left, but that episode was well and truly behind her. She smiled, remembering the mornings when they were happily married and she hardly drank and would leap out of bed ready to tackle whatever the day had in store.

Jenny sighed now, feeling as though that was a lifetime away and pulled brown opaque tights up her long legs. She hoped they would stretch enough to reach her crotch, as being an inch from six foot, she found it difficult to buy tights that were long enough. She sighed with relief as they did and pushed her slim feet into flat brown brogues. After vigorously brushing her teeth twice and gargling with a strong minty mouthwash; she sat at her dressing table and brushed her long blonde, hair into place. She applied a light foundation and a coat of mascara to her long eyelashes then popped an extra strong mint into her mouth, and ran out of the door.

It's got to stop, Jenny warned herself as she swung her Micra into the factory car park. But, no matter how many times she'd said this to herself lately, by seven o'clock that night, she knew she'd be desperate to open a bottle. On her way downstairs towards her office a number of colleagues greeted her with sarcastic comments about her late arrival, and by the time she opened her office door, Jenny's face ached with the effort of smiling. She sat down at her desk, drawing comfort from the tidy piles of folders and her daily work plan in front of her.

Jenny hadn't left work until nine o'clock the night before as she'd had to deal with a safety issue in the factory, but now she breathed a sigh of relief that her day's activities were planned with meticulous detail. The safety issue had been resolved quickly and efficiently, mainly due to the diligence of her two QA assistants. They'd spotted the problem early enough for Jenny to take action and prevent, as the production manager had said, a molehill becoming a mountain.

Quickly now, Jenny saw Laura's note and sighed. Jenny wished she could talk about her drink problem with Laura, but poor Laura had enough problems at the moment without her adding to them. Jenny speed-dialled Laura's mobile number and left a message to say she would be in the canteen in thirty minutes.

While Laura made coffee in the canteen and sat down at one of the grey oblong tables to wait for Jenny she stared around at the large impersonal room. The walls were painted cream and there were around thirty tables accompanied by grey, plastic-moulded chairs. Everyone who worked on site used the canteen for their breaks at varying stages of the day. The production staff, who began their shift at 6 a.m., tended to have lunch around midday, whereas the management and office staff had lunch at one o'clock.

Laura looked longingly at the chocolate bars in the three vending machines standing against the opposite wall. It's not the answer, a small voice nagged in the back of her mind, but her mouth watered at the thought of the thick, comforting Cadbury's. As she slid her money into the machine and waited for the bar to drop down into the receptacle she heard Jenny's voice behind her.

'Get me one too, Laura. I could do with a pick-me-up this morning.'

Laura drew her eyebrows together in disbelief. Jenny didn't usually indulge in the guilty pleasure that the rest of the office girls couldn't resist. She sat down opposite Jenny, placed the coffee mug and chocolate bar in front of her, and nodded. 'Bad morning?' she asked. 'I heard about the near miss last night and how you were all here until nine o'clock?'

Jenny grimaced. 'Yeah, but thank God we managed to stop it before Production had run the line for more than a few minutes. I tell you, Laura, my two assistants are worth their weight in gold!'

Laura smiled understandingly and hoped the tiredness in her friend's eyes was only through lack of sleep. Jenny had seemed worn out and very unhappy lately.

She patted the back of Jenny's hand. 'You must be whacked?' she soothed. 'But at least it's Saturday tomorrow and you'll be able to have a lie in.'

Jenny bit into a square of chocolate and her shoulders drooped. 'Mmm,' she sighed quietly. 'I'd forgotten how good that was.'

'Yeah, it sure is,' Laura agreed sucking her way through the smooth chocolate. 'It can't solve any of my problems, but it makes me feel better when I'm eating it, although the scales tell a different story. What's the saying? A minute on the lips, a lifetime on the hips!'

Jenny nodded. 'Come on then,' she asked. 'What's up?'

Laura remembered Phil's rejection last night and felt the bubble of anxiety build in the pit of her stomach. 'He's having an affair, Jenny,' she wailed. 'I'm convinced of it now.'

Jenny smiled and calmly folded her hands on the table in front of her. She motioned for Laura to continue.

Briefly, Laura told Jenny what had happened. 'And, it's nearly three months since we've had sex, he's hiding his mobile at night, a-and says he is going skiing with his friends in November,' she stuttered. 'I mean, he didn't even invite me but just told me he was going.'

Jenny took hold of Laura's hand and squeezed it tight. 'Look, he could have just been exhausted last night. All marriages go through lean patches. There were often times when Steve and I didn't have sex – you don't always have to be at it like rabbits,' she reassured. 'And, he probably didn't ask you to go skiing because he knows you hate it. I mean, would you go if he asked you to?'

Laura considered the question and bit her lip. 'Well, probably not. But ...'

'Well, there you go,' Jenny stated, and let go of Laura's hand. She sat back confidently in her chair.

Laura's mind quickly digested Jenny's words. 'OK, that might be true,' she nodded. 'But why doesn't he fancy me any more?"

Jenny held a hand up in front of Laura. 'Now stop this, Laura. I think you're simply overreacting,' she said firmly. 'I've known Phil for years and probably just as long as you have. He loves you to bits and worships the ground you walk on.'

With Jenny's words of support Laura felt her anxiety begin to settle. Jenny was right, of course he still loved her, and she was just being silly. Laura knew she often let problems bottle up inside her until she became irrational. Thank God, she had her dear friend to keep her feet planted firmly on the ground.

'Thanks, Jenny,' she said.

Jenny sucked thoughtfully on the last piece of chocolate. 'Laura,' she asked. 'Why don't you just ask him?'

'Well, I have asked him if there's anything wrong and he says not,' Laura murmured then swallowed hard feeling her cheeks flush. 'But, I just can't ask him why he doesn't want to have sex – it's far too embarrassing.'

Jenny shook her head and raised her fine eyebrow. 'And this is from a man you've been married to for nearly eighteen years and who you've had a baby with?'

Laura clasped both her hands together under the table to stop them from trembling. She could hear in her own mind how ridiculous it must sound to Jenny, and she tried to explain. 'If I'm totally honest, I'm not sure if I really want to know the answer,' she whispered, and leaned across the table. 'I mean, what if it's something I don't want to hear, and he is having an affair?'

Jenny rubbed Laura's arm. 'Look, honey. Not that I think you've got anything to worry about, but wouldn't knowing the answer be better than torturing yourself like this?'

The silence between the two women was suddenly shattered with a shout from the doorway.

Laura's technologist, a man called, Alex called across the room, 'Laura, we need you,' he said. 'The guys in the factory are going to start packing salmon sides.'

Jenny smiled. 'No rest for the wicked. I'm due in a meeting anyway in ten minutes,' she said. 'But I'll see you at lunch time.'

Hurrying towards the door, Laura agreed and followed Alex along to their development office. They walked through the office and out of the side door into their small development kitchen where she covered her brown curls with a hair net, and although Alex was bald, he also placed a net on his head. They put on white coats and took turns to wash their hands in the hand basin and while she sprayed her hands with anti-bacterial solution she looked at Alex.

At the age of fifty-seven Alex did most of the trials in factory and had worked in the department since the day it first opened. He didn't have an ambitious bone in his body and had always refused any offers of promotion, but when Laura had wanted to apply for the manager's position he'd supported her all the way. She trusted him implicitly and although she knew she could leave the checklist of new products up to him she still liked to look at them herself – it was simply a way of staying abreast with what was happening.

'I think the orders for salmon sides on Good Friday are even bigger than last year,' Laura said as they walked onto the factory floor.

It was a large square room with four long packing lines and numerous other pieces of stainless steel equipment. The clean fresh smell filled Laura's nostrils and she smiled. It was a miscued conception by most people that fish had an offensive smell, but it didn't. As Jenny often told new staff, fresh fish had no smell at all and it was only when it was past its sell-by date that it gave off a bad odour. But, Laura thought, smiling, as Jenny had a nose like a bloodhound when it came to inspecting fish, she knew they were all in safe hands..

Alex stood still, adjusting his ear plugs under the hair net. 'Yeah. I'd heard that too,' he said. 'I wonder why everyone eats fish on Good Friday. I've never really known the true reason.'

As they walked towards the cutting tables in the far corner of the room Laura said, 'Well, a lot of Christians prefer to eat fish on Good Friday.'

One of the butchers stood at the cutting table and boomed his hello as he slapped a three-kilo salmon onto the table as if it weighed nothing. He was a huge man and seemed to dwarf Laura and Alex, but he was also known in the factory as the gentle giant.

He grinned at Laura. 'Here we go again, eh? The start of the bloody Easter madness.'

Laura nodded and walked around the table. She smoothed the salmon side he'd cut and ran her fingers down the centre feeling for bones. 'It looks good quality. Are you happy with the salmon stock they've bought in?'

The buying of salmon didn't concern the operators as such, but Laura knew that these guys who handled it day and night would be the first to spot any problems.

The butcher nodded and smiled with a big gap where his two front teeth were missing. 'Aye, this is top notch. No complaints, Laura. It handles like a dream.'

Nodding with satisfaction Laura wandered over to the packing line where the sides were placed onto long slim plastic boards, wrapped in clear film, sealed at both ends, and then had the retailer's labels applied. It was noisier at this end of the factory floor and as the staff wore ear plugs many of them had learned to lip read rather than shout above the sound of the machinery.

The operators all greeted her with cheery smiles and comments while she watched them pack the salmon sides onto new green coloured boards as opposed to the standard black. The green boards were also made of a new material which the operators told her handled much better.

'Anything to keep you all smiling,' Laura quipped, and received a warm hug from the line manager.

The cold factory atmosphere began to make her shiver and pleased that the salmon sides were being packed to perfection, Laura hurried back to the office.

When she arrived back to her desk there was a small salad tray in front of her computer with a note from Phil. 'I've been out to M&S so I brought you a salad for lunch. XX'

Laura smiled at Phil's forethought and kindness, but then remembered last night. She drew her eyebrows together in puzzlement and tapped the side of her computer with a pencil. It didn't make sense. How could he turn away from her in bed and reject any form of intimacy yet obviously think enough about her during the day to buy my lunch. What on earth was wrong with him? She looked around the small office at Alex's chair and desk and the beige-painted walls – she shook her head in dismay.

The door to the office was propped open and she looked up to see Jenny appear in the doorway. Jenny stood with her arms folded and a smile playing around her lips. 'Hmm,' she muttered. 'And this is from a guy who doesn't love you?'

Laura smirked. 'Yeah, I know – he is thoughtful,' she agreed, and put her head on one side. 'It could, of course, be the sign of a guilty conscience.'

Jenny shook her head in exasperation as they wandered into the canteen together arm in arm.

The girls joined a table full of friends who worked in the planning and finance departments and Laura hungrily ate her salad while half listening to the conversation. She knew Phil loved her, but he just didn't seem to fancy her any more. Could it be a physical or medical problem that he didn't want to talk about?

Laura's reverie was broken by moans and groans from the women about the extra work that was starting for the run-up to Easter. Jenny reminded them all carefully that in the current climate they should all be grateful to have their jobs, and although everyone agreed, there was still a mixture of light-hearted banter.

An older lady, called Muriel, who was the managing director's personal assistant, and due to retire at the end of the year, said, 'I wish it was all over and behind us and that we'd made a good profit. Then all we would have to think about is the party.'

Jenny ate her cheese sandwich and nodded. 'I'll second that,' she said. 'However, we've got weeks of mayhem to get through first. Then its party, party, party!'

Laura thought Jenny looked much better than she had done at coffee time and she told her.

'Yes, thanks, I'm feeling much better and I'll definitely catch up on sleep tonight,' Jenny answered. 'Then I'm going to Newcastle tomorrow to shop for a new dress to wear. Are you coming?'

Laura groaned. 'There's no point because we won't be able to make it to the party this year.'

'What!' Muriel gasped and stared at Laura. 'You and Phil aren't coming?'

'No, my cousin and aunt will be here visiting from Australia and they're only stopping for one night. Mam and Dad would never forgive me if I wasn't there – she's making a special meal.'

Muriel's face crumbled. 'I wished I'd known; I could have maybe changed the date,' she offered. 'But we always have it the first Saturday after Easter, and it's very late this year.'

'Nooo,' Laura said shaking her head. 'You can't go changing dates because two people can't make it. Don't be silly. It just can't be helped.'

The rest of the women planned outfits, hair styles, and fake tans, as Laura listened enviously. It would probably do her and Phil good to be out socially, and relaxing with their friends, but Laura thought, she couldn't possibly disappoint her parents.

Later that night Laura sat at home waiting for Phil to come back from the gym. She idly flicked through TV channels, looking for something to watch. Deciding there was nothing of interest she sipped a glass of wine and glanced around the lounge-diner at the boring cream and brown décor. It was nearly five years since it had been decorated and the beige-striped wallpaper on either side of the fireplace looked tired and dated. She sighed heavily, maybe, after all our years together, she thought, that's how Phil sees me now – in need of a makeover.

They'd been together since their first year at Newcastle University where Laura was taking a consumer science degree and Phil was doing business studies. The attraction had been instant and by the end of two months they were an item. While Spice Girl Geri Halliwell wore the famous Union Jack dress, and Tony Blair seemed to be on every billboard, they rocked their way through university without a care in the world. But, as Laura had stood on the stage at their graduation ceremony waiting for her name to be called, the sickly feeling in her stomach wasn't because of nerves and anxiety – it was because she was pregnant.

Laura shook herself now as she heard his key in the front door. She took a deep breath and pressed her lips together in determination – she wasn't going to give up. Jenny was right, it was ridiculous that she couldn't talk to him, and as soon as they'd eaten supper she intended to ask him outright.

'Hiya,' he called from the hall and bounded into the lounge. 'Sorry, I'm late. I really got stuck into the weights tonight and forgot the time. Hope dinner isn't spoilt – I'm starving.'

Laura stood up and looked at his shining eyes and puffed-out chest. He looked as if he'd won Wimbledon and was waiting to collect his trophy. She smiled. 'Well, I'll rescue the bolognaise sauce and cook some fresh spaghetti. It'll only take ten minutes.'

Phil smiled. 'Great, that means I've time for a glass of wine.'

As Laura cooked, he pushed his sweaty gym kit into the washing machine and they chatted about work.

'Hey,' he asked plodding through into the dining room. 'Muriel mentioned that we wouldn't need tickets for the end of year party – what's that all about?'

Laura took a deep breath and counted to ten while placing the plates of food onto the dining table. 'I told you weeks ago about the Australian visit,' she said, sitting down opposite to him. 'It's just a shame that out of the whole year, it's fallen on the same Saturday as the party.'

Phil began to eat hungrily, twirling the strands of spaghetti around his fork and licking the sauce from his lips. Abruptly, he stopped eating, pressed his thin lips into a fine line and narrowed his eyes. 'Shit!' he muttered. 'And they can't visit on the Friday or the Sunday?'

'Nope,' Laura shook her head. 'They're only here on Saturday from six o'clock in the evening and will be leaving early the next morning.'

Silence settled between them and she began to eat. She looked at his hands expertly twirling his fork. They were lovely hands for a man; she decided, always clean and kept perfectly manicured. She remembered how his long fingers felt when they were caressing her body and she sighed with longing.

Abruptly he placed his cutlery down onto the plate with a clatter. 'Well, I'm sorry, Laura. But I'm not missing the party,' he said firmly.

Laura gasped and stared at him. She tried to breathe deeply and remain calm. Surely, he wouldn't go to the party without her? 'But Mam is cooking a special dinner for us all,' she cried.

He stood up and scraped his chair along the wood floor. 'I can't miss the party, Laura. This year is an important time for me in the company,' he pouted. 'It's expected of me and I need to be there with the rest of the managerial team.'

Phil picked up his plate and headed into the kitchen while Laura noticed him avoiding her eyes. She stared open mouthed after him.

His voice changed into the smooth treacle tone that he often used at work when he wanted something. He cajoled, 'Look, you can still go along to see the relatives and have the special meal. You don't need me to be there.'

Her insides began to churn with anger now. Who the hell did he think he was? The managerial team, indeed! She was part of that very same team, but she also knew where her responsibilities lay, and with whom. Laura wanted to scream at him.

She picked up her half-eaten meal and strode after him. 'I can't believe you're going to do this and let the family down.'

He turned to face her. 'Ah, but they're not my family.

Are they?'

'No,' she shouted glaring at him. 'But I thought I was!'

Chapter Three

The following morning as Laura sat next to her on the metro train travelling into Newcastle city centre, Jenny smiled in satisfaction. She hated shopping on her own and always valued Laura's opinion who had excellent taste in fashion and clothes. The pain killers she'd taken earlier had eased her hangover, and although she'd failed at her efforts not to open a bottle of wine, she had forgiven herself, because after all, she reckoned, she'd had a valid reason.

'I'm so pleased we decided not to drive into town,' Jenny said. 'This is much easier than finding parking spaces. And, there's no point in you staying at home alone when Phil is playing golf with Steve.'

Laura smiled feeling glad that she'd decided to join Jenny. 'Well, I figure a little retail therapy will do me good.'

Laura looked at Jenny's hunched shoulders in her denim jacket. Although it was nearly two years since Steve had left, Jenny still refused to talk about him. At first, this had created an awkward atmosphere between the four of them, especially as Phil had remained Steve's close friend, but now, they all knew how to handle the situation. However, when Laura had discussed the relationship dynamic's with her father, he was adamant that Jenny still had issues with Steve's rejection, and the fact that she wouldn't speak to him meant she hadn't gained closure.

As the metro pulled into Eldon Square Laura walked behind Jenny up the escalator into the shopping centre.

'Can we go to Debenhams first?' Jenny asked excitedly.

Laura agreed and lengthened her stride to keep up with Jenny's fast pace. It's a good job I wore my trainers today, Laura thought, looking down at the Lunar glide pink heeled trainers and smiled – they matched her Nike Capri pants perfectly. Laura was, and always had been, obsessed with shoes. She had her own cupboard with shelving to accommodate her shoes, boots, and sandals, which were what she called her collection. Phil and Peter always teased her about them, but Laura knew that the correct footwear could make any outfit stand out, and the wrong footwear could destroy whatever impression a woman was trying to create.

In the doorway of the department store, Laura stopped and inhaled the mixture of perfumes. 'Mm, I love the smell in here,' she said, looking around the beautifully designed store with sparkling bright lights.

As they alighted into ladieswear, Laura said, 'OK. Let's look in Wallis first because I know their range will be long enough for you.'

Laura smiled at Jenny as she began to look through the racks of dresses. Although Jenny moaned about her height, in a size ten with the longest legs Laura had ever seen on a woman, she envied her. Jenny also had what Laura's mam called ample breasts, and Laura had long since decided hers was the perfect figure.

Following behind Jenny, Laura also looked at the dresses and decided that even though she wouldn't be going to the party, she might treat herself. As they browsed, Laura quietly told Jenny about the row she'd had with Phil and how he planned to go to the party on his own.

Jenny stopped in her tracks. 'Nooo,' she hissed. 'That's not very fair.'

'I know,' Jenny said and shrugged her shoulders. 'No matter what you think, Phil is changing. At one time he would never have done anything like this to me,' she sighed.

Jenny put her arm along Laura's shoulder and hugged her. 'Look, he's probably just saying it. And when it comes to the day, he'll change his mind and go to your mam's with you.'

Laura could see the sympathy in her friend's eyes, and not wanting to put a dampener on the day, she brightened. 'Maybe ...' she whispered. 'Last night when he got into bed he did put his arm around me and snuggled my back for most of the night.'

'Well, there you are,' Jenny replied holding out a long white dress to show Laura. 'What do you think?'

Laura grinned. 'Perfect. Go and try it.'

Laura waited outside the changing cubicle and when Jenny stepped out in the dress, Laura whistled through her teeth.

Jenny twirled around and giggled. 'Great length and I love the gold clasp under the bust,' she said, then frowned, 'Is £150 too much to spend on a dress?'

Laura cooed, 'When is £150 ever too much to spend on a dress that fits you like that!'

Jenny grinned and stepped back into the changing room. Carefully, she pulled the dress over her head and put it back onto the hanger. She pulled her jeans up her legs and winced with period cramps as she fastened the zip. Her monthlies had gradually become more painful since the last miscarriage two years ago, and she wondered if a visit to the gynaecologist would help. She pulled the T-shirt over her head and lifted her long hair out of the collar, sighing with memories that threatened to engulf her. Not now, she breathed deeply forcing herself to stay in control. She swallowed hard, determined not to get upset and spoil her day. Those ghastly memories, she decided, could only be coped with when she had a glass in her hand.

While Jenny was in the changing room Laura wandered around the lingerie section and stopped in front of a black all-in-one cami. She fingered the silky material and the deep plunge bra that was hidden inside the front. Just because I'm missing the party, she thought, it doesn't mean I've to miss out on everything. If there was anything that would get Phil's pulse racing again it would be something like this, she knew, and found her size on the rack. She held it up against herself in the mirror and mused; did she have the courage to wear it? Well, maybe not now in the cold light of the day, she thought, but after a few glasses of wine, surely she could seduce her husband again?

Jenny appeared at Laura's shoulder and gasped. 'Wow!'

Laura grinned. 'I'm going to wear this and ply him with drink. And if this doesn't make him fancy me again, then nothing will …'

'Oh, honey. You don't need that,' Jenny stressed. 'Phil loves you the way you are.'

'Yeah, well, I don't just want his love, Jenny. I want the sex as well. Apart from the fact that it's upsetting me, I'm really frustrated and missing him – if you know what I mean,' she said winking.

Laura scurried into the changing cubicle while this time Jenny waited outside. They chatted through the thick curtain while Laura stripped off her Capri pants, T-shirt, and underwear. She stood in front of the full-length mirror looking at her body. She was the total opposite to Jenny, at just five foot three in height, and a cuddly size twelve with small breasts, she sighed heavily. She fingered the stretch marks on her stomach and shrugged her shoulders, knowing there was nothing she could do about them. She dropped the silky cami over her head, and wriggled it down. The plunge bra actually lifted her breasts, giving her a cleavage, and body of the cami was long enough to hide the stretch marks. She imagined the fishnet stockings and her high black heels, and grinned – it looked perfect.

While Laura began to put her clothes back on, Jenny started to tell her how much she liked their new Italian commercial manager, called Luigi.

Laura held the curtain across her body, but popped her head out and stared at Jenny. 'Really?' she gaped. 'You've never said before.'

Jenny lowered her head. 'I know. The more I've been with him in meetings the more I've realised he's a very special type of guy.'

Laura was gobsmacked. She'd wished many times over the last couple of years that Jenny could meet her Mr Right. Perhaps, she thought excitedly, it could be Luigi?

When Luigi had first arrived last month, Muriel had discovered that he was separated from his wife, who he'd left behind in Florence for a new sales career in England. One of the younger girls in the office had nicknamed him the Italian Stallion.

Laura emerged from the changing room, smiled and then held the cami up in front of Jenny. 'They've got this in white, too,' she teased. 'And if the Italian Stallion takes you home from the party he won't be able to resist you in this.'

They laughed their way to the pay desk and Jenny bought the same cami in white along with the fabulous dress.

Meanwhile, on the golf course, Steve swung his iron and hit the ball down the fairway. Phil clapped him on the back. 'So, how was your date last week,' he asked. 'Did you have a good time?'

Steve rubbed his jaw. 'Yeah, she was OK but nothing clicked, if you know what I mean?'

Phil nodded. 'I know exactly what you mean – it's that bloody thing they call chemistry. I feel like that about Laura now – I'm bored to death. There's nothing left between us any more, no sparkle, no attraction, absolutely nothing.'

'Christ, be careful, mate,' Steve said. 'You know the saying; you don't what you've got till it's gone. I'd hate to see you leave her and make the same mistake I did! You could end up regretting it like me.'

'I know,' Phil muttered and rammed both his hands into his trouser pockets and rattled his car keys. 'To be honest, Steve, it's only during the last six months that I've begun to realise how trapped I've felt in our marriage. Although I still love Laura, I think of her more like a sister now. And, I just can't stop looking at other women. I know it's unfair to Laura, but I simply can't help it.'

Steve nodded, and began to walk ahead slowly. 'Aye, I've noticed you doing it in the gym. It's as though we've changed places,' he said. 'Now I've realised there's no one else like Jenny. I know when I left her it was because I as desperate to have my own kids, but it's dawned on me since then that there's not much point in making babies with someone you're not in love with.'

Phil pulled his golf bag behind him and sucked in his cheeks. 'Well, it's not all my fault,' he pouted defensively. 'I mean, we were married at twenty-one because she was pregnant, and I knew it was as much my responsibility as Laura's to raise Peter, which, don't get me wrong, I've loved doing. But now he's grown up and left home I'm finding I want to make up for what I've missed out on in life.' Steve looked out into the distance and frowned. 'Just before Laura found out she was pregnant I'd been on the verge of going to London to a firm whose marketing section was second to none. Even in those days the opportunities were fantastic.'

Steve stopped abruptly and stared at Phil. 'I never knew that.'

Phil gave a snort of dismissive laughter. 'Neither did Laura, and she still doesn't to this day. I couldn't see any point in telling her at the time, especially as her dad was breathing down our necks to get hitched.

You know, Steve, as well as my marriage, I've also been smothered all of my life by my mam. She has doted on me and glowed with pride at everything I did which turned me into her little hero. So, I had to do the right thing and marry Laura, and content myself making our own family,' he said folding his arms across his chest.

Steve nodded his head in understanding. 'So, what do you want now?'

'I want to do all the wrong things,' Phil said staring down at his shoes. 'When I was down in London a few months ago I got really drunk after the presentation. Normally I'd have gone home straight after but this time I went to a club with the guys, and I ended up going home with this Swedish girl. She was something, Steve, taught me all sorts of new stuff, and she made me realise what I've been missing out on and all I want now is my freedom so I can play the field. Christ, Steve, I want some bloody FUN!'

Steve looked past Phil's shoulder and frowned. 'Shit, we're a right couple of clowns. Here's you wanting my single life and all I want is a family.' His cheeks flushed red as he kicked at the side of his golf bag and sighed heavily. 'I must have been crazy to leave Jenny – she was fantastic in bed. When she wrapped those long legs around my back and rode me, well, I've never met anyone since who could excite me like she did.'

Phil grunted and strode ahead while Steve hurried to catch up with him. 'Is Jenny seeing anyone, Phil?' He gabbled, 'I know you've said before that she's been dating online but has she met anyone special?'

'Er, I don't think so,' he answered. 'Well, not that Laura's mentioned.'

On Sunday night, with the third glass of Phil's favourite Sauvignon Blanc in her hand Laura sat close to Phil on the settee in front of the TV. She'd bravely put on the black cami and fishnet stockings under a black V-neck dress and now her whole body tingled with anticipation. With the curtains closed the only light in the room was from a standard lamp in the corner and Laura had lit three scented candles on the mantelpiece.

When Phil had returned from the gym he'd showered, and wearing only a pair of jogging bottoms, he'd wandered into the lounge, eying her stockings and black heeled shoes.

He raised a speculative eyebrow and dabbed at the sweat forming on his forehead. 'It's really warm in here?' he said, and without waiting for a reply went into the kitchen to turn off the central heating.

As he walked back towards the settee Laura re-crossed her legs, knowing the wrap part of her dress had fallen aside to reveal the top of her stocking. She could see him swallow hard as he sat back down next to her and fiddled with the remote control.

Laura stared at his broad toned chest and squirmed with desire – it seemed forever since they'd made love. The effects of the wine made her feel mellow and the whole of her insides were aching with lust and craving to have him touch her again. She moved closer to him and pushed one of her legs against his thigh. She knew he'd be able to feel the suspender and prayed silently that he would respond. When he didn't, she took a deep breath, and with her heart racing in excitement, she gently ran her fingers across his nipple and played with the small cluster of hairs. 'Hmm, this is nice,' she said. 'Just me and you relaxing together.'

He bristled at her touch. 'Look, Laura …' he murmured.

Ignoring him, she determined to keep going and drank a large mouthful of wine which made her feel light-headed and reckless. She ran her hand down his chest towards his waistband. He stiffened and slowly moved his leg away from hers.

What's wrong with him, she thought, and decided the soft, seductive approach wasn't working. Her feelings of desire overrode the anxiousness she'd felt about wearing the cami and now she was desperate for him. She decided to go for broke.

She stood up in front of him and slowly unwrapped the dress then slipped it from her shoulders. 'I bought something special for you,' she purred.

Slowly he closed his eyes and grimaced. 'Laura, I'm sorry. It looks lovely but I just can't!'

She moved towards him and slid into his lap. Laura gasped in alarm as she felt no reaction underneath her whatsoever.

Swiftly, Phil put his hands under her armpits and hauled her off his lap. 'Get up, now!' he yelled. 'Just stop it. Don't do this, Laura.'

She stumbled back from him burning with shame and humiliation and felt uncontrollable tears fill her eyes. 'But what's wrong with me?'

'Oh, love, there's nothing wrong with you. It's me – not you! I simply can't do this any more,' he said looking at her with eyes full of sympathy. He sat forward on the settee and put his head in his hands. 'I'm sorry, Laura. I'm so very, very sorry.'

She felt as if she'd been slapped across the face. Her heart thumped and she felt quite breathless as her legs began to tremble. She grabbed her dress from the floor and ran out of the lounge and upstairs into their bedroom. The tears she'd held back now began to curse down her cheeks as she kicked off the black heels, yanked the cami off, and rolled down the stockings. Oh, God, how could you be so stupid, she sobbed. He actually looked embarrassed for me, she thought as she pulled on her pyjamas.

Laura didn't want to sleep next to him and quickly she grabbed a box of tissues from her dressing table then fled next door into Peter's room. She banged the door shut and stood against it, trying to control her breathing. What in hell's name was wrong with him? It had to be something serious, but what? Surely no man could resist a woman in sexy underwear and stockings.

She took long deep breaths until she felt her heart beat return to normal and a calmness settle upon her. Her dad had taught her a relaxation technique before she went into labour with Peter, and now the thought of her dad's kind eyes and comforting arms wrapped around her made Laura long to be at home with him. Honestly, she thought, and bit her bottom lip, you're a grown woman now with a family of your own. It's about time you were able to sort out your own problems without running back to him all the time.

Laura wiped the tears from her eyes and tried to think about what had just happened in a logical and rational manner. She sat down on the end of Peter's bed and looked around the room at his posters of rock bands and Newcastle Falcons rugby team. She'd tidied the room when Peter had first moved into the halls of residence last year but when he'd arrived home for Christmas he'd been cross and rearranged the bedroom back to how it had always been.

Thinking of her son Laura smiled; even as a little boy, he'd loved routine and familiarity – it had always seemed a comfort to him. She looked at a photograph on the set of drawers and smiled thoughtfully. The photograph was taken of the three of them sitting on a beach in the sun and she tried to remember which holiday it was. But, Laura decided, there was no point in remembering previous happy times in their marriage and all the good things they'd shared when obviously they were having so many problems now.

Was Phil simply going through a mid-life crises, she wondered miserably, and if so, then surely she should be supporting him until he worked his way through it? But there again, she argued with herself, if this was true who could tell if he would find his way back to the lovable guy he once was. And at the bottom of her heart, she wasn't sure if she could weather the storm, because she didn't like the man he'd become.

Shaking her head in defeat she crawled under Peter's quilt.

By the time Laura got up the next morning and plodded downstairs, dreading the thought of facing Phil she saw a scribbled note on top of the microwave. 'I'm off early this morning because I'm going down to Asda head office in Leeds for meetings and a conference. Staying overnight but will text you later, Phil. X'

Damn, Laura cursed, although he had told her last week, she'd forgotten about the trip. As she made cereal and coffee she let her mind drift back to only last year when Phil used to hate going away for work. He'd moan and complain about staying in hotel rooms and she'd even known him drive back up the country late at night to get home.

She smiled with the memories of him creeping up the stairs desperately trying not to wake Peter and snuggling into bed behind her. He'd usually be rampant after the drive, and would slide his hands up under her pyjama top, as he told her how much he'd been thinking about her as he drove. He'd moan her name into her ear and wrap himself around her. Half asleep she'd protest her tiredness, but he'd had a certain way of fondling her into submission.

She sighed now and picked up a stray sock from the floor that had obviously fallen out of his holdall. In the past he'd usually leave the packing to her and she'd make sure he had overnight toiletries, clean underwear, and a choice of three shirts, but now it seemed as though he couldn't wait to get away and had his own bag ready days beforehand.

Later that night Laura sat in Jenny's lounge after eating supper. She perched on the end of Jenny's new white leather settee and looked around the trendy décor in her lounge. For some reason, although Laura knew both their houses were identical in size and shape, she always thought it looked bigger. Her eyes came to rest upon an enormous vase of long stemmed yellow roses which stood on top of the oak cabinet in the corner of the room. As Jenny wandered back into the lounge carrying another bottle of red wine and a corkscrew, Laura raised an eyebrow and nodded towards the vase. 'They're gorgeous! Where did they come from?'

Jenny sighed. 'They arrived yesterday from Steve,' she answered and looked down as she popped the cork from the bottle.

'*Steve?*' Laura exclaimed. 'But why? I mean, why now? Have you seen him or something?'

Jenny shook her head and poured wine into the glasses then handed one to Laura. 'No. And I've no idea why all of a sudden he's sending me flowers.'

Laura immediately placed the wine glass securely onto the oak coffee table in front of them. She had to admit the new décor and furniture looked fantastic but she wished the settee wasn't white, and uttered a silent prayer that she didn't spill any of the red wine. Laura tutted at herself for having such thoughts as she knew full well, even if she did have a mishap, Jenny wouldn't be bothered. They were too close for trivial matters like spilt wine to come between them, in fact, she thought looking at Jenny's confused expression, she couldn't remember them ever having a wrong word.

Laura asked, 'Was there a card with the flowers?'

'Oh, yeah,' Jenny retorted, 'telling me that he can't stop thinking about me, how sorry he is and that he still misses me. Oh, and wait for this, how he'd love to talk to me over *dinner*?'

Jenny sunk back into the settee and crossed her arms over her chest. She raised her chin. 'As if that was ever going to happen!'

Laura gulped at her wine and then sat back relaxing into the luxurious soft leather. She took off her glasses and wiped them on the hem of her short wool skirt. 'Hmm,' she said nodding. 'So are you going to meet him to hear what he has to say?'

Jenny didn't answer. She simply shrugged her shoulders and stared over at the flowers.

'Maybe he's hoping to soften you up a bit with your favourite yellow roses,' Laura mused feeling torn. She didn't want to encourage Jenny to see Steve for fear that she got hurt again, but at the same time if they did talk things through then Jenny might gain what her dad called closure, and it could help her move forward.

'I know,' Jenny said. 'I was furious when I read the card and was going to dump the whole lot into the dustbin, but when I lifted them from the wrapping paper and smelt the fragrance I simply couldn't. They're so beautiful.'

Laura whimpered her agreement and thought of Steve and the years they'd all been great friends – they'd had some happy nights in this room. She remembered how Steve and Phil had sat glued to the TV watching football and she and Jenny had cooked together in the kitchen while baby Peter lay upstairs in his cot. And then in later years the Christmas parties they'd organised had been the envy of all who weren't invited. She remembered one particular New Year when Jenny and Steve had insisted upon keeping Peter overnight, and she'd worn a special red dress. Phil had carried her home in the snow to stop her red shoes getting wet and they'd hardly been through the front door when he'd pulled the dress above her head and she'd cried out in ecstasy.

She sighed heavily, wondering if those days were so far away that they'd never find their way back again. Her throat gathered with a lump of tears and she swallowed hard, remembering the look of repulsion in his eyes last night when she had stood in front of him in her lingerie.

Laura felt Jenny's hand on her arm, which shattered her reverie and she let out a huge wailing sob. Choking on tears Laura told her friend what had happened and Jenny placed her arm around Laura's shoulders, holding her tightly as she cried.

'Just give him time,' Jenny urged. 'It's probably just a phase he's going through and he'll soon be back to his old self again.'

Laura sniffed and sobbed into Jenny's shoulder. 'Oh, Jenny, it was awful. I was so embarrassed! It was as though he couldn't bear me touching him and was appalled at the sight of me in the cami and stockings. He ... he made me feel like a pathetic trollop,' she stuttered.

'Now, come on,' Jenny soothed. 'You're working yourself up into a state. Phil was probably just startled and didn't know how to handle the unusual situation because you were downstairs.'

Laura sat up and dried her face with a tissue. 'For God's sake what difference does it make which room we are in? I mean, it should be easier now that Peter has gone and he's got the chance to chase me from one end of the house to the other, but for some reason it simply isn't *happening*.'

Jenny cooed reassuring noises and stroked Laura's arm.

With her third glass of wine Laura felt the upset turn into resentment against Phil and she bristled. 'Up until now I've never had any reason to try and seduce my own husband, and I'll tell you something else, Jenny. I won't be doing it again! After all, who the hell does he think he is – knocking me back?'

Jenny grinned and patted the back of her hand. 'That's my girl,' she said. 'I think you're placing way too much importance on the whole thing. Why not try ignoring him for a while and see what happens?'

Laura nodded and pulled her shoulders back. Maybe Jenny was right, she thought, sipping her wine. She'd tried her best to put right whatever was wrong between them and nothing she did seemed to have an impact on him. Their relationship had changed, she knew, and unfortunately it wasn't for the better. Laura lifted her chin and determined, 'You're right. From now on I'm just going to get on with my own life and leave him to it. I mean other men would give anything for their wives to be
 sitting in their laps in a cami and stockings.'
'Exactly,' Jenny stated emphatically.

Laura looked at Jenny's face which had a smile playing around her lips as she topped up their glasses. She felt her spirits rise. 'And, if I say so myself, I did look bloody amazing in that outfit.'

Jenny threw her head back and laughed. 'I'll bet you did,' she said. 'And I'm sure in a few weeks' time

Phil will be back to his normal self and chasing you around the bedroom in it.'

Chapter Four

At five thirty the next morning Jenny's mobile phone rang. Dragging herself from a deep sleep, she thought at first, the ringing noise was her alarm clock but realising it wasn't she clicked on the bedside light and snapped up her mobile phone. The screen name was her brother-in-law, John.

'Hello,' she managed to croak with a dry thick throat.

She could hear agitation in John's voice. 'Jenny?' He said, 'I'm so sorry to ring at this time, but Kate's gone missing.'

'Missing?' Jenny muttered sitting up in bed and shook her head to focus on his words.

'Yeah, she went out last night with some friends into Durham and she hasn't come home yet,' he said. 'I've got a flight at seven from Teesside Airport and I can't leave the kids on their own in the house.'

Jenny threw the quilt back and sat on the end of the bed. John was an airline pilot and flew mainly throughout Europe. 'I'm on my way,' Jenny said hurrying through to the bathroom. 'If the roads are clear I should be there in thirty minutes.'

As Jenny drove through the deserted streets out of Gosforth she crunched on a cereal bar and gulped at a can of orange juice to give herself a lift. She didn't dare take any painkillers on an empty stomach, but decided she'd take some when she got to Kate's house.

Laura had left the previous night after her third glass of wine, but as usual she'd fought, and lost the usual battle against having more – she'd drank another two glasses of wine on her own. As she waited for the traffic lights to change on the approach to the Tyne Bridge Jenny shivered and pulled up the zip on her padded jacket. It was still dark and in the second week of April, although they were having warm spring weather, the early mornings were chilly. Driving towards Gateshead she felt her stomach twist with worry about Kate.

As Kate's older sister by two years, she'd been a stand-in mother to her since they were taken into care. Their mother had been a drug addict and alcoholic and had died in an overdose when Jenny was only fourteen. Luckily, they'd been fostered locally, and she'd lived with a couple in Jesmond and Kate had lived with a family in Durham. Sadly, although they hadn't been placed together they had managed to see each other once a week.

Jenny pulled into Quarryheads Road in Durham and took a deep breath as she manoeuvred the car into the open driveway. John was waiting at the front door for her as she scrambled out of her car. At six foot tall with a smooth good-looking face, he was what Jenny classed a dream husband. From the first day she'd met him Jenny had known that Kate was lucky to marry such a wonderful specimen of manhood. He oozed self-assurance and confidence and had the ability to take command of any situation that befell him.

He stepped forward to greet Jenny and gave her a warm hug. She could smell his subtle spicy aftershave and for one split second she could have put her face into his neck as the need for a man's strong support overwhelmed her.

'Still no sign of her?' Jenny asked as she broke away from him and followed him into the hallway.

'No,' he sighed heavily. 'Not yet ...'

Jenny saw his flight bag and small trolley propped against the old oak banister. 'OK, so what did the police say?'

John avoided her eyes and looked down at the black and white floor tiles shrugging his shoulders.

Her heart began to pound in alarm. She asked, 'Have you not rung them?'

'No, I haven't as yet,' he hedged. 'I thought, maybe if she didn't turn up by lunch time you could ring them?'

Jenny couldn't understand what was going on and why he was reluctant to ring the police. 'But shouldn't she be reported as a missing person?'

John grimaced and put his hand on her shoulder. 'Look, come into the kitchen and you can make yourself a coffee before I dash off.'

Numbly, and with a sense of dread, she followed him into the large kitchen-diner, and saw the lunch boxes belonging to her two nephews on the black granite surface.

John fingered the blue strap on the box marked Josh. 'I haven't rang the police, Jenny, because this isn't the first time she's done it. This is actually the third time since Christmas that she's stayed out all night and has wandered back around mid-morning.

Granted, on the other occasions it's always been when I've been at home but maybe this time she's forgotten that I'm flying this morning.'

Jenny gasped and sank down onto a high red stool, gripping the edge of the bench. She felt her heart leap into her mouth and a pounding began in her right temple. 'What?' she cried. 'But why …'

Since the day Kate had married John, she'd more or less handed over the reins of caring for her sister to him. And, as Kate had settled happily into married life, having Josh and Simon with only a two-year gap between them, Jenny had laid her old concerns to rest. Now the unhappy memories of those years as a teenager began to re-surface and bubble under her ribs, making her catch her breath.

'I don't know why,' John said. 'I can't even say it's because she looks unhappy because she doesn't.

Apparently, she has a whale of a time when she goes into town with the girls. And still swears that she loves being with me too. So …'

John's face flushed as he took his blazer from the back of another stool and pushed his arm through the sleeve. He glanced up at the wall clock. 'I feel crap about this, but I really have to go,' he said rubbing the side of his jaw. He explained the schedule for the boys' morning routine and which breakfast cereal they liked, and then hurried out into the hall. 'Thanks again, Jenny. The school bus is on the corner of the street at 8.40 a.m.'

Jenny could see the concern in his eyes now and she reassured him that she'd get the boys to school on time.

He picked up his bags, kissed her on the cheek, and hurried out to his car.

As she heard his car pull away Jenny leant her back against the shiny black door and sighed. What in God's name was going on?

When Jenny waved goodbye to her two nephews on the school bus and sauntered back up to the house she rang work and spoke to Muriel. She explained that she was in Durham with her sister who ill and had her mobile if there were any problems in the factory. Jenny sighed with irritation at the morning's events. It couldn't have happened at a worse time, she thought, three days before Good Friday and the busiest time of the year.

As Jenny swallowed down the last mouthful of her toast she heard the slam of the front door and the click of her sister's high heels on the tiles in the hall. She didn't get up to greet her.

Kate sailed through the door to the kitchen and stopped dead in her tracks when she saw Jenny. She gasped, 'What are you doing here?'

Jenny looked at her over the rim of her coffee mug as she sipped the hot liquid. 'John rang me at 5.30 this morning because you hadn't come home and he needed to leave for work,' she said.

Jenny stared at Kate now as she waltzed towards her. She marvelled at the fact that Kate seemed oblivious and hadn't even flinched with the realisation that John was due into work. And, Jenny grimaced, the fact that her boys had to be looked after because she hadn't been there for them.

The sisters were both similar in appearance except Kate wasn't as tall, but she had the same blue eyes as

Jenny, which now looked dull and flat. The parting in her blonde hair was dark in contrast to the brassy yellow highlights and a stale smell of perfume clung around her. There was a small pink mark on the side of her neck and as she bent forward to plant a kiss on her cheek, Jenny's stomach heaved at the stench on her breath.

Jenny pulled back from her and took a deep breath to clear her nose of the turgid smell, and to try and remain calm. The last thing she wanted to do was come down on her as the heavy-handed older sister but she had to know what was happening. 'Where've you been all night?' she asked. 'John has been worried sick about you!'

Kate sneered and flung a black beaded clutch bag onto the table. It fell open and she reached inside and took out a packet of cigarettes and lighter. 'Look, it's no big deal. I met some friends and we got wasted and I crashed out. I can't remember exactly where,' she said and began to giggle. 'But it was a hellish night …'

Jenny sighed mainly at the sight of the cigarettes as Kate had given up when she was pregnant with Josh, but also at her sister's casual disregard for all of their feelings. 'And was this friend a man?' she probed. 'Are you having an affair behind John's back?'

Kate lit a cigarette and blew smoke up into the air. She gave a quick disgusted snort. 'No, I'm not having an affair. I'm having fun and sex with different men and do you know what – it's bloody fantastic! No questions asked the next day, just a one-night wonder,' she smirked. 'And the one last night was certainly wonderful …'

Jenny couldn't believe what she was hearing and seeing. This woman in front of her looked like a downtrodden slag, and nothing like her sister. Instantly, Jenny was back in her old role wanting to safeguard and care for her. 'Jeez, Kate,' she urged full of concern. 'You need to be careful – did you use protection?'

Kate sniggered. 'Against what?' she snapped narrowing her eyes. 'I'm usually stoned when I meet them and end up in hotels for the night. I don't want any protection against that excitement – it's electrifying,' she cried.

A heavy silence fell between them both and Jenny could hear the quiet whirl of the fridge freezer. Kate's eyes were wild and dancing around the room, her skin looked damp and pale, and a film of perspiration stood on her top lip as she agitatedly sucked deeply on the cigarette. Jenny recognised the tell-tale signs and decided Kate looked like a carbon cut out of their mother. Dreading the answer, Jenny asked quietly, 'Kate, are you using drugs?'

'Well, just a few joints here and there,' she whispered and then yawned.

Jenny caught her breath and put her hand to her throat. It was her worst nightmare come true and she wanted to scream. She opened her mouth to speak but couldn't. Her tongue felt thick and her mouth was dry with terror. All she could do was shake her head desperately at Kate.

Kate pouted. 'Well, I don't like the taste of booze but I do love the floaty feeling I get. It's such a buzz of happiness that quite frankly, it's something John can't give me any more,' she said looking indifferently around the kitchen. 'Sometimes I feel like I'm choking in here with them – it's like I'm suffocating.'

Jenny grabbed Kate by her thin forearms. She wanted to rattle some sense into her pretty stupid little head. 'How could you?' she yelled. 'After all we've seen over the years with our mam?'

Kate pulled her arms free and slouched away from Jenny towards the kettle, flicking the switch down. 'Oh, I wouldn't expect you to understand. I'm not doing anything hard like she did – it's just a little fun,' she said snidely. 'If you can remember what fun is?'

Jenny put her elbows on the table and covered her face with her hands. She knew what fun was, but it bore no resemblance to her childhood memories. She remembered the first time when she was thirteen and Kate was eleven and how they'd come home from school to find their mam lying semi-conscious on the settee with saliva running from her mouth. Her skirt was up around her waist and her knickers were around her ankles where obviously a man had just fled as the girls had bounded through the back door. She'd pulled her mam's skirt down and taken Kate into the kitchen to make them fish-finger sandwiches.

Jenny slowly looked back up at her sister and frowned. 'Surely to God, you've got some memories of the state she used to get in? Maybe, that's how our mam started by wanting a little fun and look how she ended up,' Jenny yelled. 'Now, you tell me what was funny about that!'

Kate's eyes flashed and she took a step closer to Jenny. 'Don't you dare lecture me when you're exactly the same. I've see you at parties in front of everyone sipping your wine and then when no one is looking gulping at it as though your life depended upon it!' she shouted. 'And, it was only at Josh's birthday party last month that I caught you in this very kitchen hiding behind the door, swallowing a mouthful of neat vodka.'

Jenny could feel her face flush with guilt and horror that after all her careful actions to hide her guilty secret she'd actually been seen. 'What rubbish,' she replied shifting uneasily on the stool. 'I'd had a hellish day at work and was just relaxing myself.'

'Well,' Kate pouted childishly. 'I'm just doing the same but with a few little puffs.' She began to pace around the large kitchen like a caged animal ready to spring. 'And, what I do now has nothing to do with you any more, Jenny. I've got John to look after me and I certainly don't need you checking up on me too!'

Jenny was flabbergasted. She recognised this as the paranoia kicking in after the effects of the drugs – it was how their mother used to be. 'But I'm not doing that; it was John who begged me to come through to look after your children. You do remember amongst all of this that you have two boys to care for?' Jenny picked at the stitching on the side of her jeans. 'Kate, you're doing to them exactly what our mam did to us and it sickens me …'

Out!' Kate screamed. 'Get out of my house and don't come back.'

Startled, Jenny looked up and winced at the ugly look on her sister's face. 'OK, OK, I'll go. But please try to sort yourself out, if only for their sakes and not your own,' she said sliding off the stool. 'John will only put up with so much, and it looks to me as though he's had enough.'

When Jenny stood up Kate came behind her and as she walked towards the door Kate started pushing her in the back with little shoves as she moved into the hall.

She chanted repeatedly, 'Out, out, get out.'

Jenny opened the wide door and pleaded with her. 'Get some counselling or help, Kate,' she murmured, as Kate slammed the door behind her back.

Jenny sat in her car trembling. She wanted to walk away and leave her sister in her own mess, but when she pictured Josh and Simon's little faces, she knew she still had to help in some way – but how? If Kate could only nip it in the bud now before she got too hooked then maybe, just maybe, her nephews would be spared the experiences she'd had to go through. There again, Jenny reasoned, there was one big difference, at least the boys would always have their dad, who would protect them from the horrors of drug addiction. Which, she thought, driving down towards the river, was more than they'd ever had – they didn't even know who their father was. She pulled into a car park and parked under a hanging laurel tree and sat watching the slow but steady flow of the river. She relaxed her shoulders, let out a huge breath, and allowed big hot tears to curse down her face. She recalled Kate's words about the neat vodka, and wondered if she was right. Was it in their genes, and were they both going to end up as carbon copies of their mother? Between them they were using alcohol and drugs to cope with their lives which really, she thought, had turned out much better than expected considering their poor start.

Jenny scrunched her eyes shut, trying hard to blot out the awful times, and how they had all come to an end one Monday morning. Kate had told a teacher at school how she'd had a dream that a strange man had come into her bedroom and pulled the sheet down to look at her. This admission had started the ball rolling and eventually social workers turned up at the house to question both of them and their mother was judged unfit to look after them – they were taken into care. The fear and terror that day as they were driven away from their home still burbled in her chest even now.

She'd been terrified that Kate would be taken from her and they'd never see each other again. And, at first they had been separated, but luckily Kate wasn't too far away and they managed to see each other every week, if not twice a week. She'd still worried about her timid little sister, but as it turned out Kate had a fantastic foster family who loved her dearly.

Jenny twirled her car keys around in the palm of her hand and remembered how she'd read somewhere that the experiences one has as a child would shape the rest of your life. And, whereas other children, like Laura, who had never witnessed their role model drinking and shooting stuff into their arms, wouldn't automatically turn to alcohol and drugs as a comfort – both her and Kate, were doing just that. Wearily, Jenny put her forehead on the steering wheel and wept.

Chapter Five

Laura sat in front of the computer in her office and sighed. She felt hungover after the wine she'd drank the night before at Jenny's, especially as she wasn't used to drinking mid-week. Her dad's voice came into her mind, saying 'not on a school night, ducky', and she smiled. Finding his name in her mobile she sent him a text with an invite to lunch, and as she waited for her computer to boot up, she read his reply, 'Usual table at one? Dad X'

She grinned at the thought of seeing him and looked forward to catching up. With a two strong cups of coffee behind her she tackled the morning's work and went to three meetings. When Laura heard of Jenny's absence as her sister in Durham was ill, she sighed with disappointment – she'd wanted to thank Jenny for her advice the night before.

Laura left the factory and crossed over the road to the old Victorian building, squinting with the sun in her eyes as she gazed up at the clock tower. It was a beautiful old building and, although there had been many new additions to the back of the hospital over the years, the front remained as it had been built in 1869. She entered the old wooden door and stared at the grey, square floor tiles. She remembered being a little girl and coming here with her dad at weekends if he'd been called to see a patient, and how she would hop-scotch across the tiles until she reached the star in the centre of the floor. Laura looked around the empty hall, hitched her pencil skirt above her knees, and hop-scotched to the centre. She pulled her skirt back down and giggled as she hurried along to the cafeteria.

Her dad was waiting at their table and talking on his mobile but ended the call as she approached and stood up to give her a big hug. At the sight of him wearing his old cable-knit cardigan and well-worn brown corduroy trousers, Laura bit her lip and fought back tears. She flung her arms around his neck, inhaling the remnants of Old Spice aftershave on his shirt collar, and felt as though she was twelve years old again.

'Hey, what's with this?' he murmured into her hair. 'Anyone would think you hadn't seen your old man for years.'

She sniffed, pulled back from him, and then gave him a big grin. 'It's nothing, it's just really good to see you,' she said sitting down opposite him at the brown Formica table.

'OK,' he said staring at her. 'What's the matter? You look really tired, Laura.'

Laura picked the menu up and shook her head, struggling to keep her emotions in check. 'I had too many glasses of wine last night with Jenny,' she said, and then swung around to look at a blackboard on the wall advertising the daily specials. 'I think I'm going to have the beef stew and dumplings today. I could do with some comforting carbs to help the hangover.'

After they'd chosen their meals at the counter and sat back down at the table her dad picked up his knife and fork then paused to raise an eyebrow. 'It's not like my girl to drink on a school night.'

Laura chewed a piece of beef from the stew and licked her lips. 'Hmm,' she uttered and swallowed. 'Well, Phil was away in Leeds so Jenny made supper for us and then we just got chatting and the night seemed to fly over.'

Laura felt her face flush. She wasn't sure whether it was from the warm stew or the fact that, although she hadn't exactly lied to her father, she was evading the truth.

He continued. 'Your mam was just saying the other day that we hadn't seen Phil for a while. He used to drop in for a cuppa on the way to the golf course.'

'Well,' Laura hedged. 'I don't think he's playing much golf at the moment.' She squirmed in her seat, trying to avoid his questions, but knew full well that she would buckle under his scrutiny at some stage in the conversation. Her father was a master at getting the information he wanted without direct questioning; after all, she thought, that was his job and, he was bloody good at it.

As he crunched his way through chicken salad and she hurriedly ate the stew a comfortable silence settled between them. Laura knew he was patiently waiting to hear what was troubling her, and although she wanted to tell him, she had to find a way without discussing their sex life.

'It's just that Phil seems so distant and he's ... changed,' she offered up in to the silence.

Her dad leant forwards over the table and frowned. He made a steeple with his fingers. 'We thought that too,' he said.

Laura gaped at him. 'You do?'

He nodded. 'Me and your mam think that Phil seems disengaged from us all nowadays.'

Yes, Laura thought, that was exactly the right word to describe Phil and the way he was behaving towards her, and now apparently, her family too. In a way, it cheered her slightly to know that Phil's manner wasn't all in her imaginings. She chewed the remnants of the beef and told her father about the party and how he wouldn't be coming to see the Aussie relatives.

'Phil doesn't seem interested in our usual day-to-day things any more,' she said. 'I worried at first it was because Peter had gone off to university but he says not.'

'Well, it is a big change in the family dynamics,' her father agreed. 'But empty-nest syndrome does mainly affect women. Have you mentioned any of this to Phil's parents?'

Laura smiled gratefully. 'No, I'd never thought of that,' she said.

Phil's parents lived in an exclusive area outside Newcastle called Darras Hall and were now in their late seventies. Phil had been a late baby and his mother had spoiled him every day of his life.

'I suppose,' Laura mused, 'it couldn't do any harm to talk to them. We don't tend to call in as much as we used to, but maybe you're right and a visit is long overdue.'

Her dad squeezed her shoulder. 'Well, knowing his mam she'll naturally be defensive about Phil. But, if you choose your words carefully you might be able to find out something.'

With her spirits lifted and a more optimistic outlook than when she'd earlier crossed the road Laura ran back to the factory and hurried downstairs to her office. Not for the first time in her life, she thought of her dad as a genius – he always seemed to know what to do in difficult situations. Laura sat down at her desk just as a text popped up on her mobile from Phil. 'I have an unexpected meeting tomorrow morning with two new buyers so I'll be staying in Leeds another night but should be back for supper tomorrow. X'

Laura took a deep breath and stared longingly at the cross. She fingered her lips, wishing it was a deep sensual kiss from Phil – he'd always been a masterful kisser. Laura pondered, when had he stopped kissing and touching her? She remembered the exact date when they'd last made love, but when had the intimate gestures stopped? Being married for many years made it difficult to pin-point gradual changes and she racked her brain trying to remember. He used to slide the mirrored wardrobe into position so he could watch her in her bra and panties getting dressed – when was the last time he'd done that? But Laura shook her head in defeat – she simply couldn't remember.

Laura eased herself back in the chair and folded her hands behind her head. When they were first married he used to grind himself up against her as she was stood washing dishes in the sink. She would giggle, feeling him against her, and with a quick glance to make sure Peter wasn't within view, he would push his hands up inside her jumper.

Laura groaned with longing at the thought of him doing just that now and squirmed in her chair – she missed the intimate gestures as much as the actual act of sex itself. If Jenny was right and it was simply just a lean patch they were going through she prayed it wouldn't last too long.

She bit her lip – maybe she was overreacting? She had read in magazines about marriages where couples' intimacy dwindled down to once in a blue moon. But surely, she reasoned, they were far too young for that to happen? And, if she was totally honest with herself, she didn't want to stay in a marriage with no love.

She remembered her mam once calling her communications with her dad 'dove-tail', where they knew each other so well he would finish a sentence for her and vice versa. Or, she would walk past him and he'd kiss her and give her a cheesy smile. Perhaps she'd lapsed into that pattern with Phil over the years. But the love and attraction between her parents was still visible, she thought, whereas she wasn't quite sure where Phil's attraction for her had gone – was it simply that their marriage was now on automatic pilot and he couldn't be bothered to make an effort? Or, she thought sitting forward and doodling on the side of her diary, were her suspicions right, and he was having an affair?

Laura remembered Jenny's words the night before and how they'd agreed she should try ignoring Phil's behaviour, so with her index finger she firmly pressed reply on her mobile. Slowly, she simply typed one word, 'OK' and then wavered deciding whether to add a kiss. Deciding against it she pressed the send button.

As she walked home that evening she stopped outside Jenny's front door, wondering if she was back from Durham. There was a film on at the cinema that she wanted to see and hoped Jenny would join her. But, as there was no answer when she knocked on the door she rang Peter instead. Happily she arranged to meet him in the city within the hour.

Laura stood outside the Tyneside Cinema on Pilgrim Street in Newcastle, tapping her black ankle boot against the drain pipe, hoping Peter wouldn't be late. The film would begin soon and after reading the reviews she was looking forward to seeing it. An arm quickly went around her shoulder from behind and Laura jumped in surprise. Peter had approached from the opposite entrance and he grinned at her as she stood up on her tip toes to plant a kiss on his cheek. They hurried inside and settled themselves in their seats with a bucket of popcorn and cans of coke.

'How's Dad?' Peter asked as he placed his can in the holder on the chair.

She stared at her son's bitten fingernails. 'Oh, he's fine,' she smiled. 'He's down in Leeds tonight or I'm sure he would have come along too.'

Laura was conscious that her voice sounded edgy, although she was doing her level best to keep it happy and carefree. The last thing she wanted was Peter to worry that something was amiss.

Peter snorted. 'Ha! No he wouldn't – Dad isn't the remotely bit interested in sci-fi.'

The lights began to dim and Laura grabbed a handful of popcorn. From an early age Peter had always been fascinated in space travel, as was depicted here, and she fondly remembered their trip to America when he was twelve. She whispered, 'I was just remembering the day at Kennedy Space Centre.'

Peter nodded and ran a hand through his dark brown hair to stop it falling into his eyes. 'Yeah,' he nodded. 'That was a fantastic trip.'

While the adverts were showing, Laura studied his profile. He looked so much like Phil it sometimes overwhelmed her, but the resemblance stopped with his looks. He had none of Phil's personality. Where Phil was ambitious and pressured himself in his career with an overriding wish to make as much money as possible, Peter was creative, steady, and laid-back. He was studying music for his degree and had played the piano and guitar from his teenage years. When Peter had first applied and been accepted for the course Phil had tried to dissuade him. Phil had worried that Peter's options in the job market would be limited without a decent academic degree behind him, but she had taken Peter's side in the arguments because more than anything else, she wanted him to be happy.

The following evening as Laura lifted a beef stew out of the oven she heard Phil's key in the front door and braced herself. She hadn't seen him since the embarrassing moment in the lingerie and she dreaded him mentioning Sunday night. Laura knew that her husband of old would certainly want to discuss such an upsetting episode between them, but she wasn't too sure what this new Phil would do.

She cursed under her breath and tried to smooth down her hair, knowing the heat from the oven would have made her fringe frizzy.

'Hi there,' he said, and pecked her cheek. He threw his bag onto the floor and then crouched down and opened the zip.

Laura turned to look at him with oven gloves on her hands. 'Hello,' she said pleasantly, but could hear how stilted her voice sounded. She pressed on. 'How was Leeds?'

Phil began to push his dirty laundry into the front of the washing machine which was close to her legs as she stood at the cooker. His physical presence made her shiver with longing for him to touch her. If only he would run his hand up the inside of my leg, she thought while stirring gravy in a saucepan. She shook herself back to reality and listened to his account of the meetings, and the hotel, and then for one split second Laura thought she caught a whiff of stale perfume emanating from his shirts.

Deciding she was becoming paranoid Laura tried to ignore her irrational thoughts and concentrated upon serving dinner. As they settled down at the table to eat she told Phil about her trip to the cinema with Peter.

'It was fantastic,' she gabbled. 'The special effects were amazing, and we both thoroughly enjoyed the cinematography.

'Hmm,' Phil grunted. 'I would have thought that Peter might have grown out of that space ship rubbish by now.'

Laura looked at the irritation in Phil's eyes and instantly felt her temper flare. She could cope with him making her life a misery, but she sure as hell wasn't going to sit by quietly while he slagged off their son. She grimaced. 'Well, you would know exactly what your son liked nowadays if you made an effort to spend more time with him!'

Phil swallowed a mouthful of chicken and sighed. 'Look, it was only a throwaway comment. I didn't mean it like that,' he said. 'God, you're so bloody tetchy!'

She took a deep breath and tried to steady her nerves. She wasn't going to get anywhere if she lost her temper, and although she had decided to get on with her own life, she still needed to keep communications open. Laura took a sip of wine and shrugged her shoulders.

A lengthening silence began between them and she struggled to think of conversation other than Peter and their marriage, which she now realised appeared to be on more of a slippery slope than ever.

Phil broke the silence. 'So, how's it been at work? Have we started the usual Good Friday panic?'

'No, well, not yet,' she said and smiled. 'But it'll probably kick off tomorrow knowing our luck.'

'Right,' Phil said. 'I just wondered because of something Luigi said yesterday about a new guy working in the planning department.'

Laura puzzled to think what he meant. 'Nope, I didn't hear any gossip,' she said shaking her head. 'So, was Luigi with you in Leeds?'

Phil nodded and finished eating then stared around the room. Laura decided he looked as if he had his feet in the starting blocks and was getting ready to run. It wasn't a look of unhappiness in his expression, she thought, more of disenchantment as if he was struggling against the boredom of her company.

'Talking about Luigi,' she said, forcing as much lightness into her voice as she could muster. 'Did I tell you last week that Jenny really likes him?'

Phil drew his eyebrows together and frowned. 'She fancies *Luigi*?' he exclaimed. 'No, you didn't tell me that.'

Laura thought by Phil's expression that this liaison wasn't a good idea, and she wondered if he knew anything detrimental about the Italian. She needed to find out for Jenny's sake because the last thing she wanted was to see her friend hurt again. 'Why is that a shock, Phil? Do you know something awful about him? I mean, was he playing around in Leeds or something?'

Phil looked horrified. 'No he wasn't!' he shouted back.

Laura knew she'd touched a raw nerve and wondered if it had been Phil who was playing around in Leeds. She took a deep breath and tried to remain calm. 'OK,' she muttered. 'There's no need to shout.'

Phil got up and began to clear the plates from the table. 'Sorry,' he murmured. 'It's just that Steve told me last week that he still missed Jenny and is hoping to try and win her back.'

Laura gasped – she couldn't believe the transparency of men at times. She shook her head and tutted. 'Jenny will never give Steve another chance,' she stated emphatically. 'I know for a fact she couldn't forgive him for leaving her after the two miscarriages.'

Phil nodded while he carried the dishes into the kitchen as she sipped the last of her wine.

'And, I don't blame her,' Laura retorted. 'When the doctors told Jenny it would be highly unlikely that she'd ever be able to carry a baby to full term and she gave Steve the option to leave – well, the last thing she expected her husband to do was walk out!'

Phil stood in front of her with his arms hanging limply by his sides and a twisted smile on his face. 'Yeah, you're right, but he was stupid enough to believe that he would meet someone who could give him loads of babies. It's because he is from a big family that he's always been desperate to have his own kids,' Phil mused.

'He's an idiot,' Laura said getting up from the table. 'As my dad would say, life can't always be mapped out to perfection, and Steve should have been mature enough to realise that before he broke Jenny's heart.'

Phil yawned. 'Oh, yeah, and your dad knows the answers to all of life's problems,' he sniped, then wished her goodnight and wearily climbed the stairs.

Laura sat at the table with her head in her hands remembering how devastated Jenny had been when Steve left shortly after losing her baby daughter. Laura had spent night after night in Jenny's lounge sitting with her arms around her friend as she'd sobbed her heart out. In fact, she'd spent so much time with Jenny that Phil had eventually complained and reminded her that she had a husband and son at home that needed her just as much as Jenny did.

The next morning at work, Laura stood in the development kitchen in a white factory coat and hair net. Alex had a dental appointment, and as they had received a request for samples of prawns to go out to the Co-op head office, she had decided to make the sample packs herself. It was a small oblong kitchen with two work surfaces on one side and on the opposite wall there were two big stainless steel fridges and a freezer. It wasn't as large as some developments kitchens she had seen in other factories, but as there was only herself and Alex in the team it was a perfect size for them to work alongside each other. It was simply Bijou, Alex often said.

Listening to 'Because You Loved Me' on the radio Laura suddenly felt overwhelmed as she remembered Peter's birth and their first home together. Phil had been the proudest of fathers and much to the amazement of both their families he had become proficient in nappy changing and making up bottles with an expertise that even she had struggled with at first. While she had moaned that all her clothes smelt of baby sick he never once complained and took to bath times and sleepless nights as if he'd done it all his life. As a young mum Laura had been anxious and nervous with the responsibility and had hoped that all the well-worn platitudes – it'll come naturally to you once he's born – would be true. Phil had been an anchor of solid support. When her mam had offered to look after Peter and she'd returned to work part time until he was eight years old, Phil had encouraged her all the way. And, on the day her old manager retired Phil had taken Laura by the hand to personnel and sat next to her until she completed the application form.

Laura sniffed back tears and set twelve empty packs on the granite work surface. Who could believe that their marriage would turn out like this, and how far apart they now seemed, she thought sadly.

After Phil had gone to bed the night before she'd cleared and stacked the dirty dishes into the dishwasher then lain in a hot bath. By the time Laura reached the bedroom he was snoring slightly, mouth open, with the covers thrown aside. She'd stood looking at his toned tanned chest and stripy boxer shorts, and longed to lie on top of him again then have him take her to dizzy heights. His body was so familiar and the temptation had been excruciating. But the memory of how he'd rejected her on Sunday night stopped her reaching out to him, and she'd sighed with sadness, likening it to a form of torture. As she'd turned to get into bed she'd noticed his grey wallet sticking out of the pocket in his jacket that hung on the wardrobe door. It was where he usually kept his expense receipts, and although she'd managed to resist the temptation of his body, she hadn't been able to resist looking inside the wallet. There'd been a receipt from a restaurant in Leeds for two starters, two main courses, and two bottles of Chardonnay at lunch time.

Laura pulled a pair of disposable gloves onto her hands and examined the prawns she had brought from the factory. She conscientiously checked the grade and quality while weighing the necessary 300g of prawns into each pack. As she worked Laura tried to shake the idea from her mind that Phil had had lunch with another woman in Leeds. The sensible side of her mind reassuringly whispered that his guest could have been Luigi and she was worrying herself unnecessarily. But there were also senseless doubts and notions scattering around the other side of her mind that Phil was cheating on her.

With the samples labelled and placed in the chiller Laura headed along to the canteen for lunch. She looked forward to seeing Jenny who was now back in work.

When she walked into the canteen Jenny waved to her from the end of a table where some of the office girls and Muriel were eating their lunch. Laura inhaled a mix of tuna salads and egg mayonnaise sandwiches, and sat down opposite Jenny.

As Laura looked at Jenny she gasped in concern at the look of sheer exhaustion in Jenny's blue eyes – she looked as though she hadn't slept for a week.

'How's your sister?' she asked.

Jenny swallowed a mouthful of salad and nodded. 'Much better,' she said, and began to explain an imaginary flu bug that Kate had suffered from. 'I'm just hoping the boys don't get it now.'

Everyone agreed and comments were made about how it couldn't have come at a worse time. The general chatter centred upon how big the Easter orders were and Jenny assured them all that so far everything was ticking over nicely.

Inevitably, the girls began discussing their outfits for the party and Laura told everyone about Jenny's fabulous white dress. Oohs and aahs were exclaimed loudly as Laura embellished Jenny's attributes and how beautifully it fitted her.

Jenny blushed at her compliments and thanked her. 'Oh, I wish you were coming, Laura,' she said. 'It won't be the same without you and Phil.'

Muriel gasped. 'But I thought you were coming now?'

Laura looked at the older woman and wondered if her memory was going. 'No, Muriel,' she said slowly. 'We've been through all of this before – remember – we have the relatives here from Australia?'

Muriel looked offended and patted the back of her grey perm. 'I know that,' she sighed. 'I'm not daft! But when Phil bought a ticket from me this morning I figured there'd been a change of plan.'

Laura's eyes widened and she felt her cheeks burn. She stared down at the palms of her hands as if all the answers she needed were secretly written on them. 'He … he bought a ticket?'

An uneasy silence settled between the women and Laura felt their eyes boring into her. The bastard, she seethed, how could he? She took a deep breath and quickly tried to think of a comment that would cover over the confusion when suddenly the door swung open.

One of Jenny's QA assistants quickly approached the table. 'Jenny, you need to come now. Someone in the planning office has missed off an order and we are four hundred packs short of breaded cod fillets!'

'Jeez,' sighed Jenny. 'I spoke too soon. I'll have to run.'

As Jenny got up from her seat she passed by Laura and squeezed her shoulder in support. 'We'll talk later,' she whispered.

By one in the afternoon another line had been set up in the factory to pack the extra fish needed, but as most of the morning shift had already left, the production manager urgently requested help. Muriel and the MD hurried around the office staff and extra people were drafted into the factory to man the line. Laura put on her white coat, hair net, and washed her hands, then went straight out onto the factory floor.

Phil, Luigi, and three of the commercial team, alongside Jenny's QA technologists, were all standing on the line packing fish into trays. The line leader gave Laura a place to stand at the end of the line and she saw Phil smile at her. The knowledge that he'd gone behind her back and bought a ticket for the party incensed her and she glared at him. With the noise in the factory she knew he wouldn't be able to hear her, and she felt embarrassed enough at his actions without, as her mam would say, airing their dirty washing in public, so she remained silent. But when his eyebrows knitted together as he stared at the scowl on her face Laura knew he sensed her annoyance. Phil shrugged his shoulders and carried on chatting to Luigi who stood next to him.

Laura ignored Phil and chatted to the QA technologist next to her. They joked about how different everyone looked in factory clothing, and in an atmosphere of camaraderie and amusement, they all worked in unison to meet the deadline rather than let the customer down. As everyone left the line at the end of the run Laura walked quickly to catch up with Luigi and asked him if he'd enjoyed his visit to Leeds.

With smiling deep green eyes Luigi turned to her and grinned. 'Yes, thank you. Your husband – he is very good company,' he said, holding the plastic flap curtain open as they left the factory area. 'And, he is excellent at his marketing job. He is always on the watch for new opportunities and drives the category of products with such gusto!'

Laura smiled and nodded 'Yes, he does. But I hope he didn't tire you out.'

'Well, it was much drinking, but, as it was only for one day I managed to, how do you say, survive?'

Laura couldn't help but smile even though her mind was digesting the fact that Luigi hadn't been with Phil to share the meal in the Leeds restaurant.

Luigi removed the white hair net and shook out his jet black hair. His olive skin seemed to glisten under the bright strip lighting in the corridor, and as Laura looked at him and thought about his impeccable Italian manners and easy-going personality, she could see what Jenny liked about him.

When Laura reached her office she took a long deep breath, removed her factory safety shoes and slipped her feet into her favourite black, three-inch heels. High heels always gave her the added boost she needed to her confidence and as she pulled on her black jacket she lifted her chin then smoothed down the fitted sleeveless dress. She had thirty minutes to get ready for a presentation.

The PowerPoint slides were ready and she flipped on the computer standing in the corner of the office with the overhead projector. She'd invited the commercial director, and his team, Jenny, Phil, and Luigi to show them her ideas for the company's

Christmas party lines. Alex had made ready the samples the day before and she carried them from the kitchen into the office, arranging them on the table with plastic forks and napkins. After a quick visit to the ladies she stood and looked at herself in the mirror. Try and put all the thoughts of Phil out of your mind for the next hour, she determined – this is your time to shine. It was, she smiled confidently, why they paid her the great salary. The commercial director and MD had often told her she excelled at thinking of new ideas outside of the box, and it was these ideas that made the money.

Laura strode into the office just in time to see everyone gathering around the screen. Excited chatter ran amongst her colleagues and jokes were being made about the slip up in the planning office.

'Ah, don't take the piss, you lot,' she said, happily basking in her their camaraderie. 'As my dad often says, everyone has to start somewhere.'

The MD, a huge man in his sixties with an old fashioned thick moustache clapped his hands together. 'I know we shouldn't, Laura. But to make such a gaff in your first week especially at this time of year! Well, we just can't help it.'

Laura grinned and turned to face everyone standing in a semi-circle apart from Phil who sat perched on the corner of her desk, swinging one leg.

'Laura,' Phil smirked. 'That dress is far too small for you – it makes you look fat.'

Gripping hold of the flicker switch Laura raised her eyebrows at Phil and took a deep breath. Why the hell, she seethed, did he think it was OK to embarrass her in front of their friends? Luigi stood next to

Muriel who sat on the only office chair. He said, 'Ah, but it shows off your curves really nicely.'

The whole group burst into good-humoured laughter and she grinned at Luigi, grateful to him for rescuing her. There was a gleam and shine in Luigi's eyes that danced attention on her and for a split second Laura looked behind to see if another woman had entered the room. She couldn't believe such thoughtfulness was directed at her. Laura heard Phil huff and puff at the laughter, but as she knew it was time to call the presentation to order, she turned her back to him and began.

Laura described and showed everyone a new supersized green lip mussel she had sourced from one of their regular suppliers and handed them around the group to taste. She worked through her slides of costings, delivery dates, specifications, and new recipe ideas, which included an exotic seafood medley. Ooohs and ahhhs of delight were expressed as the different aromas and flavours from Asia, India, and Mexico filled the room. Large plump tiger prawns and pure white calamari rings glistened in colourful dressings and marinades as everyone tasted and commented upon their own personal favourites. Holidays and different seafood combinations were relayed, and as Laura knew from past experiences who were the outspoken talkers in the group, she gave them a few minutes before moving onto her next product. Laura knew how to give people free reign to enjoy themselves and join in with the tasting panel, but at the same time, she also knew how to keep her presentation to a strict schedule. Prawns wrapped in filo pastry, smoked salmon mousse shapes and sizes were tasted and discussed, and finally she showed her new variations to the habitual Christmas Day starter of prawn cocktail.

When Laura passionately explained her ideas of including champagne, brandy, and white rum into their Christmas portfolio prawn products the excitement grew to fever pitch with everyone talking at once. Jenny raised her hand and wanted to know how they would control the addition of alcohol through the factory. Great hilarity was expressed with ideas of marking bottles and casks to keep record of how much was being used in the products and images of the staff lying around drunk for days before Christmas were laughingly portrayed. However, much to Laura's delight the MD loved her fresh ideas and uptake on the traditional prawn cocktail product and Laura basked under his admiration.

'Yeah, you've come up with some great ideas,' Phil said, smiling at her.

She looked at her husband and shrugged her shoulders. 'Thanks,' she murmured knowing he was trying to make up for his earlier embarrassing remark. As she turned her back she wondered exactly how much sincerity lay in his compliment.

The MD made to leave the office. 'I don't know where we'd be without you, Laura. Keep up the good work,' he said and patted her shoulder before heading towards the door. 'Phil,' he warned. 'You'd better look after her – she's our little gold mine!'

Phil hurried behind his boss fawning and agreeing with him, and Laura briefly wondered if her troubled relationship with Phil was being noticed throughout the company.

At seven that night when Phil arrived home from the gym Laura was ready to do battle. Her stomach churned with anxiety, but she was determined to get some answers from him. She hadn't prepared any food as she had no appetite, and had decided, if Phil was man enough to look after himself in Leeds, he was capable of feeding himself at home.

'Hi,' he called entering the hall and sniffed the air. 'Is there no dinner on the go? I'm starving.'

She walked across the lounge towards him. 'If you want food I suggest you look in the kitchen,' she snapped.

Phil plonked down into the armchair next to the piano. 'OK …' he said. 'And what was that awful look for in the factory this afternoon?'

Dressed in a plain white T-shirt and jeans Laura folded her arms across her chest and stood in front of him. It was what her dad would call the defensive position, but she was past caring. Phil's behaviour at home was bad enough, she thought, but humiliating her at work was a different matter. 'Muriel told me you've bought a ticket to the party next week?'

Phil looked up at her. 'Yes, I have,' he said. 'But we've already talked about this and I told you I need to be there.'

'Nooo,' she said through clenched teeth. 'We haven't agreed on anything. You said you were going and I said you should be coming to meet the relatives.'

Phil laid his head back against the chair and sighed with impatience. 'So, now you're telling me what I can and can't do?'

Laura fumed at his arrogance and the indifference in his sigh. It was as if he couldn't be bothered to talk to her, or she simply wasn't important enough to waste his time on. She took a deep breath. 'No, Phil. I've never done that and although I'm trying to understand this upset between us I will not have you belittle me at work!'

'What?' he yelled. 'How can buying a ticket belittle you? I think you're overreacting, Laura. All you had to do was tell everyone that you are going to meet the relatives and I'm going to the party. What's wrong with that?'

'Because I didn't know, and it made me look stupid in front of everyone as if I don't know what my husband is up to,' she said and ran her sweaty hands up and down the side of her jeans. 'Which, I don't, Phil. I feel like I'm living with a stranger – especially after the upset on Sunday night.'

'Upset?' Phil asked raising an eyebrow and sitting forward in his chair. 'Ah, so that's what we're calling your underwear charade, is it?' His hands gripped the arms of the chair and he put his head on one side. He snorted loudly. 'So, because we're having a few problems you've decided if there's no sex there's no dinner?'

Laura's heart began to thump and her whole body tensed. How dare he make fun of her – he obviously didn't care a jot about her feelings or the months of anguish he'd put her through. She yelled. 'Don't you speak to me like that!'

Within seconds Phil slumped back down into the chair. He looked deflated like a balloon that had burst. 'I'm sorry,' he said. 'Look, it's been a long day and we're both tired and saying things we don't mean. Let's call a truce, love. You know I hate arguing.'

He stood up, took a step towards her, and then rubbed the sides of her arms. For a split second Laura thought he was going to wrap his arms around her and make it up to her like he'd always done in the past. Usually, he'd take her to bed and make love with gentle tenderness – she sighed in longing at the memory.

But instead he walked past her, rubbing his stomach. 'God, I'm hungry,' he mumbled, and then spun around. 'How about I'll nip out and get us a pizza?'

Laura's mood softened. Wanting to meet halfway she walked towards him. Maybe if she swallowed a little pride too it would help. 'OK,' she soothed and draped her arms around his neck. 'I just want us to get back to normal, Phil. I miss you.'

He pulled back from her, untangled her arms from his neck and grabbed his jacket from the chair. 'I'll run out for the pizza,' he muttered hurrying towards the door. 'Won't be long.'

It was just before ten when Laura heard Phil arrive home. By this time Laura had climbed into bed and when he came upstairs to look for her she feigned sleep with the sheet over her head.

Chapter Six

On Friday afternoon Laura finished work early and drove through Darras Hall, heading towards Phil's parents' house. She'd mentally prepared a conversation and some vague questions which, she hoped, might throw some light on the dilemma she faced.

She saw Phil's father, Michael, who was an older version of her husband, peeking from behind the curtains as she pulled up outside the large, five-bedroomed property. During the last year Michael had been diagnosed with the beginnings of Alzheimer's disease, and as an intelligent, retired bank manager, it was tragic to see him suffering. Naturally, both herself and Phil had offered to help support his mother, but she'd flatly refused, insisting she could cope alone.

Mavis Johnson was one of the tallest women Laura had ever met. Phil had once told her that his mother was six foot two inches, which made a stark contrast to Michael who was only five foot six. Though most people's height appeared to decrease as they got older, Mavis at the age of seventy-seven was defying this law of nature. She still stood tall, and erect, with her wide shoulders pulled back as Laura entered the elegant lounge. Laura kissed her mother-in-law on the cheek and nodded at Michael who scurried past her to make tea while she perched on the end of the chaise lounge in the window.

'So, my dear,' Mavis said. 'To what do we owe the pleasure of this visit?'

Laura took a deep breath. Mavis had never been the easiest woman to get along with and Laura knew, although Phil had regularly disputed the fact, that she would never have been her first choice of a daughter-in-law. Laura gazed around the dual-aspect room wondering for the umpteenth time while they didn't have a comfortable settee. It was a large room but the only furniture they'd ever had were two stand-alone chairs, and the precarious seat she now sat upon. The chaise lounge was the seat that all visitors were shown to and in the past it had seemed steadier as Phil or Peter would sit on the opposite end to her.

Now, it tilted dangerously and she shuffled further into the middle. 'Oh, I was just passing this way and thought I'd drop by to thank you for Peter's Easter card and money,' she said.

Mavis sat back down in her fireside chair which was covered in faded tartan fabric and gave Laura a smile that didn't quite reach her eyes. She crossed her long, thin legs. 'It would have been nicer to see Peter,' she huffed slightly. 'And then he could have thanked us himself.'

Silently, Laura counted to ten. And if you were, or ever had been, a little more loving towards Peter he would come more often, she thought, but instead she smiled back at Mavis. 'Well, he's really busy with exams at the moment, but I know he was delighted with your generous gift which will buy the extra books he needs.'

Michael shuffled into the room and placed the tea tray onto a small table. Mavis watched her husband with a scornful expression in her tight jaw as he spilt a little milk out of the delicate china jug onto the gold leaf tray.

Laura immediately leapt to her feet to help him, but was ushered back down by Mavis as she tutted at her husband and then cleaned the tray with one of the napkins neatly folded on the side. Laura felt sorry for her father-in-law and gave him a big smile as he slunk down into the chair at the opposite side of the fireplace. Maybe her mother-in-law would prefer a servant to carry tea trays and run after her all day, Laura thought vindictively, and then chastised herself – she'd never get anywhere with this attitude.

Laura smiled and sipped her tea. She complimented Mavis on how well they both looked and invited them for tea on Easter Sunday, although as soon as the words were out of her mouth, she knew Mavis would decline.

'Oh dear. I think we have a bridge party that day,' Mavis said tilting her head to one side at her husband. Michael, who at Laura's invitation had lifted his eyes up to her, now dejectedly dropped his shoulders and stared at his feet. Laura knew Phil's dad would have loved, even in his confused state, to join them, but as ever Mavis ruled the roost.

'Now that is a shame,' Laura said, knowing full well that neither of them had been out socially since the day Michael was diagnosed. She also knew Mavis would think his confusion was shameful and something to be hidden away from their haughty, upper-class circle of friends. Laura thought this attitude was more shameful in itself.

During all of the years she'd been married to Phil she could only remember them coming twice to her home and once to her parents' house. Laura wanted to tell Mavis that even if Michael was having a muddled-up day it wouldn't matter one iota, because he would fit in well if her own mam was having one of her outbursts. Laura smiled at the thought of them trying to mingle together in her parents' lounge.

While Laura was lost in thought, Mavis had begun on one of her crusades about how marvellous Phil was at everything he did, and was planning to do in his career.

The old woman's eyes shone as she talked about her son. 'Phil could have made quicker and much better advances if he'd been working down in the capital,' she said. 'Staying in the North-east has done nothing but hold him back.'

Laura could feel Mavis's beady eyes boring into her, and she knew, although Mavis hadn't said as much, that she held Laura and Peter to account for this. Laura sighed and stared down at her blue laced pumps. She finished her tea, realising that the visit had been a pointless exercise. Even if Phil had opened his heart and poured out all of his troubles to his mother, which Laura knew he would never do, Mavis would sooner die than tell her anything. She stood up to leave and thanked Mavis for the tea.

Michael got up and sprightly followed her out of the lounge while Mavis didn't leave her chair. Laura chatted briefly to him as they returned through the enormous hallway towards the wide Jacobean door. She paused to look around at the once opulent, but now jaded décor – he must feel like a prisoner, she thought.

Laura took hold of his wrinkled hand. 'Michael, if ever you want to come over to see us – just ring. And either me or Phil will come and collect you.'

Michael lowered his head towards her shoulder and whispered, 'Phil is trapped, you see. He feels trapped and wants to be free.'

Laura frowned, wondering what he was talking about. She bent closer to him inhaling his expensive old cologne, and muttered, 'What do you mean, trapped?'

Michael's dark brown eyes danced and he put a finger to his lips. 'He was far too young at the time, and I offered him some money when he got that girl pregnant at university so he could run away and be free, but she …' he said nodding towards the lounge door, 'took it off him and told him he had to do the right thing and marry her.'

Suddenly, it dawned upon Laura that Michael was talking about her. Oh, my, God. She trembled.

Mavis called Michael's name from the lounge and jerkily he opened the door. 'Toodle pip,' he said, then gently but firmly hurried Laura through the door.

Once outside on the wide concrete step Laura's heart began to pound and her legs quivered as she walked across the gravel drive towards her old red Mini. She knew Michael, or maybe both of them, would be peering from behind the drapes as she climbed into her car. Laura gripped the steering wheel in an effort to steady her shaking hands and slowly drove back out onto the road.

Laura drove steadily further down the road and found a place where she could safely pull in for a while – she needed to think. Had she misheard Michael? Was he definitely talking about her? Laura thought back over the whispered conversation two or three times until she was convinced that what she'd heard was true. His mind could be fluctuating between the past and the present, she decided. Phil had told her after his last visit that Michael was getting worse, and on that particular day, Michael had been watching a film about Dunkirk and actually thought he was in one of the boats!

Laura sighed. However, if Michael was talking about them, then unless Phil had got another girl pregnant when they were at university, he must have meant he'd been trapped by her.

She bit her lip and swallowed a lump in her throat. Knowing Phil had been offered a bribe to run away and leave her to bring up Peter alone was horrendous. Had Phil accepted the money before Mavis found out and took it off him? Or, had he flatly refused to take it because he loved her and wanted to get married?

Laura remembered the evening after graduation as they'd lain together in the park, basking in a late summer sun and she'd told him she was pregnant. His eyes had widened in trepidation at the news. But, when she'd wrapped her arms around his chest and looked up at him asking what he thought they should do, he'd relaxed his shoulders and hugged her tightly to him.

'We'll be fine,' he'd said. 'If we get married straight away no one will know.' And then they'd discussed silly names for boys and girls. Not once, Laura thought now, was terminating the pregnancy or splitting up ever discussed. It had been, she'd always thought, just a natural progression in their relationship and something that would have happened in due course after they were married.

Laura picked at the stitching around the cover on her car seat; had she been so besotted with him and blinded by love that she hadn't, as her mam would say, been able to see the wood for the trees? Questions raced through her mind now as she gazed down the quiet tree-lined road. With all the problems they'd had lately, she'd been holding on to her lovely old memories, but perhaps the past hadn't been quite so rosy for Phil. She shook her head and imagined what Jenny would say when she told her – so you're going to take notice of an old man's ramblings above the years of happy marriage you've had with Phil? Laura grimaced and started the car.

Laura hadn't said a word about the visit to his parents, mainly because she still wasn't speaking to Phil after he'd crawled into bed smelling of pizza and red wine on Wednesday night. She was convinced now that he was having an affair. Even if her thoughts were irrational, she decided, no one could dispute the fact that it didn't take two hours to buy a pizza and that he'd obviously been somewhere to drink the wine. Jenny had tried to reassure her that Phil could have called in to see Steve or a friend while waiting for the pizza, but Laura didn't share her sensible reasoning and optimism.

Now, at nearly seven o'clock she was planning to drive over to her parents' house in Fawdon to meet the relatives from Australia, and Phil was going to the party at the Gosforth Park Hotel. Laura sat on the end of the bed fastening silver stud earrings as she watched Phil getting dressed in the corner of the bedroom. She could smell a different Calvin Klein aftershave hanging around him after his shower and she watched him fasten the buttons on a new white pleated-front shirt. The black tie and new Paul Costelloe black dress suit fitted him to perfection.

Laura gaped at him as he admired and preened himself in front of the long-length mirror, turning one way to another to check his appearance. She shook her head in disbelief and stared at the back of his shoulders, wondering where her husband had gone. In the past Phil would have complained at the request to wear a dress suit and bow tie, but now it seemed as though he was loving it. And, Laura thought, as much as she missed her old Phil, this swanky new Phil did look absolutely gorgeous. She swallowed hard, desperately wishing that she was going with him to the party. After a spray of Angel perfume behind her ears Laura checked her clutch bag and snapped the clasp shut with a note of irritation. It wasn't that she couldn't appreciate the fact that at his age Phil wanted a new look, but what was increasingly hard to accept was the fact that his new image was to impress other women and not her.

Laura left the bedroom in silence and grabbed her car keys from the table in the hall. Slowly, she pulled out of the cul-de-sac and began to drive through the quiet streets. In the dimming light she thought about Phil's stance, and the arrogant way he'd stood in front of the mirror, and let her mind drift back to when Phil had first started work at the company.

Following a few lucrative marketing deals and projects, Phil had quickly made his name and his confidence soared. With this continued success he'd developed a cocky tone to his voice, and on more than one occasion in the canteen Laura had heard the word arrogant linked to his name. But when they were alone in bed together lying facing each other he would let all his defences down and was still the loving vulnerable guy she'd fallen for at university. He would whisper his fears to her and tell her about his dreams and ambition to be the best at his job. She would hold his head on her chest and run her hands soothingly through his hair, reassuring him that, in her eyes, he was already the best.

Now, as Laura thought over the last five or six years she realised the arrogant swagger didn't diminish when they were alone together, and how it now seemed to be a permanent feature of his personality. And, where once he'd encourage and support her own management role, the demeaning note in his voice when he talked about her capabilities now at work was irritating to say the least. What had happened to that sweet lovable guy, she wondered, and maybe, along with everyone else she'd got so used to thinking of him as Mr Nice Guy, she hadn't noticed that maybe he wasn't any more?

As she drove onto Ancroft Way and pulled up outside her parents' 1940s detached house, she prided herself with the fact that the rest of the family hadn't noticed the strained atmosphere between her and Phil. Or, if they had it wasn't mentioned. Peter had been home for Good Friday and Easter Sunday and they'd spent much of the time with her dad. Both herself and Phil had been into work at varying stages, but had managed to share the family lunch followed by the traditional gorging of chocolate eggs.

Peter worshipped his grandparents and Laura smiled remembering the camaraderie and fun he'd had teasing her dad. Laura climbed out of the Mini, smoothed her dress down, and took a deep breath. She owed it to her parents to be cheerful and welcoming to her aunt and cousin.

By nine o'clock and after a lovely meal all of the family insisted Laura should leave and join Phil at the party for the last few hours. Her heart leapt with joy and she tried to quell the butterflies that were fluttering around her stomach as she sped away from her parents' home towards the hotel. She grinned at the thought of surprising Phil and her friends by turning up unexpectedly, and although she wasn't dressed in anything as glamorous as Jenny's long white dress, her short black lace dress was ideal for dancing and her black strappy sandals were as ever, the perfect match.

Within ten minutes she pulled up outside the hotel, parked the Mini and hurried towards the white canopy with Marriot Hotel in black lettering on it. As she passed the reception desk she told the guy she was looking for her husband, and he waved her through to the function room. Fluffing up the back of her curls and pasting a big smile onto her face she swept inside.

It looked beautiful, with large round tables covered in white linen tablecloths and high-backed chairs with pink silk bows fastened around them. A Robbie Williams song blasted out onto the dance floor as she weaved her way in-between the tables calling out greetings to her friends who mostly looked decidedly tipsy, and in some cases very drunk. The tables were cluttered with empty glasses and wine bottles as young waiters and waitresses made valiant efforts to clear them away.

Laura scanned the dance floor but couldn't see Phil. She did however, catch sight of Muriel trying to teach one of the young factory workers how to dance the tango and she giggled. Suddenly an arm squeezed around her waist and she turned to look into the shining green eyes of Luigi.

She smiled. 'Hey there. Are you having a good time?'

Luigi grinned and looked her up and down. 'I am,' he said. 'And the night has just got a whole lot better.'

He was flirting with her and Laura grinned. 'Have you seen Phil?' she asked looking over his shoulder.

'Ah, Phil,' Luigi drawled. 'He left after the meal. His head, was thunderous …'

Laura drew her eyebrows together and frowned. 'Oh right,' she said. 'That's strange because he didn't have a headache earlier.'

'Maybe it was all the red wine he drank,' Luigi stated. 'Can I get you a drink?'

Laura nodded and when Luigi went off towards the bar she spotted Muriel leaving the dance floor. She hurried towards her. 'Muriel, have you seen Jenny?'

'Hello, my lovely,' Muriel said swaying slightly. 'Ah, the poor lamb couldn't make it. Her sister is ill and I'm not sure if she's gone through to Durham again.'

Laura leant back from the powerful smell of whisky on Muriel's breath – she thanked her and guided her carefully back to her seat.

In a split decision Laura decided to leave and go home to see Phil. She didn't believe for one minute he'd left because of a headache and she desperately needed to know what was happening. As she slipped out of the room she quickly pressed his number in her mobile, but by the time she'd ran back across the car park her call had gone straight to voicemail. Once again Laura sped off in her car. She was fuming at his behaviour and sudden departure from the party. Even if his head had been thunderous as Luigi said, he should have made more of an effort to stay. After all, she grimaced; he had been the one who was desperate to be there and had let the family down with his insistence. Filled with disappointment Laura cursed him under breath knowing that now, she too had missed out on all the fun.

As soon as Laura pulled up outside their house she knew Phil wasn't there. They always left the landing light switched on when they were out for the evening – if he'd returned and gone to bed, he would have turned it off. Even so, she ran through the front door and still checked in every room as her heart pounded with trepidation and fear. Her mind began to reel as she imagined him in a nightclub or with another woman. Frantically, she knew sitting at home waiting for him to come back wasn't an option – she needed Jenny.

Laura kicked off her sandals and slipped her feet into an old pair of trainers. She pulled on a fleece jacket and set off to run around the cul-de-sac to Jenny's house. A glimmer of hope surged through Laura as she looked up and spotted the soft glow of Jenny's bedside lamp through the thin voile at the bedroom window. Laura came to a halt, breathing a sigh of relief that she was obviously back from Durham. She needed Jenny's calm reassurance more than she'd ever needed it before.

Laura rang her door bell twice but couldn't hear any movement from inside. Maybe she was still in Durham but had left the bedroom light switched on? She glanced at her watch, and then stepped back into the garden to look up at the window. Laura saw a fleeting shadow behind the voile and instantly knew there was someone in the room. If it was Jenny then she would have run down the stairs by now. Maybe it was an intruder and she was being burgled? Laura began to hammer on the door loudly now and with the other hand she pressed Jenny's number on her mobile.

Just as Laura raised her fist to hammer on the door again it suddenly swung open and Jenny appeared. She looked distraught and was pulling a short robe across herself and trying to tie the belt around her waist as her hands shook.

Laura gasped at the sight of Jenny. Her hair was dishevelled; her eyes were glazed and bulging, and with a strong smell of alcohol clinging around her breath and mouth, Laura could tell she was very drunk.

Jenny swayed and grabbed the bottom of the banister to steady herself. 'Wh ... what's wrong?' she slurred and then tried to stare at Laura as if she was having trouble focusing.

'Christ, Jenny,' she whispered. 'What have you been drinking?'

There was another noise and soft padding footsteps coming from above on the landing and Laura quickly understood that Jenny wasn't alone. It couldn't be Luigi as he was still at the party, she thought, but could it be Steve?

Laura frowned and gingerly stepped up onto the first stair looking upwards as she put her head on one side to see who it was.

Her mouth dropped open and she fought to catch her breath as she looked up at her husband.

Phil was naked and standing looking down over the banister rail. An eerie silence settled between them as Laura blinked her eyes and shook her head wildly – she couldn't believe what she was seeing. Panic and terror bubbled up inside her stomach as she stared dumbly at him. Laura retched and put her hand over her mouth as she swallowed down bile. Her knees began to wobble and her shoulders shook, she stepped back and grabbed at the letterbox to stop herself from falling.

Phil took a step forward whispering her name and then the silence was shattered as Jenny began to wail, 'Oh my God, I'm so sorry,' she sobbed. 'I'm so ... sorry, Laura.'

Ignoring Jenny, Laura continued to stare at Phil until he turned and ran back into Jenny's bedroom. 'Wait, Laura,' he called. 'Let me get dressed and explain …'

Laura's mind began to take in the situation. She snarled loudly, 'You godforsaken *bastards!*'

Laura glared down at Jenny who had slumped down onto the bottom stair–– her robe parted to reveal the white all-in-one cami she'd bought when they were shopping in Debenhams.

Laura shook her head in disbelief. There was a dark purple love bite on the side of Jenny's breast and Laura buckled at the thought of Phil sucking it. A wailing growl began in the pit of Laura's stomach, and she turned to run. She screamed at the top of her lungs, 'Noooo …' and set off running along the street as though the devil himself was behind her. Tears cursed down her face as she sobbed and chocked at the horrific image of her husband and best friend being together.

With trembling hands Laura managed to get the key into the lock and opened the door then ran into the lounge and flung herself down onto the settee. She buried her face into a cushion and howled into the darkness like a wounded animal feeling actual physical pain in her chest. It couldn't be happening, she cried, Jenny wouldn't and couldn't do that to her?

Jenny's head was actually swimming. She struggled to focus and began to drag herself up the stairs one at a time on her hands and knees. Half way up, she felt Phil's hands under her armpits as he hauled her up the last few stairs and carried her through onto the bed.

'Are you crazy?' she sobbed. 'You stupid idiot – why did you come out of the bedroom?'

He didn't answer but made soothing noises and talked to her as though she was a child. He smoothed her hair down and wiped the tears and secretions from her nose with a tissue.

'I … I didn't know who it was,' he said. 'And I was worried.'

His hand on her hair was irritating and she brushed it away from her face as she closed her eyes and felt herself float into a drunken stupor.

Phil whispered, 'It'll be all right, darling. I'll go and talk to Laura. It'll be fine, you'll see and then we can be together properly.'

Jenny groaned and let the darkness and blessed oblivion take over. She slept deeply at first but then from around five in the morning she woke up every hour seeing Laura's tragic face in her dreams. Finally around ten o'clock Jenny felt a hand on her forehead and she opened her eyes. Phil was sitting on the side of the bed holding a mug of hot steaming tea.

The pain in her head was horrendous and her dry lips were stuck together. At first Jenny thought they were in the hotel room in Leeds. But, no, she decided, looking around the room; he was here in her own bedroom. She groaned with the simple effort of moving her eyes and head.

'Bad head?' he asked placing the mug onto the bedside table. 'I'm not surprised. That Russian vodka is powerful stuff.'

The memory and realisation hit Jenny like a truck. Laura's traumatised face slammed back into her mind and she squeezed her eyes shut to try and block it out. 'Oh my God', she moaned, 'what have I done?'

Phil brought her painkillers and water as he chatted easily then hurriedly showered and dressed. 'I'm going straight around to see Laura. I'll pack a bag of clothes, and then move in here with you,' he said.

Jenny tried to speak but couldn't seem to form the words from her lips. She raised herself up in bed and the quilt slid down to waist as she gulped at the glass of water. An aroma of sex, sweat, and stale perfume wafted up her nose making her want to retch. Jenny stared down at the white cami which was now askew, revealing one of her breasts.

Phil hurried to the bed and looked down at her. 'It'll be fantastic, Jenny. No more sneaking around to see each other and we can be together all day and night like we've dreamt about,' he muttered, and bent down to fondle her.

Jenny stiffened in shock and turned her face to the wall. It's not my dream, she agonised, the thought of Phil being here 24/7 appalled her.

Lifting his head up Phil crooned, 'Look, I'll be as quick as I can. You jump into the shower but stay in bed and as soon as I get back you can ride me again like last night. Wow! You were amazing. I've never had sex like that before – you were like a real she-devil.'

Jenny groaned as the early memories of the night flooded into her mind and remembered how she'd lifted his arms above his head and made him clasp hold of the white metal bedstead. She'd ground herself on top of him biting his neck in ecstasy, but then the memories were blurred as she'd drank more vodka.

'I'll not be long,' Phil said striding from the room, at which Jenny sighed with relief.

The sun streaming through the curtains in the lounge woke Laura. Her face was pushed into a velvet cushion on the settee and at first she couldn't remember where she was or why she felt different, but all she knew was that she wasn't in her own bed. She lifted her face and looked around the lounge in semi-darkness then shivered with cold. As she sat up and shook her head the memories of the night before crashed mercilessly into her mind and she automatically started to sob. She needed the toilet desperately and dragged herself from the settee and upstairs to the bathroom. The memory of Phil naked and Jenny with her breasts exposed actually made her retch and after using the toilet she stood up and ran cold water into a tumbler. Laura gulped the water thirstily which eased the dry soreness in her throat and then slowly she lifted her head up and looked into the mirror.

Laura cried out in horror at the sight of her face. The velvet cushion had left a streaky imprint on her cheek, her usual bright chestnut curls were dull and plastered around her face, and a trail of saliva wound down her chin. But it was her eyes that were the biggest shock. They were so swollen and puffy that they were practically closed. Laura started to cry once more but filled the sink with hot water and washed her face with soap. It took two attempts to remove the blackened smudges of mascara from underneath her eyes and the soap stung when it mixed with the hot tears that fell uncontrollably from her eyes.

She plodded into the bedroom, stripped off her black dress and underwear, and pulled a night shirt over her head. Laura crawled under the duvet shivering with cold and what, she thought, her dad would probably call shock. With the foul images in her mind she tried desperately to go back to sleep, but although the shivering subsided sleep eluded her.

Her mind spun with horror at what she'd seen – how could either of them do this to me, she wept. With an already sodden tissue she wiped her face, and took a deep breath trying to rationalise her thoughts. She thought about Phil's behaviour in the last few months and knew that finding him with another woman, if she was truthful, was what she'd expected. Therefore, the confirmation, although torturous, was not the biggest shock. But Jenny's betrayal, to use one of Peter's expressions, was mind-blowing.

Laura startled as she heard a key turning in the front door. Was it Phil or Peter? Knowing Peter was hiking in Aberdeen with university friends she relaxed her shoulders. She didn't care one iota what mess Phil saw her in, but she couldn't bear her son to see her like this.

'Laura?' Phil called and she lay still hearing his footsteps hurry into the lounge and kitchen diner. Then as she heard his footsteps running up the stairs she braced herself and pulled the quilt over her head.

'Oh, you're there,' he said resolutely as he made his way quietly around to her side of the bed. 'Are you asleep … Laura?'

She didn't know what to do. She wanted to ignore him and prayed he would go away. Knowing she would have to face him at some stage Laura lifted the duvet down from her head, but still faced the window and didn't turn her head.

'Are you OK?' he asked gingerly then laid a hand on top of the duvet over her shoulder.

Suddenly a rush of hatred and anger surged through her. As if he bloody well cared, she raged, and pushed the duvet and his hand away from her. She sat up in the bed and faced him. 'What is it to you?' she snarled.

'Get your hands off me!'

Phil jumped back and gasped, 'Christ!'

Laura glared at him. She could see the look of distress in his eyes at the sight of her ravaged face. She looked him up and down as he stood with his arms hanging by his sides in his crumpled dress suit and white shirt. The shirt had a red wine stain down the front and wafts of stale alcohol made her stomach heave again. Desperate not to vomit in front of him she swallowed hard. Laura was determined not to break down and pulled her shoulders back. 'Yes, go on, take a good look,' she sneered. 'Take a look at the mess you've left behind.'

He stripped off his jacket and plonked down on the end of the bed. 'God, I'm sorry,' he muttered then sat forward and put his head in his hands. 'You should never have found out like that – it was appalling. We just got so drunk that I forgot the time and I thought you'd be at you parents until late.'

Laura wanted to hoot. He wasn't actually apologising for having sex with her best friend but was making excuses for being caught out. 'Oh, I'm sorry for spoiling your plans. How inconsiderate it was of me to burst in on you both like that.'

His chin quivered and he croaked, 'I should have told you weeks ago but I just didn't know how.'

He looked up at her and he held open the palms of his hands as though begging for forgiveness. In the past, this was the look that had always won her over; she could never bear to see him low-down and vulnerable. It was what she'd always thought of as his little-boy-lost look, but now she recognised it for what it was – simple cowardice.

The hairs on the back of her neck stood up and her heart began to pound as adrenalin surged through her body. She jumped up off the bed and stood in front of him with her hands on her hips. 'You spineless creep,' she erupted. 'It's bad enough what you've done but to come here looking for sympathy is simply pathetic.'

Phil got up and threw his jacket into the laundry basket then pulled out a large holdall from the bottom of the wardrobe. 'I'm leaving, Laura. It's over. There's nothing left between us and I can't go on pretending any longer,' he stated. 'I'm crazy about Jenny and have been for weeks now so I'm going to move in with her.'

Laura's eyes followed him around the room. 'Well, you can get that stinking jacket out of the laundry basket,' she yelled. 'I'm sure as hell not doing your dry cleaning for you!'

Her mind reeled with the confession that he'd been with Jenny for weeks. When he'd first sat on the end of the bed Laura thought he was going to say it was a one-off night of drunkenness with Jenny and he wanted to be forgiven. But this, she knew, was so much worse. She watched him throw underwear and socks into the holdall then pull down a handful of shirts and trousers from the hangers. Silence hung between them. The only noise in the room was the tinkle of the empty coat hangers.

Laura knew this might be her only chance to find out what had been happening. She took a deep breath and asked, 'How long?'

'What?' He said turning to face her.

She folded her arms across her chest and glowered at him. 'How long have you been seeing her?'

She watched him draw his eyebrows together as if he was pondering over a query at work. He shrugged his shoulders. 'What does it matter?'

Laura took a menacing step towards him wishing she could find something to hit him with. She knew she'd look ridiculous if she pounded on his chest with her fists but as she clenched and unclenched them she really wanted to strike out.

She shrieked, 'I asked you how long you've been sleeping with her?'

Phil picked up the holdall and headed into the bathroom where with one sweep of his arm he cleared all his toiletries into the bag. 'About six weeks …'

Laura followed him onto the landing as he hurriedly made his way downstairs pulling the zip along on the holdall.

He turned before reaching the front door and looked up at her. 'I'm sorry,' he said. 'I'll always care about you, but only like a sister. And, I know that's crap but I just can't help it.'

And with that, he opened the door and left.

Chapter Seven

Jenny stood under the shower and let the hot water pour down over her head. Her mind was reeling with emotions of fear and dread, but mainly of self-hatred and loathing. She lathered her body with soap hoping to scrub away the smell from last night and poured an excessive amount of shampoo onto her hair.

She dressed hurriedly in an old jogging suit and flew into the bedroom, stripping the sheets from her bed. Her heart raced as quickly as her mind as she tried to decide how to get rid of Phil. She didn't want him here, and couldn't understand how or why he thought that moving in with her would be an option. She knew with certainty that she hadn't signed up for anything long term – after all, they'd only ever said it was a bit of fun, hadn't they? She tried to recall the times they'd had sex and if she'd ever told him she wanted more, or that she loved him? Jenny knew however, that this was a fruitless exercise because she'd always been plastered with alcohol and sighed – she only wanted him when she was drunk.

And, it didn't necessarily have to be him, she thought, stripping pillowcases from the pillows. She didn't love Phil; in fact, she didn't have any real feelings for him. She gathered the linen into a bundle and paused; if she was totally honest with herself she didn't care who the man was, and if it hadn't been Phil it could have been anyone. As long as she was drunk and in charge of the sex that's all she'd wanted – that's what made her feel powerful and in control –

she made the rules and they had to abide by them. Phil had told her during their first time together that she was irresistible, and all the men at work were in awe of her. This had made her feel a hundred feet tall. And the next morning when she'd thought it through, she'd decided that Phil was the perfect choice – he wasn't a stranger and at least she would be safe with him.

Jenny hurried downstairs and bundled the bedding into the washing machine, set the controls, and poured soap powder into the drawer. As she watched the sheets twirl around in motion she thought she could see Laura's tormented face peeking out at her amongst the bedding. She cried out aloud in fear as her vision blurred and she caught hold of the bench to steady herself. She felt as though she was on a roller-coaster at the fair ground.

With trembling legs she went through into the lounge and sat down heavily on the leather armchair. A feeling of pins and needles spread across her chest and sweat formed on her forehead. Was she having a heart attack, she thought, and tried to take deep breaths praying the panicky feelings would pass. She looked around at the newly painted white walls with strips of aubergine patterned wallpaper and then at the white leather settee. She tried to think clearly and logically, but the panic bubbled up in her throat and she knew she wasn't in control of her thoughts. She squeezed her eyes tight shut dreading the moment when Phil would come back – maybe she could lock the doors and not let him inside?

All of a sudden, the front door opened and Jenny realised Phil had left the catch up when he'd gone out earlier. Damn, she cursed, and put her hands over her face.

'Hey there,' he said cheerfully and ran across the room to her. 'It's all sorted. Laura is OK and I've left her.'

He threw his holdall to the floor and dropped down onto his knees by her chair. 'Now we can start and live our own lives,' he soothed. 'Hey, I thought you were going to wait in bed for me?'

Jenny peeked through her fingers and spied his bag on

the floor – where was he going to put his clothes? She didn't want his things in her wardrobe, especially not in Steve's side. Her heart began to thump again and she felt as if the walls were closing in on top of her. 'Get away from me,' she shouted. 'I don't want you here! I never asked you to come. This is my house, it's not Steve's, and it's certainly not yours!'

Phil pulled back and sat on his hunkers shaking his head. 'But I thought …?'

'You thought?' Jenny yelled. 'It's always about what you lot think, isn't it?'

The telephone started to ring and after a few seconds Phil got up and walked across the lounge to the oak cabinet. 'Shall I pick it up?' he asked.

Jenny nodded and sat forward. 'Whoever it is,' she mumbled. 'I don't want to talk to them.'

'It's your sister,' Phil said and carried the cordless receiver over to her.

Jenny put the receiver to her ear and as soon as she heard Kate's voice she started to sob. Jenny's mind was foggy as she heard Kate apologising for being horrible to her when she'd been in Durham. She tried to remember if that was last week but couldn't seem to focus. 'I … I can't stand it any more, Kate,' she said, and then began to babble. 'I know I shouldn't have done it, but when I left yours I drove up to Leeds and had sex with Phil all night in a hotel. I had to get drunk, I simply had to. We were banging each other senseless and I just couldn't stop. I … I could hardly walk the next day. And, it's just … well, I've never once thought of Phil as Laura's husband. He … he is just a man who I need sex with – it's got nothing to do Laura. I love Laura as much as I love you and I wouldn't hurt her for the whole world. But now I have and she hates me …'

Phil stood at the door to the lounge with his mouth gaped open.

The tears were streaming down Jenny's face but still she babbled on, 'Phil is here now, but I don't want him. I only need it when I'm drunk, and he won't go away. Please make him go away, Kate. I think I'm like Mum was now. I … I'm being driven by the devil!'

Jenny closed her eyes, dropped the receiver down on the carpet and laid her head back against the leather chair.

Phil could hear Kate shouting Jenny's name and he picked up the receiver.

Kate said to Phil. 'Tell Jenny I'm on my way. And don't leave her alone until I get there.'

When Kate knocked on the door and flew through into the lounge Phil stood aside looking the two sisters.

Kate flung her arms around Jenny and cuddled her tight, making soothing noises into her hair. 'You're alright now, darling,' she stated firmly. 'You are going to be fine.'

Jenny had given her a card with David's number at St Nicholas on it, and his secretary assured her that Laura's dad would pull a few strings and get someone out to the house as soon as he could.

Kate then looked over at Phil hovering in the doorway. 'Maybe you should leave for a while,' she suggested. 'Don't worry, I'll look after her.'

Phil nodded and taking the spare key from the pot on the hall table he quietly left the house.

After phone calls the following day a locum psychiatric nurse sat next to Kate on the settee. Jenny was sitting in the armchair opposite to them and he clasped his hands together as he listened to Jenny's ramblings.

Jenny fiddled with the toggle on her jogger pants. 'I remember when we were taken into care the social worker asked me to explain how I felt,' Jenny mumbled. 'I was only fourteen but I can still remember what I said. It was : "nobody wants us, no one loves us, and I'm scared".'

Kate began to cry and the nurse leaned over to squeeze her hand. 'And is that how you feel now?'

Jenny nodded and looked past them both towards the window. 'Jack and Susan were a lovely foster couple and they got me through college and university, but I always felt like a visitor in their house. And then Steve married me and we got this house and just as I was beginning to feel as if this was my home I failed again because I couldn't give him the babies he wanted and he left. I feel helpless and like a reject because I can't carry a baby,' she said sobbing. 'It's awful when I'm with other women and their children because I'm embarrassed that I can't do it.'

A dreamy soft expression flooded over Jenny's face as she carried on. 'I had two girls' names and three boys' names chosen, but we didn't need them because they all died.'

Kate stared at the nurse with tears in her eyes. 'I've never ever seen her like this,' she whispered. 'Jenny is always in control and she is the one who sorts everyone else out.'

The nurse drew his fine eyebrows together. 'Hmm, that's very often the case. I think she is having some sort of breakdown. I'm going to arrange for her to see a psychiatrist, but in the meantime I think she looks exhausted and needs a sedative to get some sleep along with a course of anti-depressants,' he said looking around the room. 'Is there anyone here to look after her?'

Kate shook her head. 'No, but I'll take her through to Durham and look after her there.'

Chapter Eight

After Phil left Laura hauled herself up from the landing and plodded back along to the bedroom. She felt exhausted as if she'd been boxing someone in a ring and had ended up the loser. Which; she supposed, was exactly what had happened. Her eyes were stinging, and although she tried to stop crying the tears flowed relentlessly as she crawled back under the duvet. It was unbelievable, she thought, after all their years together her marriage was over within a few cruel sentences.

When she thought about Phil and Jenny's deception, the betrayal, she decided, was nothing short of crucifying. During the weeks when she'd imagined Phil being intimate with another woman it had made her feel physically sick, but now she knew he'd been having sex with Jenny, it was nothing short of disgusting.

She thought about the new Phil who had changed so much over the last few months and sighed, but at least, in a crazy way, he'd been consistent in his rejection of her. Whereas Jenny, she thought, wiping her wet cheeks with the back of her hand, she had been lying to her all the time while offering comfort and support. She recalled their latest conversations and Jenny's words which now came back to haunt her. Laura shook her head and tutted, how could Jenny have told such bare-faced lies? They'd been friends since university and she'd always thought she knew her best friend better than anyone else. But obviously not, she raged. Laura blew out a deep breath and shook her head remembering how she'd cried to Jenny that Phil didn't fancy her and had no interest in sex. No wonder, she seethed, and all that time Jenny had known the real reason why Phil didn't want her in bed! Laura cringed and swallowed hard, feeling ridiculous when she thought of the things she'd confided to Jenny. She remembered the day they'd bought the lingerie in Debenhams, and Laura cried aloud, for god's sake, how crass was that? Jenny buying underwear to wear for her husband!

Laura sobbed herself to sleep again, but by late afternoon she woke with her stomach groaning in hunger. She dragged herself out of bed and wandered downstairs into the kitchen, sighing as she opened the fridge. She had neither the energy nor spirit to cook and then spotted the two Easter eggs sitting on top of the cupboard. The chocolate eggs were given to them by the company every year and Laura eyed the Crunchie and Mars Bar eggs indecisively. To hell with it, she thought, picked up both eggs and went back upstairs to bed. She decided upon the Crunchie first and peeled back the gold wrapping, broke up big pieces from the outer chocolate shell, and then unwrapped one of the Crunchie bars from inside. The mixture of honeycomb toffee sugar centre and smooth Cadbury's chocolate was delicious and she moaned in pleasure.

The silence in the house seemed deafeningly lonely and she switched on the portable TV in the corner of the bedroom to see an old Hitchcock film just beginning. She'd watch this, she thought, and hopefully try to keep the horrid memories from her mind for a while. By the time the credits rolled at the end of the film, in-between spats of sobs and tears, Laura realised with shame that she'd eaten both chocolate eggs and felt physically sick.

Laura actually stayed in bed most of the weekend, but invariably as with any type of shock, normal day-to-day life kicked-in, and she knew she'd have to get through events. As she lay on the settee with a slice of cucumber on each eye to reduce the swelling, she moaned aloud, 'Six weeks!' How could they have been seeing each other for that length of time without her noticing? Probably, she decided, because they were both much cleverer than her and not for the first time she cursed her own naivety and trusting nature.

A tinkle on her mobile showed a photo-message from Peter. The photograph was taken at the top of a mountain he'd just climbed. She cooed in amazement at the lovely spring colours of the landscape and decided to ring him. Not wanting to spoil any of his Easter break Laura decided not to tell him what had happened until he came home the following weekend. She forced cheerfulness and an upbeat tone into her voice while they chatted, but when he asked twice if she was OK, Laura realised he must know something was amiss. Scolding him, she insisted that she was fine and everything was okay but frowned with uncertainty when she clicked off her mobile because she wasn't sure she'd convinced him.

Usually on Sunday nights Laura ironed their clothes for the following week and just as she habitually dragged the ironing board out of the kitchen cupboard she stopped abruptly. How on God's earth could she go into work tomorrow morning as normal when Phil was living with Jenny? She slumped over the ironing board and covered her face with her hands. Up until now Laura had been living in the moment, but now it began to dawn upon her what the fall-out would be from their affair.

I can't do it, she whimpered, I'm simply not capable of going into work and seeing them both together. Laura knew that Phil had the confidence to front it all out without a moment's hesitation, and she also knew that she wasn't that brave – she would crumble into a heap. Laura rang Muriel and told her that she had the flu and wouldn't be in to work until she felt better then choked back tears as she listened to Muriel's concern and suggestions of cold-relief remedies.

By the following afternoon and after hours of conditioning herself not to cry, the swelling in her eyes had subsided. The feelings of acute pain were mellowing now into overwhelming periods of misery and she desperately tried to keep herself busy in the house. After catching up with chores she slumped down onto the settee with a coffee and stared around the lounge at the tired décor and curtains which were faded in large patches.

Her marriage to Phil was over; she kept repeating this to herself like a mantra, while sipping the coffee. All of a sudden, she wondered what would happen to their family home. Would it have to be sold? Or, could she afford to do what Jenny had done when she'd bought Steve out of his share of their house. The thought of Jenny made her swallow hard and she felt tears prick the back of her eyes. No, Laura determined, no more crying over either of them, they simply weren't worth having sore eyes again.

She got up and opened the oak bureau and dragged out all of their mortgage and house documents.

She froze as her mobile rang. Phil's number appeared on the screen and she answered the call.

'Hi,' Phil said. 'I was just ringing to check on you because you phoned in sick and everyone is asking after you. Are you OK?'

Laura shook her head incredulously at his casual manner. It was as though nothing had happened and their lives were normal. 'Yeah,' she sneered. 'Spookily enough I didn't feel like breezing into work this morning to see my husband drooling over my best friend. Strange that, isn't it?'

She heard Phil take a deep breath of impatience. 'Look, you're being ridiculous. Nobody at work knows anything about us, and they never will hear it from me. And, Jenny is through in Durham.'

Laura pulled her shoulders back and lifted her chin. If
he could be non-committal about their marriage, then so could she. 'Well, I'm not coming into work until I feel up to it. And, I don't want any further contact either from you or Jenny. The only time I will speak to you both will be on a purely professional basis about work-related issues.'

'But you can't do that.' Phil said. 'What about Peter? Have you told him yet?'

'Ah,' she sniped. 'At last you've remembered you have a son. Well, I haven't told him anything as yet because I don't want to spoil his trip in Scotland but I will do when he arrives home on Friday.'

Laura smoothed down the velvet criss-cross pattern on her lounge trousers waiting for his reply.

She knew he would be choosing his words carefully and could imagine him rubbing his jaw. 'What are you going to tell him?'

As Laura imagined the hurt on their son's face when she told him what his dad had done she felt her temper rise. 'I'll tell him the truth like I always have done,' she stated.

'But you can't!' Phil exploded. 'I mean, it's obvious that you need to tell him that our marriage is over, but you don't have to tell him all the rest?'

Laura was incensed. 'Oh, I see. You don't want me to tell him that you're shagging my best friend and living with her!' she yelled. 'So, what happens if he walks past the house and see's you both in the lounge together?'

'That won't happen at the moment,' Phil said. 'Look, can't you just give us all some time to figure this out?'

Laura took a deep breath. 'And why the hell should I? If you'd thought anything about me and your son you wouldn't have done it in the first place ...'

Phil clicked the connection off his mobile and Laura screamed with frustration into the silence of the room.

The following morning Laura felt incensed with anger and empowered to do something. She dragged the ladders from the garden shed and armed with a scraper she began to remove the wallpaper from the walls in the alcoves. She'd already decided that even if she was financially able to buy Phil's share of the house, she didn't want to because the thoughts of passing Jenny's house every day was grotesque. Laura also knew that if the house had any chance of selling it would need to be updated and quickly. In her old jeans and scruffy black trainers she furiously scraped long pieces of paper from the walls. Every time she came upon a stubborn piece that was stuck hard to the wall she imagined Jenny or Phil's face, gritted her teeth, and hacked viciously with the scraper until it loosened.

I'll have a fresh start somewhere on my own, she thought, maybe one of the new flats down near the quayside. And, as long as it has a spare bedroom for Peter, and it's not too far from my parents, it'll be fine.

Her mobile tinkled with a text message and hurrying down from the ladder Laura gasped in shock when she saw Jenny's name on the screen. Slowly, she opened the message and read, 'I can't begin to tell you how sorry I am. Could I come to see you and apologise properly? X'

The two-faced bitch, Laura fumed. She ground her teeth together and typed in reply, 'Drop dead!'

By early evening Laura had nearly finished stripping the whole room and was struggling with the last piece in the corner behind the piano when she heard male voices talking outside the front door. Quickly she turned the volume of the radio down and scrambled up from her knees. She gasped in surprise to see her father and Peter standing in the doorway of the lounge.

'What are you doing here?' she exclaimed. 'I wasn't expecting you home until Friday.'

Peter walked into the lounge and dropped his rucksack on the floor then stared at her.

Her dad followed him into the room and perched on the arm of the settee. 'Peter was worried that something had happened and rang me. I've just picked him up from the train station,' he said.

Jenny threw the scraper down onto the floor. 'Well, that's just silly, Peter,' she muttered. 'There was no reason to miss out on the rest of the week. Everything's OK. I'm fine.'

Her dad stood up and held out his arms. 'You're not fooling anyone, love,' he said. 'I can see by your face that something horrible has happened.'

Laura felt her shoulders droop. All the tension and frustration that she'd tried to work out of her system with the vigorous scraping made her body feel weak and her legs began to shake. As hard as she tried she couldn't stop tears filling her eyes. She ran to her dad who enveloped her in a bear hug and stroked the back of her hair.

With his strong arms around her Laura felt relief wash over her like she'd done as a little girl when he'd reassured and comforted her. He would make it all right, she thought, her dad could work miracles. He gently manoeuvred her to the settee and sat down next to her without removing his arms and made soothing noises into her hair.

Suddenly, Laura remembered her son and raised her head. 'Peter?' she mumbled.

'He's OK,' her Dad reassured. 'He's making us all a strong cup of tea.'

With her face buried in his shoulder she began to cry and told him the whole story. He listened while she explained how Phil had left the party with an apparent headache and how she'd raced home to find him missing, and then how she'd fled to Jenny's house. She stuttered and babbled about how he'd been naked upstairs on the landing and just as she was going to tell him about Jenny's drunken state in her underwear, she heard Peter slam the mugs down onto the coffee table. Laura froze.

Dear, God, she thought rapidly, she shouldn't be saying all of this in front of Peter. She shook off her dad's arms and sat up drying her face with the sleeve of her T-shirt. She cursed under her breath knowing how much it would hurt Peter to hear about Phil's disgusting behaviour.

'Oh, just ignore me. I'm babbling rubbish,' she said and smiled weakly. 'This tea will help though. I'll drink this and get a grip of myself.'

Peter stood in front of them with his hands on the hips of his jeans. His lip curled as he stared at her. 'So, Dad was upstairs naked and bonking another woman?'

Laura cringed and sipped the hot tea. Her mind raced quickly trying to decide what else to say. She couldn't lie and invent another woman, but she couldn't possibly tell them it was Jenny. Peter worshipped Jenny, and from being a small boy he'd thought of her more like an aunty than just his mam's best friend. The look of abhorrence and hurt in Peter's eyes was dreadful and Laura frantically tried to think of a way to smooth things over. 'Look,' she said. 'I'm probably exaggerating and have got myself worked up over nothing.'

Peter stepped forward and shouted, 'Stop treating me like a five-year old! Who was the woman?'

Laura's insides were quivering and she shook her head.

'It … it doesn't matter now,' she stumbled.

'Mam!' he yelled. 'Who was the other woman?'

'It … it was Jenny,' she whispered looking down at her hands clenched together in her lap.

Her father gasped and groaned in shock, and Laura felt him shaking his head in disbelief next to her own.

Peter's eyes widened in shock and he sucked in a loud gasp. He shook his head and shouted, 'So, he's been shagging Aunty Jenny behind your back?'

Laura watched Peter's nostrils flare. His young face twisted into a thunderous glare. 'The bloody scumbag!' he bellowed, stormed out of the lounge, and crashed the front door behind him.

Laura shrugged her father's arm away as he tried to hold her back. She jumped up from the settee to run after Peter.

'Leave him, Laura,' he warned. 'Let him work it out in his own way.'

Laura started to pace while her father removed dust covers and dragged the furniture back into place. She tried to drink the lukewarm tea but her stomach was churning. She should never have blurted everything out like that in front of Peter – she should have thought of her son's feelings before her own. And now he might do something crazy, and then it would be all her own fault. Laura had never seen him look so angry – he was always so very mild mannered.

'Oh, Dad. Where's he gone?' she cried and grabbed the bottle of brandy from inside the bureau. She picked up two small glasses. 'I need something stronger than tea.'

Her father chortled, 'Girl after my own heart,' he said, took the glass of brandy and gulped it down. 'You know I can't talk about work or my patients,

Laura. But all I can say to you is that in my opinion Jenny has many

unresolved issues and is a very troubled soul.'

Laura raised her eyebrow with puzzlement at her dad's words. What did he mean, she thought, surely to God he wasn't defending Jenny?

Just as Laura felt the warm effects of the brandy soothe her fluttering stomach she jumped at the sound of a key in the front door. 'Peter?' she called and turned towards the lounge door.

Peter bounded into the room rubbing the knuckles on his right hand that was clenched into a fist. 'That feels better,' he said eyeing the brandy bottle. 'Can I have one of those, Gramps?'

Laura gasped at Peter's pale face and the sweat standing on his top lip. Dreading the reply, she asked, 'What have you done?'

'I've been round to Jenny's. Luckily Dad was just getting out of the car and I caught him off guard. He smiled at me as though nothing was the matter, so I punched him in the nose as hard as I could,' he said. 'And I hope I've broken it!'

Laura's Dad chortled as he handed his grandson a glass of brandy. 'That's blooming marvellous. You've saved me a job,' he joked. 'Because I was going to do the exact same thing.'

Chapter Nine

The following morning Laura made breakfast for Peter in an effort to bring some type of normality back to their lives. With a promise from her son that he'd stay home to study and not go near Phil again Laura set off to see her parents. She climbed into her car and checked her lipstick in the mirror. Laura knew her dad would have told her mam everything by now, and she didn't want them to worry more than necessary. Laura had lain in bed the night before, unable to sleep. Her mind had wavered between fretting about Peter's reaction to what had happened, and her own steadfast resolve not to be a victim in Phil and Jenny's affair.

Her decision to sell the house and start again on her own was still foremost in her mind and in some weird way; she hoped the breakdown of their marriage may turn out to be the making of her. She'd spent far too many years depending upon Phil and her dad, she thought, and this was her chance to prove that she could be as confident and strong in her personal life as she was in her professional career. Laura fastened her seat belt with a determined click, and from now on, she decided, there would be no more dithering and waiting to hear other people's advice and opinions. She would make her own decisions and whether they turned out to be right or wrong, so be it.

As she drove around the cul-de-sac towards Jenny's house she kept her hands clenched firmly on the steering wheel and stared ahead, not once looking to the left at the house. If they were in there together she didn't want to know let alone catch a glimpse of them.

The sun shone brightly in a cloudless sky as she pulled up outside her parents' house and swung her legs out of the car. Dressed in denim shorts and blue-laced pumps, she adjusted her blue T-shirt shirt and tugged it down to the waistband of her shorts. Pulling her shoulders back and lifting her chin she strode purposively down the path to the front door.

'Oh, my darling girl,' her mam wailed the minute Laura stepped into the hall. Laura swallowed hard and braced herself ready for her onslaught. The heavy scent of beeswax hung around the hall as Laura crossed the oak parquet flooring. She opened the lounge door and stepped gingerly into the room. In the past, Laura had often wondered how two such different people could get together in the first place let alone marry one another, because as sensible, calm and steady as her dad was, her mam was the total opposite.

Easily excitable, and prone to overreacting and worrying about trivial matters, Margaret Stephenson sat in her fireside chair suffering from what Laura often thought of as an attack of the vapours. When Laura had read the classics at school she remembered comparing her mam to Mrs Bennett in *Pride and Prejudice*. Laura hurried to her side. Margaret was only five foot in her stocking feet and now at the age of sixty-seven she seemed to be as wide as she was tall.

'Good God,' Margaret sighed heavily. 'Your dad has just told me about Phil!'

Laura slid onto the broad arm of the chair and nodded. 'I know, Mam. It's horrible.'

Margaret pulled a grey cardigan together across her big chest and looked up at Laura with tears flooding her eyes. She shook her head in bewilderment. 'I mean, what the hell's got into him?'

Laura heard her dad clattering dishes in the kitchen sink and breathed a sigh of relief, knowing her mam would be easier to handle when he was around. For as long as she could remember Laura had always worn a brave face for her mother, because she couldn't cope with her emotional outbursts. And, although they were less frequent now as they'd grown older, and although she continually reiterated the fact that she loved them both equally, Laura knew her relationship with her dad was much closer.

From being a small child the noise of her mam's wailing and loud crying had scared her and she'd clung around her dad's legs for shelter. But, as much as he'd reassured her that it was just her mam's way of expressing herself, by the time Laura was a teenager she did everything in her power not to cause any upset. She distinctly remembered being terrified of telling her mam that she was pregnant and had cowered behind her dad when he'd broken the news. But, Laura recalled, her mam had surprised her by being very matter of fact and had stood by her throughout. 'You're not the first woman it's happened to, my love,' she'd stated emphatically. 'And, you sure as hell won't be the last!'

Laura draped her arm along the chair behind her mam's shoulder and squeezed it. 'I don't know, Mam. Apparently, it's been going on for six weeks behind my back,' she murmured and then gradually, in between choking back tears, she told her most of the story.

Margaret shrugged Laura's arm from her and got up out of her chair to begin pacing around the room. Laura noticed her black pleated skirt gathered into the ample folds of her large bottom and she managed to tug it free as she walked past her without Margaret realising. 'And, that Jenny!' Margaret stressed. 'I thought she was supposed to be your best friend!'

Margaret stopped at the oak mantelpiece and picked up one of her figurines to inspect. Using the hem of her cardigan she quickly polished the already spotless Lladró flower and replaced it into position then swung around to face her. 'Dear God, if she's meant to be a friend I'd hate to see your enemy,' she said. 'When I think how I opened our door and welcomed that girl into my home! Well, I simply can't believe she would treat you like this.'

Laura sighed just as her dad entered the room carrying a tray with three mugs of coffee. He kissed Laura on the top of her head as he passed by her and set the tray down onto the circular table. 'Now, Maggie, don't start winding yourself up. We've already talked about it this morning and we don't know the background to Jenny's behaviour in this situation. Our Laura needs support at a time like this, not weeping and wailing.'

Margaret folded her arms under her large bust and grunted. 'Humph, am I crying, Laura? No, I'm most certainly not. In fact, I've a good mind to go around to her house and give them both a piece of my mind!'

Startled, Laura jumped up. 'No, Mam. There's no need for that,' she gabbled, horrified at the thought of her tackling Phil and Jenny. 'It'll just show me up even more and I'm embarrassed enough already.'

Her dad smiled wickedly. 'Now, that would be a sight to behold,' he said. 'My money's on your mam any day of the week. She'd make mincemeat out of both of them!'

Margaret began to giggle and pushed her husband's arm affectionately. 'Stop it, David. This isn't the right time to mess about. We have to think seriously about what we're going to do and make a plan.'

'A plan?' Laura muttered with a churning stomach. She didn't like the sound of this and gave her dad a beseeching look.

He cocked his head to one side. 'Oh, but that's not necessary, Maggie. Laura already has her own plan, haven't you, love?'

Standing with his coffee mug in his hand behind his wife he mouthed the word, decorating, to Laura who nodded and told them her plans to re-decorate the house.

'Hmm,' Margaret considered. 'Out with the old, and in with the new. Now that is a good idea if you can you afford it?'

Laura nodded. 'I make more money than Phil does, Mam,' she said. 'And, I don't think he is in any position to argue about money at the moment. But I will see a solicitor.'

Laura had her mam's eyes and now they stared back at her glistening with pride. 'That's my girl,' she said. 'If you find a wallpaper you like I'll come over and hang it for you.'

Laura thanked her, finished the coffee and with their words of encouragement ringing in her ears she drove off to B&Q in the outskirts of Newcastle.

As Laura wandered up and down the aisles looking at colours of paint and wallpaper she sighed with indecision. Usually, she would look at things first and then get Phil's opinion before making a decision, but going forward she knew this was something she would be doing alone. As she stopped in front of an aubergine print which reminded her of Jenny's new decor she bit her lip. Maybe she should follow in Jenny's footsteps and hire a freelance interior designer to give her some ideas? Laura fondled the soft aubergine cushions and swallowed a lump in her throat as she thought of Jenny. No, she thought adamantly, I know I can do this myself. Jenny had used the designer because with a technical and methodical brain she openly admitted to never having any creative juices. But, I've got plenty, Laura determined. At work she was never short of new ideas for food, therefore, she reasoned, it was simply a matter of applying the creative side of her mind from food to decoration.

Laura paused in front of a duck-egg blue emulsion with a matching feature wallpaper and all the necessary soft furnishings. She smiled. In the past Phil had often said that blue was a cold colour, but this wasn't and had a warmth to it that she liked. It was fresh and light, and as the lounge windows were south facing the room was always flooded with sunshine – it would be perfect. With this decision made and her purchases in the trolley Laura's confidence grew and she headed to the bedroom section.

Suddenly, she stopped in her tracks and wondered if Phil had ever brought Jenny to their house and into their bedroom? No, she reasoned, he wouldn't do that – would he? Laura knew that once she had the thought in her mind she would need to take some definite action to stop thinking about it, and decided to order a new bed and bedroom furniture. This, she hoped, might wipe out the possibility of her old memories being sullied. Laura didn't want any trace of Phil left in their bedroom, and she chose a soft lemon colour and alabaster paint. She loved the calming colours together and bought new bed linen, curtains, and cushions to give it a whole new look.

As Laura made her way through the car park pushing the overloaded trolley she heard a man's voice call her name and swung around to see Luigi hurrying towards her. Damn. She was off sick with flu and she shouldn't appear well enough to be out shopping. Could Luigi be trusted to keep her secret? She shrugged her shoulders and decided the only way to find out was to ask.

'Hey, there,' she said smiling.

Luigi couldn't believe his luck. He'd spent hours since the night of the party worrying why Laura had disappeared so quickly and wishing there was a way he could see her. The sensible side of his brain told him she was a married woman, who was indeed married to his work colleague, but Luigi also knew that Phil was not a good man. He'd seethed with rage watching Phil cavort himself around the night club in

Leeds and then disappear into a back room with a lap dancer, which in his opinion showed a total lack of respect for his lovely wife. He'd thought long and hard since then, but knew it wasn't his place to tell Laura, and until she realised this for herself, there wasn't much he could do about the situation.

Luigi walked up to her and took the handles of the trolley to push it the last few yards to her car. 'This is too heavy for a little woman like you.'

'Oh, I'm stronger than I look,' she said then bit her lip. 'Actually, Luigi, I had to telephone work and report sick yesterday with the flu – which was a little white lie. I'm, well, I'm having a few problems at home at the moment, and ...' she paused, trying to decide how much more to say.

Luigi nodded and could see how uncomfortable she looked at this admission that her home life wasn't good. He wanted to reassure her that he was a friend who understood and who she could trust. 'Aah,' he muttered. 'Not to worry, it can occur to us all. I myself was guilty of this offence in Florence before I came here. My wife was not the easiest woman to negotiate with.'

Laura smiled and once again she saw the glint and twinkle in his green eyes as he stared at her. Did he look at every woman like this, she wondered, or was it just her? She giggled. 'Thanks, Luigi. I will be back to work soon,' she said beginning to unload her purchases into the back of the Mini.

He lifted the big tins of paint for her and placed them in the boot. 'Do not worry, Laura. Your little white lie is safe with me. I have my lips sealed.'

Laura stared at his full lips and wondered what they would feel like covering hers.

Luigi felt the attraction slam into his chest like a sledge hammer. He too stared at her face and at the soft grey eyes behind her glasses – he knew he hadn't been wrong. Since the first time they'd talked together he'd known she had a special quality and aura around her. And, when her shameful husband had embarrassed her by calling her fat in her lovely dress, he'd wanted to take him outside and hit him hard. That wasn't the way to treat such a beautiful woman, he thought, she should be treasured and honoured every day of her life. As she'd talked through her presentation Luigi had been mesmerised by the underlying strength she possessed and the professional way she held herself together after such a demeaning comment. She might be small and dainty, he thought, but she certainly had plenty of gusto.

Laura shook her head and cursed herself for day dreaming. She thanked him and walked alongside him wheeling her trolley over to the designated bay where Luigi rescued his own trolley.

He pointed to the small brown boxes in his trolley. 'I am delighted today,' he said. 'The shop ordered some Italian tiles for my bathroom and they've just arrived.'

Laura smiled as he opened the top box and lifted one out to show her.

'Oh, they are beautiful,' she said awestruck by the intricate gold weave through the cream and light brown design. Sighing, Laura thought of the plain white tiles in her bathroom with the grubby grouting.

Luigi nodded. 'Yes, so every time I shower I'll feel like I'm at home in Italy,' he said.

With inappropriate thoughts of standing close to him under a shower Laura blushed.

Luigi noticed the colour flush to her cheeks and wondered if she could possibly be thinking the same as him.

Laura handed the tile back to him and abruptly bid him goodbye then scampered back to her Mini and drove swiftly out of the car park.

As Luigi waved to her he whistled under his breath.

Laura, he whispered, feeling her name around his tongue and loving the sound of it. It suited her well.

By the end of the following week Laura had made great headway with the decoration and her mam had arrived to hang the wallpaper. She held the paste bucket for her mam who slapped thick paste onto lengths of the patterned wallpaper with her chubby hands and stubby fingers. Laura had finished decorating the bedroom which stood ready for the new bed and furniture.

The lounge walls had been painted and now Laura watched her mam expertly adding the last few lengths of paper to the feature wall. For as long as Laura could remember, her mam had done all the decorating at Ancroft Way. Laura's grandfather, who had died when she was a baby, had been a professional painter and decorator and had taught his daughter well.

'It's just a matter of time and patience, he used to say to me while I watched him,' Margaret said proudly. 'He certainly was a perfectionist at every job he tackled.'

Laura nodded, holding the bucket steady as her mam dipped the brush into it for more paste.

Laura had actually enjoyed having her at the house over the last two days and whereas often in the past she had struggled with conversation, now they'd chatted freely and easily. The radio played quietly in the background and Laura had a good lunch planned for them. Laura had tried her hardest to steer the conversation away from Phil and Jenny, but now her mam studied her from under a heavy dark brown fringe.

'I saw Jenny sitting on her garden wall this morning as your dad drove us here,' she said.

Laura raised an eyebrow. 'OK,' she said. 'Well, that's where she lives, Mam. So, I reckon that's where you would see her.'

Laura bit her lip aware that she sounded sullen and cheeky. 'Sorry, Mam,' she uttered looking down at the thick grey paste. 'I didn't mean it to sound like that.'

Margaret cocked her head a little as she climbed the ladder holding the rolled length of paper in one hand. 'I was bitching about Jenny to your Dad, who as usual cannot badmouth a person to save his soul. But, he did make one comment – he said that getting over a miscarriage wasn't easy, and that poor Jenny had had two losses to come to terms with.'

Laura gasped and looked up as with a handful of kitchen roll her mam smoothed out bubbles under the paper until it was flat. Margaret proceeded back down the ladder.

Laura pouted. 'So, Dad thinks that because Jenny has lost two babies it gives her the right to shag my husband?'

Margaret winced at the coarseness of her daughter's language, but shrugged her shoulders. 'You know your father; he can always come up with an excuse for anyone's troubled behaviour. But, I agree with you, it doesn't give her the right to do that, especially not to a friend,' she said. 'Miscarrying a baby isn't easy and I know exactly how she feels, but heavens above, if every woman went off the rails when that happened where would we be?'

Laura swallowed hard – her mouth dried with shock at her mam's words. She furrowed her eyebrows together. 'What do you mean, you know how she feels?'

Margaret's eyes filled with sadness. 'I lost a baby eighteen months after you were born,' she said. 'And it's something that never leaves you.'

'What!' Laura exclaimed. 'But why haven't you told me – was it a boy or girl?'

'A little brother,' she murmured picking up another length of wallpaper. 'But I was only four months gone when it happened. It was during the night while your dad was away at a mental health convention in London.'

Laura grabbed hold of her mam's hand that was ready
on the ladder to haul herself up with. She could feel the smoothness of her wedding band sunk into the fat on her fingers. 'Well, how did you cope?' Laura asked amazed at this revelation. 'I mean, who looked after you?'

'Your gran did. She kept you overnight while I was at the hospital and then stayed with me for the rest of the week. It happened quite regularly and was just something women had to get on with. There was none of this counselling malarkey then,' she said.

Laura whistled through her teeth. 'I bet Dad was devastated …'

Margaret began to climb the ladder again. 'He never knew I was pregnant,' she said airily. 'I didn't realise myself until two weeks before that, but I'd decided to wait until he came home to tell him. And when the baby died I figured there wasn't much point in upsetting him unnecessarily,'

'What?' Laura said gaping at her. She couldn't believe how blasé her mam was being about it all. Or how she could keep such a big secret from her dad – she'd thought they were really close. But, as Margaret descended the ladder again Laura saw her eyes were wet with tears. 'Oh, Mam,' she said with a sad ache in her chest. 'I wish you'd told us about it.'

'Well, it wasn't an easy time,' she said. 'You must remember I was seven years older than your father and his posh family in Hexham thought I wasn't good enough for him. You see, I was the underdog from the day we were married.'

Laura sighed. 'But Dad has never treated you like that
– he worships you.'

'Yes, he does,' she said with a dreamy expression in her eyes. 'But I figured that his parents would think of me as a failure.' Margaret rubbed her hands down the sides of her straight brown skirt. 'And I couldn't see the point in talking about something that no one could do anything about,' Margaret sniped. 'Come on, hold the bucket up,' she said. 'There's only two more lengths to go and we're done.'

As her mam smoothed the last length of wallpaper to the wall Laura thought back to her childhood and wondered if her mam's emotional outbursts where born out of insecurity. Laura also realised how privileged she was that her mam had shared this with her. Maybe it was something she only wanted to tell another woman and in her own clumsy way she was trying to help her understand

Jenny's behaviour. Did Jenny think of herself as a failure? Laura bit her lip, wondering why women punished themselves like this. A miscarriage was something beyond their control and just a simple act of nature.

When Margaret stood back down from the ladder Laura put both her arms around her and hugged her tightly.

'Stop that now,' Margaret said standing back and admiring her handiwork. 'Lovely job, even if I say so myself. It's a beautiful paper to hang.'

Laura could see the smile in the corner of her mouth and knew although she was being a little abrupt; she too had enjoyed their special moment. This trifle of an endearment was the most she could expect, but Laura knew in her mam's own way, she loved her dearly.

With the slam of the front door as Peter arrived home the moment was lost, and Laura thanked her mam profusely. The room was transformed with the light duck-egg blue colour scheme, and all three of them decided it looked amazing.

'Hey, Mam, we'll have to get you onto one of those property make-over shows on TV. You're becoming a whiz at this interior design stuff,' Peter teased on the Sunday night. He'd stayed at home during the last two weeks, but now he was preparing to go back to the halls of residence, and she was returning to work the next morning.

Laura grinned at him as she pushed a second pile of clean underwear into his holdall. 'I know,' she said. 'And the great thing is that I've loved doing it all.'

She perched on the edge of the settee and looked around the room. 'It should have been done years ago, but getting your father to do any decorating was impossible,' she mused to herself. 'I never dreamt I'd be able to do anything like this on my own.'

Peter snorted. 'Yeah, decorating isn't really in the same remit as shagging other women!'

Laura sighed at his bitterness and put her head on one side. 'Ah, love. I know it's been a hell of a shock, but he wasn't always like this. Why not try to remember the happy times you had with him?'

Peter pulled the zip along on his bag and grunted.

Laura hated to see him troubled and upset, but as her father had said, Peter would come to terms with it in his own time, and she knew she would have to be patient.

As Peter pulled on his denim jacket Laura felt torn in two. She'd loved having him at home and he'd been a tremendous support. It had also given her the drive to establish a new life-after-Phil routine, which if he hadn't been there, she wasn't sure she would have made such an effort. At the same time, however, she wanted him to get on with his own life and hated to see him worried about her. For the first few days after he'd punched his father Peter had followed her around the house, not so much in person, but with his eyes. If she'd left a room Laura knew his eyes had looked up from the TV or book he was reading and didn't return until she came back. This wasn't what she wanted for him and hoped in a few months they'd both get used to this new two-some unit. She also hoped that he would re-build his relationship with Phil, but sighed, knowing it was too early for this to happen.

'OK,' she said, hearing her father's car pull up outside the house. 'Whatever you've forgotten I can always drop off through the week.'

Laura had offered to drive him into the city, but Peter thought it would be better to go with his grandfather. And now that she felt a lump of emotion gather in the back of her throat, Laura knew this was probably for the best – she'd hate to blubber in front of his university friends.

Peter moved to the door and ran his hand through his thick hair. 'Will you be OK going back to work in the morning?'

Laura stood up on her tip toes and pecked his cheek. 'I'll be absolutely fine,' she said. 'There'll be so many emails in the morning it'll probably take me until lunch time to lift my head up.'

He hugged her close and then grinned as he went through the door. 'Make sure you text me tomorrow?'

'I will, and don't you be worrying about me. I'm OK.'

Chapter Ten

Just before eight o'clock the next morning Laura sat in the car park outside the factory, taking a few deep breaths. She'd mentally rehearsed answers to the questions that people might ask about her sick leave and what she would say to Phil, if and when she saw him.

Suddenly, a tap on the window of her Mini startled her. She turned to see Alex's bald head and familiar face grinning at her, and she opened the car door.

'Hey, Laura, it's great to see you back,' he said. 'I've missed you.'

As she locked the car door and walked with Alex babbling at break-neck speed about all the happenings, Laura sighed with relief – she was going to be all right.

In their office Laura booted up her computer and half listened to Alex's news, but then lifted her head up sharply at one piece of information.

'Well, at first, we all thought you and Jenny must have the same bug as she's been off sick since the weekend of the party, too,' he said. 'But you'll know all about her – is she any better?'

Laura nodded her head and made a mental note to remember that nobody knew what had happened. It was normal for them to think that she would know how Jenny was, she thought, as they were, or used to be, the best of friends. She mumbled a non-committal answer and bent her head to look at the inbox on the screen. 'Oh, God,' she groaned. 'Four hundred and twelve emails!'

Alex made coffee and left her to work. At eleven Muriel rang and asked Laura to go upstairs to her office and complete the return-to-work paperwork. As Laura made her way through the main office she glanced to the right and noticed Phil's office was empty. She sighed heavily – this was going to be a tricky conversation. Everyone would assume that she would know where Phil was and she cursed him and Jenny again for putting her in this situation at work.

When she sat down opposite Muriel in her small windowless office, Laura thought of her dad who had advised her to tell the truth. Instead of fabricating events, or telling more lies, which she was useless at, he had thought it best to tell the truth when necessary. Laura decided to confide in Muriel.

'You still look a little peaky to me,' Muriel said staring at Laura. 'And, you've lost weight.'

Laura smiled at the concern and kindness shining in the older lady's eyes. 'I'm fine, thanks,' she said. 'But I do need to tell you something in confidence.'

'My dear,' Muriel said sitting forward in her chair. 'Whatever is said in this room stays between these four walls.'

Laura watched Muriel twirl a pearl necklace around her bony fingers and she took a deep breath. She told Muriel that Phil had left and what with the shock and upset she'd not been able to face coming into work. 'So, we are now separated, Muriel,' she said. 'I'm really sorry for saying I had flu and wondered if you could put me down for two weeks unpaid leave.'

Muriel gasped. 'Dear God,' she flustered. 'I'd thought for a moment you were going to tell me that you were pregnant! Of course – I'll sort the paperwork out.'

Laura sighed and began to play with a pencil that was lying on Muriel's desk. If only, she wished. If only Phil hadn't changed and they were still as happy as they'd always been and none of the rotten stuff had happened. She felt Muriel's thin hand cover her own and squeeze it hard. Laura winced slightly at the strength in her old hand.

'Laura,' Muriel said. 'I've known you both for too many years now to remember. And, I'm saying this from the bottom of my heart – I'm truly sorry to hear that.'

Laura looked up and smiled. 'Thanks, Muriel. But until I have time to get my head around what's happened I don't really want everyone to know about it and have to talk about him.'

Muriel's telephone began to ring and she apologised then picked up the receiver. This gave Laura a few moments to think about her next words. She couldn't see any reason at this point to tell her that Phil was with Jenny because it may only complicate matters and if Jenny was still off sick, it would give her more space to make further decisions. She'd play the rest of the week by ear, she thought, and see what happened. Laura sat back in the chair. The office was warm and stuffy and a slight aroma of Ana Ana perfume hung in the air and she ran a finger around her white shirt collar as she began to perspire.

'Sorry, honey,' Muriel said. 'It's the boss wanting more coffee.'

Laura smiled and relaxed knowing the worst was over and signed the paperwork Muriel had ready.

Muriel muttered, 'Well, at least this week won't be so bad for you with Phil being down in London at Sainsbury's.'

Laura nodded. 'We're not really talking, Muriel, so I don't know what he's up to any more. And, to be honest I don't want to know.'

'Of course,' Muriel said. 'Well, he's not back in the office until Thursday which will be easier for you. It's going to be strange for us all getting used to this, but never fear, we'll manage. And if there's anything I can do to help – all you have to do is pick up the phone.'

Laura thanked her and stood up to leave. She longed for fresh air and felt slightly claustrophobic in the cramped space.

Just as she headed towards the door Muriel asked, 'Oh, Laura, how's Jenny doing?'

Laura stopped in her tracks not knowing what to say. 'Well,' she hedged.

'Isn't it awful? I got such a shock when her sister rang and told me she was having treatment for severe depression. Kate said it could take months for her to be well again.'

Laura nodded and hurried from the room. Outside the office she took big deep breaths of air and then slipped into the toilets. Her mind raced as she tried to digest the information about Jenny and she began to put the pieces together. Obviously, her dad had known something about Jenny's condition, although Laura knew he would never divulge patient information. And, she thought, reaching back in her mind to Sunday's conversation with Phil, he'd said Jenny was in Durham.

She took a paper towel and dampened it under the cold tap to rub across the back of her neck while mixed emotions flooded through her. Up until that night, which was how she now referred to it in her mind, Laura would have been terribly worried about Jenny if she was really ill. In fact, she probably wouldn't have left her side. But now, she thought, shaking her head in confusion, how was she supposed to feel – did Jenny's dreadful behaviour wipe out the other twenty years of friendship? It was a natural instinct to worry about Jenny, but then at the same time she still hated her for what she'd done with Phil. She swallowed hard and threw the paper towel into the bin. How in God's name, she raged, am I supposed to cope with all of this?

Laura's answer came through work. At a meeting in the afternoon with the MD and Luigi she learned that the company had been invited to bid for a large chunk of business with a new customer in Ireland. She was asked to work closely with Luigi on this special project to develop a new range of fish and seafood. They left the office together and Luigi followed her downstairs.

Laura felt like skipping down the stairs – this was just what she needed to help keep her mind off Phil and Jenny. 'My mind is buzzing with ideas,' Laura said smiling.

Luigi grinned. 'Then I will come to your office now and we can buzz together?'

Laura looked at the mischievous look on his face and burst into laughter. 'OK,' she said. 'Let's get buzzing!'

Phew, Luigi thought, the gods are smiling down on me at the moment. If there was one person in this company he would love to spend time with every day it was Laura. From the day he'd shown her the new tiles in the car park he hadn't been able to stop thinking about her. She had, as the English said, got right under his skin. The attraction he'd felt as she looked back into his eyes had startled him. He'd never experienced love, or passion, at first sight before.

'Thank you for not telling anyone about my shopping trip,' Laura said over her shoulder as she reached the bottom step before him.

He smiled. 'Laura, I told you then, and I want you to believe me when I say this. Anything you want to tell me will always be confidential. I'm not, and never have been, a tell-tale.'

She grinned and casually touched his shoulder, 'Thank you, Luigi.'

'I have it right, yes? The word is tell-tale?'

Laura began to walk towards her office. 'Perfect,' she said.

As Luigi followed her into the office he thought about the way she'd said his name. It sounded warm and friendly, maybe even inviting, as though there was more to come. The gentle touch of her small hand on his shirt had sent waves of tingling through his body and he breathed deeply. You need to take care, he warned himself; you could be heading into trouble with feelings like these.

With a mug of coffee each Laura cleaned a table in the corner of her office. She pulled files out of cabinets, recipe books from overhead shelves, and magazines from racks. 'Right, shall I start buzzing first?' Laura teased.

Luigi threw his head back and laughed. 'It's good to see you laugh again, Laura,' he said. 'Your face has looked sad for too long.'

He looked into her gentle grey eyes and sighed – her soft and compassionate nature seemed to envelop him and he longed to be closer to her. She was so very different in every respect, he thought happily, to his wife and the many Italian women he'd known in the past. There was no haughty confidence surrounding her as there was in her friend, Jenny. Luigi remembered when he'd first arrived and how Jenny had given him a come-on look, but her hard manner had reminded him so much of his estranged wife it had made him shudder and he'd kept his distance.

Laura nodded and thought how right he was. She couldn't remember the last time she'd actually laughed out loud and it felt good. Especially, she thought, as the laughter was with him. She'd thought about the day in the car park many times over the last two weeks and had decided when their eyes locked together and she'd felt all the hairs on her arms stand to attention, it was merely in her imagination. And, she'd reassured herself, that the feelings of desire were completely normal as she had months of pent-up frustration on board without an outlet. The thought of a good-looking man standing under a shower was enough to turn any woman's head.

Laura shook the thoughts from her mind, and began listing the popular fish species they had to work with that met the Irish budget – she opened a recipe book and they both became engrossed in their work and discussions.

By six that night Laura finally lifted her arms above her head and stretched. Her back was aching with sitting on the hard plastic office chair but she felt exhilarated with the plan they'd put together.

Luigi too stood up and rolled his shoulders sighing heavily. 'These chairs are not good for the spine,' he said. 'And I'm a little too heavy at the moment.'

Laura looked at his slight pot-belly hanging over the waistband of his navy trousers. He'd already removed his jacket and the pale green shirt he wore seemed to accentuate the deep green of his eyes. At five-foot seven, Luigi was what she would call chunky, but not fat. She could see his strong biceps filling the sleeves of his shirt, and a broad manly chest that tapered down to slimmer hips. She smiled. 'You're not too heavy,' she reassured him.

He raised an eyebrow. 'I think you are being too English and too kind,' he said. 'It is the food, you see. When food has the great flavour I cannot resist it!'

'I'm a little like that myself,' she replied. 'I suppose it's the downside to working in the food industry. We are surrounded by food; we talk about it all day.'

Luigi nodded thoughtfully. 'But, your husband has great restraint. No matter how good the food is Phil can stop himself and say, enough! He is also a fan of the gym and staying fit.'

At the mention of Phil, Laura felt her spirits dip and she began to stack the books and magazines into piles. 'Hmm,' she muttered.

Luigi could have kicked himself. He could see by the mention of her husband she had closed up in defence, and he cursed his stupid thoughtlessness. If Laura was having problems at home the last thing she would want to do is talk about him at work. He had to make amends, because he didn't want to leave a lovely afternoon together in a bad light.

'So, tomorrow you will make these recipes and we can taste them?' Luigi asked gently laying a hand on her shoulder.

Laura could see concern in his thoughtful expression and smiled. 'Yes, I'll get some sea bass and sea bream from the factory and we'll get started.'

Luigi walked towards the door. 'Ah, sea bass, *bellissimo*!' he cried.

Clearing the table, Laura giggled and switched out the lights then left the office.

The following morning Laura wandered along the corridor towards her office door and stopped outside Jenny's door. She fingered the name plate and sighed – it felt strange to be here at work without Jenny. The rage she'd felt towards her was beginning to ebb and she was left feeling thoroughly mixed up and confused. Laura missed popping into Jenny's office for a quick chat, and had, without realising it over the years, become dependent upon her friend's shoulder to cry on. Laura sighed, Jenny had been her main-stay and it was only now that she understood the reason behind one of her mam's favourite expressions, you don't know what you've got until it's gone.

Laura bit her lip, and felt tears prick at the back of her eyes. How could Jenny have gone behind her back and lied to her? Day after day it rankled at her because they'd both been through so much together.

Laura remembered their university days and how she'd been the shy, anxious fresher whereas Jenny had been full of swagger and confidence. With a bundle of books under her arms one morning Laura had hurried down the stairs into the open courtyard then stumbled and gave a small yelp as all the books scattered to the ground. A crowd of third-year students had howled with exaggerated laughter at her until Jenny stepped up next to Laura, gave the older students a mouthful of abuse and bent down to help Laura pick up the books. She had been her saviour that day and had continued in the same way ever since. As Laura had got to know Jenny she'd realised the swagger was a false bravado born out of the embittered childhood she'd had. David and Margaret had welcomed Jenny into their family and more than once Laura had heard her dad say, Jenny didn't know how to express or cope with affection because as a child she'd never been shown any. At the end of the three years Jenny was like the sister she'd never had.

Laura headed into her own office now and slumped down at the desk. She crossed her arms over her chest and rubbed her arms, wishing she had someone to hug her. It suddenly dawned upon her that after nearly three weeks she wasn't actually missing Phil half as much as she missed Jenny. How could that be, she thought, he was, and still is, my husband, but his betrayal doesn't hurt as much as Jenny's did.

Laura shook her head and decided to put it out of her mind for the rest of the day. She removed her jacket put on a white coat and hair net and strode into the development kitchen. With the radio playing and a mug of hot coffee Laura began to collect all the ingredients she needed. Alex joined her and took the list of fresh fish she needed into the factory, returning with bags of sea bass, bream, and prawns.

At the sound of a voice calling, Laura looked up from the bench to see Luigi standing in the doorway. Her heart gave a little leap at the sight of his familiar face.

'Can I come in?' he asked grinning.

Luigi felt a surge of heat radiate through his chest and a lightness of his limbs as he looked at Laura. She had the recipes they'd scratched out together the day before spread out on the work bench and he could feel the relaxed working atmosphere between her and Alex permeate through the kitchen. Whatever upset she was going through at home, he thought, she obviously wasn't letting it affect her work, and Luigi decided it was a characteristic he really liked.

'Of course you can,' she said.

Alex handed Luigi a coat and hair net to wear and he removed his black jacket placing a carrier bag onto the counter. Laura noticed he was wearing a plain T-shirt and casual chino trousers and as he pushed an arm through the white coat she nodded in satisfaction – she'd been right, his bicep muscles were twice as thick and strong as Phil's were.

'I'm pleasantly surprised,' she said as Luigi joined them. 'Not many of the commercial team ever venture into the kitchen or factory areas. But it's good to see you are obviously interested in the products you'll have to sell.'

Luigi stood next to her at the work surface and removed a bag of Carnaroli rice from the carrier bag.

'I brought you this to try in the risotto stuffing. We love it in Italy and I thought you'd like to try it?'

Luigi stood beside her and inhaled her smell. It wasn't a fragrant or perfume aroma, but more of a clean freshness that clung around her neck and shoulders. He stared at the nape of her neck and longed with such passion to touch her that he had to breathe deeply and distract himself.

Laura looked at the rice and began to read the description on the back of the packet. 'OK,' she nodded. 'Tell me all about it.'

Luigi grinned. Any other professional might have brushed aside his intervention preferring to stay with their own tried and tested, but obviously Laura was open to new ideas and tolerant of people's suggestions. 'Well, it is a white rice grown in the Italian towns of Novara and Vercelli, near Milan. We think it is the finest rice to make risotto because of the short, how do you say, plump grain?'

Laura nodded and smiled with understanding then raised an eyebrow gesturing for him to carry on as she peeled the skin from a garlic bulb.

'Well, it absorbs much more liquid than other rice's which makes the risotto rice fluffy and it is never ...' Luigi grappled for the English word, 'sticky?'

Laura nodded thoughtfully, 'Ah, so, is it in the same family as Arborio rice?'

She smiled at the boyish eager expression on his face and could hear the pride and affection in his voice as he spoke about his home country – she wanted to encourage him to become more involved in the project and take part.

Luigi nodded excitedly. 'Oh, yes. The grain is larger but when it has cooked it has the lovely creamy texture because of the extra starching.'

Alex took the bag from Laura and offered to wash the rice, but Luigi shook his head. 'No thank you, Alex. It is imperative not to wash the rice grains before cooking. The high starch allows the rice to keep its shape during the slow cooking of risotto while it absorbs the flavours.'

Alex nodded and began to gather the other ingredients for the risotto-style stuffing.

Luigi smiled loving the fact that, not only was he next to Laura, but they both seemed to welcome and accept him as part of their little team. He thrust his chest out and planted his legs further apart. 'And, you see, the major advantage is that the rice, when it is removed from heat, will remain at its same texture rather than soften minute by minute like Arborio rice does.'

Alex filled a pan with cold water. He said, 'Now that will be a huge benefit especially to busy chefs who can easily get distracted whilst cooking.'

They all agreed and Laura winked at Alex who she knew was doing his best to make Luigi feel welcome. Why that was, Laura thought, she wasn't too sure, but all the same she was glad Alex liked him too. Alex had never made a secret of the fact that Phil wasn't his favourite person in the company, and she'd noticed of late, that if

Phil did venture into their office, Alex always made a hasty retreat.

Laura crushed the garlic bulb and turned towards Luigi, 'Do you want to chop these onions and spinach?'

Luigi smiled and Laura felt her body swoon a little as she stared into his shinning green eyes. She'd always thought that once a person, male or female, had a white mop cap covering their hair they all looked the same, and it was often difficult to determine, exactly who they were. But, she decided happily, no one could ever confuse Luigi with anyone else – his eyes were his most striking feature.

Luigi stretched his arms out in front of him and cracked the knuckles in his fingers. 'Of course,' he cried. 'I'd love to help.'

Laura looked down at his chunky fingers and the fine black hairs on the back of his hands. They were masculine hands, not like Phil's delicate ones, and she wondered briefly if Luigi had a gentle touch. As she lifted her eyes to look into his she felt a frisson of attraction pass between them which made her shiver. My God, she thought, it felt like an electric current running through her body from the hair on her head to the end of her toes.

The noise of the telephone in the office ringing broke her reverie and out of the corner of her eye she saw Alex hurry through to answer the call. Quickly, she reminded herself that she was at work, dragged her eyes away from Luigi, and shook the thoughts from her mind. He certainly was a good-looking man, she thought, trying to concentrate on blending the Mediterranean seasonings. But, she cautioned herself, after what she'd been through over the last few weeks having feelings for a new man was the last thing she needed. With her professional head back in place, she conceded, this was neither the right time, and it certainly wasn't the right place.

Surely, Luigi thought, she had felt that moment between them? His blood was thumping through his veins at a great speed and the longing just to touch her hand was driving him mad. He cursed his Italian blood and passionate nature while at the same wondered why she had backed away and lowered her eyes. It was only then he noticed that Alex had slipped back into the corner of the kitchen. Hmm, Luigi nodded in understanding, Laura was indeed the consummate professional at all times, which made him appreciate her all the more.

Aromas of basil and rosemary filled the kitchen and Luigi sniffed loudly. He babbled a few complimentary words in Italian. 'Ah,' he breathed. 'It is as though I am at home cooking in my own kitchen!'

Laura smiled and marvelled at how harmoniously they worked together. At home she'd hated having Phil in the kitchen: their personalities had clashed, but more than anything, she resented being ordered around by him. Luigi, she decided, had a more easy-going personality and seemed to be completely laid back. Laura mentioned his ease in the kitchen and he told her about his large family in Florence.

'I'm surrounded with women!' he cried and pulled a comical face at Alex. 'My mamma is lovely but she is very bossy, and my two sisters are much worse!'

Laura nodded, 'You must miss them dreadfully?'

'No, we talk all the time. I speak to Mamma every other day,' he said throwing his arms up into the air. 'And my sisters never stop texting me.'

At lunch time, they tasted sea bass stuffed with Mediterranean vegetables and spinach. 'If I close my eyes I could be eating in a trattoria in Florence!' Luigi stated confidently.

Laura assessed the clear crisped skin on the whole sea bass and colourful stuffing settled snugly in the centre. 'Hmm,' she said. 'I think we need to drop the amount of stuffing by ten per cent if we are to hit our costings. But I love the combination of flavours with the tender flakes of fish. Let's hope the Irish like the concept of eating a whole sea bass. Sometimes in this country people are still put off by a whole fish with the head and eyes.'

Luigi threw his head back and laughed. 'Ha! I am still getting used to the strange English traditions! You are so very different to the rest of Europe.'

They continued onto other recipes and settled upon a sea bream coated and stuffed with cream cheese and orange zest to show as their second favourite product. Some dressings were removed or altered until they were all satisfied, and amidst cries from Luigi of *delizioso*, they were all pleased with their morning's work.

During the next few days Luigi became a regular visitor to the development kitchen and Laura's office, and she now thought of him as a good friend. She'd tried to stop staring into his eyes in an effort to keep her feet firmly on the ground, however, there were still times when the sound of his voice or the remains of his spicy aftershave hanging around the room made her squirm with pleasure. And, as hard as she tried she couldn't help looking forward to his visits and decided as she lay in bed one night, he genuinely was a special guy. Laura also noticed that Luigi was a tactile person and once she had got over her initial reserve and became used to the European custom of kissing each other on both cheeks, she relaxed into his company.

On Thursday morning after a meeting in the office Luigi hung around waiting for everyone to leave and when they were alone he gave her a gentle hug, thanked her, and told her their new product range was magnificent. Laura felt herself glow with a warm affection for him.

After he'd left the office and without thinking she grabbed her mobile to text Jenny about Luigi's hug and kisses. After typing one word and with a sickening thud she remembered what Jenny had done and letter by letter she deleted the text.

Laura slumped down onto a chair and sighed in dismay.

She wanted to tell someone how she felt about Luigi and how she wondered if he felt the same way towards her. It was going to take more than a few weeks to curb the habit of talking everything over with Jenny, she thought wearily. And, in a crazy way, she also wanted to talk about Phil. How sad to have no one that I can trust with my secrets, she thought, staring dumbly at the computer screen. And, even though she reasoned that Jenny had been the one who'd betrayed her confidences and secret thoughts, she still missed her.

She shook her head wondering how that could be, and felt a deep sadness fill her insides.

She wanted, no she needed, more than anything else, the answers to questions that constantly tumbled around in her mind. She lifted her shoulders in pride knowing she'd rather die than lower herself to ask Phil, but then she groaned, the only other person who knew these answers was Jenny.

Had Phil always fancied Jenny and over the years had Laura blindly missed the signs that were obvious to everyone else? Or was it only a recent fling as Phil claimed it to be? One of her major worries was that the affair had being going on when the four of them had been such great friends. But, she puzzled, that couldn't be true because Jenny had been totally in love and devoted to Steve. They'd married the year after she had married Phil and they'd both been each other's bridesmaids. Laura frowned, and the biggest mystery that she couldn't fathom was how Jenny was attracted to Phil. Laura knew what Jenny's taste in men was – Phil certainly didn't fit the bill.

Laura's stomach twisted with agitation, or was it hunger, she pondered, and glancing at the clock realised she'd been lost in thought far too long. Her father would be waiting for her to have lunch. As she headed out through the main doors into the sunshine Luigi was stepping up to the doors.

'Hey there,' she said smiling. 'What are you up to?'

With his black jacket casually slung over his shoulder, and a forlorn look around his eyes he told her how hungry he was and how little he was looking forward to a ham salad.

Laura felt sorry for him and took a deep breath. She would probably live to regret this, and knew she shouldn't be encouraging him whilst at work, but what the hell, she thought, and said. 'Well, if you want to come over to the hospital you can eat lunch with me and my father?'

Luigi clapped his hands together in delight. 'Ah, Laura, I would like that very much. I would be honoured to meet your father.'

Laura smiled as they waked easily through the car park together.

Luigi sat opposite David and sighed with happiness. He could see now where Laura got her personality from – her father, he decided, was an exceptional man. True to Italian family values Luigi held a huge respect for David as the head of the family. He also felt in awe of him as David explained his medical career and how, even after forty years, he still got such a buzz out of helping people turn their lives around. As Laura and her dad gently swapped friendly banter Luigi sensed the special close relationship she had with him. A sudden moment of melancholy swept over him making him realise how much he missed his own father. He'd been dead for eight years now, he told Laura and David, but there wasn't a day that passed by when he didn't think of him.

Luigi turned to look at Laura and saw her bite her lip. He'd got used to this little quirk of hers now when she was thinking about something, and it suddenly dawned upon him that he couldn't bear the thought of never seeing her again. Within a week of working closely together, and although he'd managed to keep his feelings for her away from work, he knew she was a very special woman.

Up until Luigi mentioned his dead father, Laura had been enjoying herself so much the time had ran away with her. The friendly relaxed atmosphere, coupled with a glass of red wine and beef chasseur, had made all three of them quite light-hearted and gay. There weren't many people that her dad didn't get along with, she decided, after all talking was a large part of his job, but she could tell within minutes of introducing him to Luigi that he liked him immensely.

She touched the side of Luigi's arm. 'I'm so sorry to hear about your father,' she commiserated. 'It must be especially hard for your mother while you are away from home?'

Luigi nodded then smiled. 'It is fine really,' he murmured. 'Thank you for asking, but my mother has remarried and is happy with another man now. Although, there is, how do you say, no loving lost between me and him.'

Laura giggled at his phrase and her Dad chortled.

'Well,' David said, 'As long as your mother is happy that's the main thing.'

'Yes, thank you,' he said politely. 'My father was a great man too and ran his own shoe-making business all his life as his father before him. But my oldest sister took over the business which was a great relief to me as I wanted to make my career elsewhere and loved the idea of travelling.'

David said, 'Ah, you should get along very well with my daughter then who has a *healthy* obsession with shoes – it has cost me a small fortune over the years.'

They all laughed and Laura pushed her dad's arm playfully.

David asked, 'And, how did you end up working here in the North-east? Not that we aren't delighted to have you, of course.'

Luigi shrugged his shoulders. 'Two things really, I studied in Rome and then Paris and then following my father's advice I returned home to Florence to work and married my childhood sweetheart, Adrina, who was also his best friend's daughter. Within six months I realised we had nothing in common and for the first time in my life my father's advice had been proven wrong.'

'Aah,' David muttered in his steady matter-of-fact tone.

Luigi nodded, 'Then things turned from bad to worse when my wife left with another man, and my mother's new husband moved into the house. We started the divorce proceedings and I knew then it was time to find a new life for myself and when I applied for jobs I had the choice of a job in Kent, or here, so here I am.'

'Well, I'd say that Kent's loss is our gain,' David replied and winked. 'Wouldn't you, Laura?'

Laura sighed happily. She could feel Luigi's black trouser leg against her thigh as without realising and being so engrossed in his story she had inched further along the grey plastic seat next to him. The heat seemed to radiate through the thin cotton skirt she wore and her heart swelled with sympathy for him.

He too had suffered at the hands of deceit and betrayal, and instead of pulling her leg away from him she sat perfectly still, loving his presence and fighting the urge to climb into his lap and wrap herself around him. Laura nodded in agreement towards her dad and Luigi feeling her cheeks blush with contentment.

The next morning as Laura sat at her computer compiling recipe sheets and costing figures for the products they'd developed, she marvelled at what a good week she'd had. At the end of their lunch break her dad had invited Luigi to Ancroft Way on Sunday to sample a traditional North-east Sunday lunch and the thought of seeing him again made her tingle with anticipation.

Last night when she'd climbed into bed she'd gone over everything Luigi had told them about his family, and especially his wife. Apart from the turmoil she'd just been through with Phil, it was the main reason why she'd made herself pull back from Luigi. She knew first-hand how it felt to be the cheated wife at home wondering where her husband was and who he was with. It was a helpless, horrible feeling that she wouldn't wish upon any other woman. So, to find out that Luigi's wife was the one who had left him and there were no children involved cleared her conscience. Not, of course, she thought, that they'd done anything yet to feel guilty about, but she hoped, no she prayed, that one day in the future they might.

Earlier, Laura had told Peter via text that her week hadn't been as bad as she was expecting, and how neither Jenny nor his dad was at work. But, later that afternoon when she heard the office door open and looked up to see Phil standing in the doorway, she knew she'd spoken too soon.

'Got a minute?' he asked, sliding around the door and closing it quietly behind him.

Phil looked tired, pale, and anxious. He chewed the inside of his cheek as he stood in front of her with his hands thrust deep down in his pockets.

Laura knew it was common courtesy to ask him to sit down but she didn't want him to, in fact, she didn't want him anywhere near her. 'Phil, I'm really busy,' she warned.

'Yeah, I've heard about the big drive for the Irish business,' he said. 'I just wanted to let you know that things haven't worked out as expected with Jenny. And last week I moved into a flat in Jesmond for the time being.'

Laura dropped the pencil she'd been holding and stared at him. 'You've left her?' Laura asked struggling to understand.

Phil shuffled from foot to foot. His shoes made a squeaky noise on the laminate floor. 'Yeah, apparently Jenny cannot forgive herself for what she's done to you and it's sort of coming between us,' he said. 'I wanted you to know where I was because I was hoping Peter would ring me or come to visit.'

Laura shook her head incredulously. She couldn't believe that it had only lasted for a few weeks. She glared at him, remembering the hurt and pain he had put her through which now seemed pointless. 'So, you've destroyed our family over a trivial fling? I thought you were supposed to be crazy about her?'

Phil sighed with obvious irritation. 'Look, our marriage is over, Laura. No matter who I'm with or not with. I hope you can understand that.'

Phil slid a piece of paper across the desk towards her. 'That's my address. And I know Peter was upset with me when it happened, but I hope when he calms down he will want to come and see me.'

Laura took a deep breath. She wanted to lash out at him, but clenched her hands together under the desk in an effort to stay in control. She also knew that in the future, Peter might want to spend some time with the worthless piece of crap that was standing in front of her now. She sighed knowing her son had to come first. 'I'll give him the address, Phil, although I think it's way too soon. But that, I suppose, will be up to him,' she stated.

Phil nodded. 'Thanks,' he said. 'I know I've treated you badly, Laura, but please don't poison him against me.'

Laura seethed. Even at a time like this, the only person Phil could think about was himself. She tutted her annoyance and shook her head in dismay. It should be obvious to him that she would always put Peter's wellbeing before her own feelings. Phil cast his eyes down. 'Sorry, that was a stupid thing to say I know you wouldn't do that.'

'Exactly,' Laura stated. She raised her shoulders, wanting to let him know that she too, was moving forward. 'Also, I want to put the house on the market straight away.'

He raised an eyebrow in surprise. 'You do?'

'Yes,' she pouted. 'You're not the only one who wants a fresh start.'

Phil nodded his agreement and quietly left the office while Laura put her head down on her forearms and blew out a noisy breath of relief. It had been nearly three weeks since she'd seen him and Laura shook her head in amazement at how little she actually felt. Phil had been the love of her life, and now, within such a short space of time, she could hardly bear to look at him.

She threw the costing sheet she'd been working at aside and gulped at her bottle of water. Should it be taking longer than this to get over him, she wondered, or, maybe this was what people called delayed shock and suddenly it might hit her? But at the moment, every time she thought of Phil, the image of him standing naked on Jenny's landing haunted her and she quickly brushed it aside. Perhaps in years to come she thought, she would remember him how he used to be – a sweet and loving husband and the father of her son.

As Laura got ready to leave for the weekend, two of Jenny's QA assistants came into her office to ask a favour. Apparently, they were all worried about their boss and they asked Laura if she could drop off a bouquet of flowers and a get well soon card to Jenny's house. They knew Laura lived in the same street as Jenny, and hoped it wouldn't be too much trouble. Laura's mind raced. She wanted to refuse, but couldn't think of a reason quickly enough, and had to agree.

Shortly after six, Laura drove into the peaceful cul de sac and looked at the front of Jenny's house for the first time in days. She pulled up at the kerb and decided now that she knew Phil wasn't there things were easier.

Usually Laura was the type of person who disliked and avoided confrontations if at all possible, but there was a large part of her that wanted to scream and shout at Jenny. Laura's heart began to race and she cowered with the thought of more emotional upset. Quickly, she wondered if she could leave the flowers on the step, ring the doorbell, jump back in the car, and hurry back to her house without seeing Jenny. But, she reasoned, the flaw in this plan was that if Jenny was still in Durham then the flowers would wilt and die on the step which would be grossly unfair to the QA assistants who had bought them.

No, she breathed deeply, she would have to ring the doorbell, hand them over, and then she would leave as soon as possible.

Chapter Eleven

Jenny stood in her kitchen, looking out of the window onto her small back garden, deciding the grass needed to be cut. She gulped large mouthfuls of cold water in an effort to quench the dryness in her mouth. It was one of the side effects of the anti-depressant tablets she was taking and the psychiatrist had told her that it could take four to six weeks before she would feel the benefits. However, her general mood had lifted slightly already, and at her counselling sessions, the therapist had commented upon her improved outlook. With the help of the sedatives she was now sleeping throughout the night and although she knew it would be a long time before she chased all her demons away, the need for alcohol to dim the pain was beginning to lessen each day.

She rinsed the glass in the washing-up bowl, and sighed remembering the mess she'd been in three weeks ago after the dreadful night of the party. If there was one image, she thought, which would haunt her dreams for the rest of her life it would be the devastation in Laura's eyes and her tiny crumpled face. The therapist had twice tried to get her to talk about Laura, but Jenny had shook her head, squeezed her eyes shut, and fought against the racking sobs that threatened to engulf her. Jenny remembered her foster mother and a phrase she'd sometimes used: if I live to be a hundred, I'll never forgive myself, and sighing now Jenny knew exactly what it meant.

Laura was just always there. Through all the big occasions in her life, good or bad, Laura had stood by her. When she'd been crying and clinging to Steve after the loss of their first baby Laura had emptied the nursery, taking the cot and Moses basket back to her own house to store in the loft, and returned clothes and equipment to the stores from where they'd been bought. And, if she thought even further back in time, Laura's family had also taken her under their wings when she was eighteen and at university. She remembered the warmth of their welcome every time she entered their house with Laura – it had felt more like home to her than even her foster parents' house.

And this is how I've repaid them all; Jenny cringed with shame. She'd told her counsellor that the guilt she would have to live with seemed insurmountable, but he'd reassured her that she would, in time, find a way through it. Jenny wasn't convinced. It was only now that the treatment was beginning to work and the effects of the alcoholic fog she'd been living under was wearing off, that she was able to think more rationally. Out of all the men in the area why in God's name had she chosen Phil? She must have been temporarily insane. The memories of the drunken sex and her hysterical out-of-control behaviour still frightened her, and she knew whatever treatment the psychiatrist advised she would complete willingly because she never wanted to feel like that again.

However, Jenny thought, if there was one tiny good thing to come out of this whole sorry mess, it was that she was close to her sister again. Jenny smiled, thinking of Kate and how she'd been her saviour taking her back to Durham and putting her to sleep in the guest bedroom. Kate had woken her at intervals insisted she ate and drank, and then walked her like a zombie to the toilet and back to bed.

'It's as though you've lost three days of your life asleep in the bedroom,' Kate had said when Jenny was finally dressed and wandering around their house. Jenny had agreed and although she was, and always would be, eternally grateful for Kate's help, she'd insisted upon returning to her own home. The loss of control had been a major incident in her life and she'd needed the chance to attend the counselling sessions with her own thoughts. At Kate's home she had to wear a brave face when her nephews were around.

'I just need the space and time to think about what's happened to me and why I've had the breakdown,' Jenny had reassured Kate. 'And, it'll be much easier for my doctor's appointments and counselling sessions.'

But Kate hadn't looked convinced and had wanted Jenny to stay a while longer. Kate frowned. 'But you shouldn't be on your own at a time like this. Not unless you want to be back with Phil, of course?'

Jenny had shuddered with revulsion. 'No. That's one mistake I'll never make again. As soon as I get back I'll insist that he leaves,' she'd stated.

And she had. Kate had driven Jenny back home and although the discussion with Phil hadn't been easy, Jenny had surprised herself by quietly but firmly insisting he leave her house and check into a hotel.

Jenny wandered back into the lounge now and settled on the settee to watch the evening news. She turned the remote control over and over in her hand, remembering the embarrassing scene with Phil.

'But we can make it work. Just give us a chance,' he'd begged, trying to wrap his arms around her.

Jenny had flinched at the contact. His cloying smell of aftershave brought back memories of them sweating and writhing in bed together and she'd shuddered uncontrollably.

'No, Phil. It won't work. I don't want to be with you or anyone else,' she'd said. 'I just want to be on my own.'

She'd watched his face turn pale and his eyes narrow at her rejection. He'd removed his arms and then traced her lips with his index finger. 'Come on,' he cajoled. 'Let's drink some vodka and you can wrap those big lips around me again.'

Appalled at the thought that she couldn't exactly remember where she'd had her lips Jenny had taken a step back from him and shaken her head.

Phil had stepped towards her and grabbed her arm. 'Please, Jenny. Come upstairs to bed. I want you to go on top like you did before.'

'*No!*' she'd shouted and folded her arms across her chest as if in self-defence. 'I'm never going to drink again. Now, please leave. Go upstairs and pack your things.'

While Phil had been upstairs packing she'd hurried into the kitchen and retrieved bottles of vodka and wine from her hiding-places. Slowly, but with steely determination she'd poured every last drop down the kitchen sink and then heard Phil clash out of the front door.

Now, at the tinkle of the doorbell Jenny started and jumped up from the settee. Who could this be, she thought, hurrying through into the hallway to open the door. When she saw Laura standing on the step holding an enormous bouquet of flowers, she caught her breath.

'*Laura!*' The sight of her best friend brought a huge lump to her throat and she swallowed hard. Laura's small vulnerable face and gentle eyes behind the clear frames of her glasses was too much for Jenny and she couldn't stop her eyes brimming with tears.

If Jenny had been surprised to see her friend, Laura was even more shocked at Jenny's appearance and gasped loudly.

Laura stared at Jenny. Her face and neck looked gaunt as she had lost so much weight. Her cheeks were hollowed and her collarbones prominent under the grey V-neck T-shirt she wore. Her usual blonde sleek highlights were long since gone, and her parting was grey with an overgrown fringe which Jenny now swept aside with her fingers. Laura noticed the spots on her forehead and her bitten finger nails which were picked down to the quick.

Jenny dabbed at her wet eyes with the back of her hand and opened the door further. 'Oh, God, it's so good to see you – please come in,' she said stepping back slightly.

But Laura was still having trouble collecting her thoughts. Although Muriel had told her that Jenny was ill with depression she hadn't, for some reason, expected her to look any different. As Laura looked into Jenny's dull and lifeless eyes, the only words she could think of to sum up her friend's appearance were that Jenny looked like a shadow of her former self.

Laura looked down at the bouquet of flowers she was now clutching fiercely around the soggy paper and stems. She stuttered, 'No, I ... I can't. I don't think I can cope with this yet. But these are from the guys in your office.' 'Oh, how lovely,' Jenny murmured.

A glint of light come into Jenny's eyes as Laura thrust the flowers and card into her friend's hands. Laura was in a quandary and bit her lip – she felt way out of her depth and didn't know how to cope with the situation. She'd just expected Jenny to look and sound the same, and if anything, Laura thought, she'd expected to feel angry at her friend. She'd imagined them shouting and arguing, but now Laura felt defenceless and knew she couldn't lash out at someone who was obviously so ill and suffering.

Jenny moved the bouquet cradling it in the crook of her arm. 'Please, Laura,' she begged. 'Please just give me the chance to talk to you. Even if it's just for five minutes?' Laura weakened and gingerly made to step inside.

Jenny smiled her thanks and turned to walk through the hall then into the lounge with Laura following behind her. Thank God, she thought, at least Laura was coming in and she prayed she would get the chance to explain. I could make coffee, Jenny thought, which might prolong Laura's visit and give me more time. Jenny stopped in her tracks as she'd heard Laura's high-heeled shoes pause on the wood floor in the hallway. She turned and saw in Laura's eyes the memory of what had happened there a few weeks ago. Jenny put her hand on Laura's jacket sleeve, 'Please, Laura. Come in and sit down. I'll make us some coffee.'

Laura followed her into the lounge – she mumbled 'Not for me, thanks. I'm OK.'

Ignoring Laura's words Jenny flustered into the kitchen and switched on the kettle. Will I be able to make Laura understand, she thought, pouring milk into mugs. Her counsellor had said that talking about herself wouldn't be easy and could be painful, but she set her jaw, determined to give it her best shot. She missed Laura every day and even if Laura got up and walked out at the end of it all, at least she'd be able to console herself with the fact that she'd tried.

Laura heard Jenny opening the fridge door and perched on the end of the settee, staring around the lounge. She still couldn't get over how dreadful Jenny looked and struggled to remember any other occasion when Jenny had let herself go like this. Even after she'd been in hospital following her miscarriages she hadn't looked as downbeat as she did right now. Phew, Laura thought, blowing air out of her lungs; this first encounter certainly wasn't anything like what she'd imagined it would be.

Jenny returned to the lounge and placed the coffee mugs on the table. Laura noticed Jenny's hands trembling as she sat down next to her. It was on the tip of Laura's tongue to ask for a glass of something stronger, but then Jenny started to tell her about the binge drinking and how she'd been on the verge, or possibly still was, an alcoholic.

'My head was in such a mess,' Jenny said looking down and picking at a thread on the side of her grey jogging pants. 'There were some days I was so hungover I simply didn't know what I was doing.'

Laura gaped at her. 'But why didn't you talk to me about it?'

'Well, it all started so gradually,' Jenny said taking a deep breath. 'I used to sit here on my own at night and think my life seemed a whole lot better after a few glasses of wine.'

Laura remembered when they were in their twenties and Jenny was with Steve. 'But you didn't used to drink much compared to us three,' she offered.

'I know,' Jenny nodded. 'You, Phil, and Steve could always drink twice as much as me and to tell the truth back then I never really liked the taste of wine. God, I wish that had been the case now then I wouldn't be in this mess,' she said wistfully.

Laura looked past Jenny's shoulder towards the window and the purple zig-zag in the curtain material. She shook her head. 'But if you'd told me I might have been able to do something to help?'

Jenny sighed heavily. 'I couldn't. You had enough to worry about over the last few months with Phil.'

Laura bit her lip at the mention of her husband's name. Without being able to stop herself, she pouted. 'Yeah, and all that time I was worried that he was having an affair – it was you that he was doing it *with!*'

With downcast eyes Jenny began to pick at her nails. 'I never meant to hurt you, please believe me, Laura. If I could do anything to turn the clock back I would.'

Laura stared at Jenny and felt the hurt and temper bubble up in her chest. 'You know, Jenny, it's the lies that I just can't get my ahead around. And the fact that after all the years we've been friends you could you do that to me.'

Jenny's shoulders curled over her chest. 'I'm sorry,' she mumbled. 'I'm truly, truly sorry.'

Suddenly the urge to be outside in the fresh air overwhelmed Laura and she stood up to leave. 'And of course, I never suspected a thing or thought for one moment the other woman could be you. I was stupid enough to trust you!'

Jenny's shoulders began to quake now with repressed sobs. She turned her distraught face up to Laura and grabbed her hand. 'Please, oh please, just let me try to explain. You see, I felt that I was split into two different women.'

Laura narrowed her eyes and frowned. She wrestled her hand free from Jenny's grasp and sat back down onto the settee. 'What do you mean?'

Jenny took a deep breath, 'Well, there was me, Jenny Campbell, QA manager, confidently running my department and sorting out everyone's problems. I was your best friend and a popular member of the team. But there was also another woman inside me that every now and then got seriously drunk, and craved total abandonment. For some reason I wanted to feel released from what I had become. I wanted to be, well, a seductress, for want of a better word, And, I wanted to be fantastic in bed.'

Laura drew her eyebrows together. 'A seductress! But why would you want to be like that?'

Jenny shrugged. 'I don't know. At the time I just wanted to be great at sex and I needed the men I was with to want me above all others,' Jenny uttered dropping her chin to her chest.

She could feel her top lip moisten and her mouth dry. She picked up the coffee mug and gulped at the coffee. 'The counsellor says because I couldn't control losing my babies I needed to control other areas. And because I felt like a failure as a woman I wanted to excel at the one thing in relationships I could do well – which is having sex.'

Jenny could see the look of bewilderment on Laura's face as her delicate features twisted in an effort to understand. Jenny's grey T-shirt stuck to her back as she perspired and her stomach whirled in agitation. The counsellor was right, she thought, talking about herself wasn't easy. She wasn't used to baring her soul and admitting to this ridiculous behaviour, and felt her befuddled state of mind was embarrassing. But, Jenny reasoned, no matter how pathetic she sounded, if she could make Laura understand that none of the hurt she'd caused was intentional then it would be worthwhile.

She pushed on, 'I ... I thought I was going to end up like my mother! And, the counsellor reckons it is a result of not being able to cope with Steve's rejection that drove me to it. In my mind I know Steve left me because I wasn't up to the job of making babies and because I'd failed at the simplest female task, I wanted to make up for it.'

Laura whistled through her teeth and shook her head. 'No wonder your head was all over the place.'

Laura knew all about Jenny's dreadful childhood. Often when people first met Jenny they thought she had a hardened personality. But Laura knew this was just a barrier of defence and underneath Jenny was as vulnerable and lovable as she, who had been spoilt by her doting parents. Laura sighed now as she saw the turmoil in her friend's eyes knowing how much Jenny had wanted her own children to indulge and give them everything she'd never had.

Jenny nodded. 'The depression was like a black fog and I couldn't see a light at the end of the tunnel,' she croaked. 'And, the worst thing out of all of this, Laura, is the way I've hurt you. Losing you far outweighs any remorse I've ever felt for Phil.'

Laura winced at the mention of her husband's name. She could feel much of her hurt and anger towards Jenny being replaced with sympathy now. And, she thought, I'd have to be made out of stone not to feel sorry for her in such a state. But Laura was determined to get some answers to the questions that had tormented her. She pulled her shoulders back. 'OK, but why go with my husband – why Phil?'

'Oh, Laura, it didn't matter who it was,' Jenny said wringing her hands together in her lap. 'Before Phil I'd been with another man who I'd met on a dating site. We just had sex then never saw each other again. Then, I figured that one-night stands with strangers weren't safe and when Phil came on to me one night, I decided in my drunken stupor, that he was as good as any other man.'

Laura sucked in her breath and gulped. 'So, Phil came on to you?'

Jenny nodded. 'It was after the day we went to Newcastle Races and then all ended up here, but you'd gone home with toothache.'

Laura tutted at the happy memories of the day and how they'd pranced around in oversized silly hats placing £5 on horses with funny names whilst the guys told them off for wasting money. She sighed now, knowing those happy memories wouldn't remain so. In future if she ever remembered that day, it would now be thought of as the day her husband shagged her best friend. But, Laura reasoned, she had to open her eyes to the fact that although Jenny hadn't been an innocent victim in this affair, it had been Phil who had made the first advance.

'Hmm,' Laura breathed. 'You know, Jenny, when it first happened I was looking for someone to blame and was convinced it had been the other way around and you'd been flirting with him.'

'Nooo,' Jenny said. 'I had been drinking all day and one by one everyone left the party and there was only me and Phil left. He made a pass at me but I was so drunk …' she paused and shook her head. Jenny stared down at her hands that were clenched around her knees. Her knuckles were white with the pressure of gripping them so tightly and she began to rock gently backwards and forwards.

Laura watched Jenny's movements and wondered if she was reliving the first time with Phil. 'Go on – tell me!' Laura urged.

'It's horrible,' Jenny whispered. 'But, I didn't even realise it was Phil until I woke up the next morning and saw him lying across the bottom of my bed.'

Laura remembered Phil's excuse of how he'd crashed out on Jenny's settee with another two people from work who'd slept on the floor. She swallowed hard berating herself for being so naive and gullible and never questioning his excuses.

Jenny muttered, 'It's disgusting and I'm so ashamed I can barely think about it now.'

'So, what did Phil say the next morning?' Laura asked trying hard not to imagine them in bed together. 'Was he worried that you'd tell me about it?'

Jenny squeezed her eyes shut – she couldn't tell Laura. It would be re-opening painful wounds yet again and she'd already hurt her enough. She released the grip on her knees and sat up straight to drink her coffee. A huge ball of misery had gathered in the back of her throat and it ached as she swallowed. She shook her head and held her hands around the mug as if to draw comfort from the warm mug.

'Tell me!' Laura shouted. 'I need to know.'

Startled at Laura's voice Jenny's hands shook and she spilt the lukewarm coffee on her jogging pants. She rubbed at the stain knowing she had no choice – she'd have to tell Laura the truth. Warily she pursed her lips. 'No, he didn't seem bothered. He just said, 'Let's keep this between ourselves and maybe we can do it again sometime?' He told me he'd had sex with a young Swedish girl the week before in London and she'd shown him some fantastic new tricks, an ... and he wanted to try them out with me.'

Laura's mind reeled. Maybe she was getting more answers than she had wanted or had indeed expected. She laid her head back against the settee, feeling the cool leather behind her hair and closed her eyes. The affair with Jenny had been bad enough, she thought, but it had never entered her head that she wasn't the only woman he'd cheated with. What type of man was he? It was as though she'd been living with a stranger over the last few months. A wave of tiredness swept through her and she sighed wearily – Phil sounded like some type of sex-fiend. How many more women had there been, and how long had he been doing this? Jenny had started explaining again and although Laura knew she should be listening there was a large part of her that didn't want to hear any more.

Jenny pleaded, 'Laura, you have to believe me, I never thought about Phil other than the few occasions we had drunken sex. I can promise you that. The other drunken woman I became didn't even register that he was your husband and that I shouldn't be doing it,' she murmured then felt her cheeks burn. 'I blamed the alcohol and told myself I wouldn't have done it if I'd been sober, and became an expert in keeping my thoughts in two separate camps. I've asked the counsellor if it meant I had a split personality, but he told me not, and that we all have different ways of coping.'

Jenny got up and began to pace around the room. Laura still had her eyes closed and Jenny prayed she was listening because she desperately needed her understanding. Whether she would ever have her forgiveness was another matter, but at the moment all she needed was for Laura to believe her. She pushed on, 'Every time we'd had sex I made sure I was up and away before anything was said – believe me there was no lovey-dovey pillow talk.'

Laura sighed, opened her eyes, and stared at Jenny. 'Well, Phil told me the morning after the party that he was crazy about you. Therefore, you must have had some conversation or type of relationship other than the sex?'

Jenny stood still. 'Honestly, Laura. The only other time we were in this house together was the night of the party when he turned up at my door,' she said and shook her head in defiance. Jenny knew Laura would want to know all the details because it was what women did – she would be exactly the same herself. Feelings within a relationship, Jenny thought, were just as, or even more, important than the actual physical contact. She wondered what Laura's reaction would be if she bad-mouthed Phil? For herself, she had no respect left for him, but she did wonder if Laura would defend his previous good character?

Deciding it was best to be totally honest, Jenny said, 'It was the way he behaved the next morning that finally made me snap because I didn't want him here,' she pouted. 'I'd never told him he could come here so why he suddenly thought he could move in was beyond me. He'd always just called it a bit of fun.'

Jenny was gabbling now trying to get the words out of her dry mouth and lips as she remembered that morning and the panic attacks she'd gone through. 'I … I couldn't bear the thought of him living here with me in my house. And that's when I felt as though these walls were closing in on me and I couldn't breathe.'

Laura looked up at Jenny pacing and agitatedly rubbing the sides of her arms. Laura mellowed, 'Jenny, please sit down. You're making me dizzy.'

Spent of all emotion Jenny slumped back down on the settee. 'And that's when I had the breakdown and our Kate came and took me through to Durham. I've never touched a drop since then and now I'm more frightened of alcohol than anything else.'

Laura laid a hand on Jenny's shoulder. 'It's okay, I can see now it wasn't all your fault,' Laura soothed. 'Are the counselling sessions helping?'

Jenny gasped and sobbed with relief at Laura's first contact since she'd arrived. It overwhelmed her and she relaxed her shoulders. She didn't deserve her friends kindness and generosity, but that was so like Laura, she thought, and loved her all the more. 'Oh, yes. Talking to the counsellor helps and he is trying to get me to put the past into some type of perspective. Next week we are going to work on the resentment I feel towards Steve, and then following that it will be coming to terms, if I can, with the loss of m … my babies.'

Laura smiled, 'Rocky road ahead, then?' she said, 'Shall I make us some tea?'

Laura could almost feel the tension and stress lift from Jenny's body as she left her hugging a cushion and headed into the kitchen. A few moments alone would give her time to pause and take stock of what she'd learnt. Jenny had committed serious wrongs, but it wasn't all her fault and she must have been, and maybe still was, acting irrationally and totally out of character. She was to be pitied, more than anything else, she thought pouring hot water into Jenny's white teapot – she clearly hadn't been in her right mind for months now.

Laura returned with the tray and white cupola pots as Jenny always liked it set out, and then joined her to sip the hot tea.

Jenny took a sip from the cup and pulled a face. 'Urgh! It's got sugar in.'

Laura grinned. 'I think you need it. My dad always reckons it's good for when you're upset,' she said. 'And, I think you could do with a pick me up.'

'Your dad is a great man,' Jenny mused. 'I think he may have had a say in getting me some help quickly. For which I'll always be eternally grateful.'

Laura nodded. 'He's been a rock during the last few weeks, especially with Peter,' she said.

Jenny's mouth fell open and she touched her throat. A fat tear slid down her cheek. 'Oh, God,' she asked. 'Does Peter hate me now?'

Jenny had been trying to hold herself together so far, but Laura could tell now that the thoughts of Peter were too much for her. From the day Peter was born Jenny and Steve had doted upon him. When he was eight years old they'd even taken him to Disneyland Paris for a weekend, and every time Jenny went shopping she'd buy him toys, until Phil had a quiet word with Steve and asked them to stop spoiling him. They'd been the best babysitters anyone could wish for.

Laura shook her head. 'No, of course he doesn't. You know Peter – he hasn't got it in him to hate anyone. He's not too keen on his dad at the moment, but I'm hoping he'll come around in time,' she said, patting Jenny's knee.

Jenny smiled gratefully and rubbed the tear from her cheek with the back of her hand. 'Peter's not daft and has probably worked out what a creep Phil really is,' she said. 'You know, Laura, when I came back from Durham and even though he could see what a state I was in,' she said gesturing around her body in circular movements. 'He still wanted to have sex and was pulling me by the arm to get me upstairs again!'

Laura shook her head and tutted in disgust with the thought of any man hitting on an ill woman. 'He's a spineless, selfish coward,' she seethed.

Jenny nodded and drank her tea. 'Maybe he needs some medical help too,' she pondered more to herself as they both lapsed into their old comfortable silence. The only background noise in the room was the quiet signature tune of *EastEnders* starting on the TV.

Laura realised the time and stood up. While she'd been at work that day her mam had waited in for the delivery of her new bed and furniture and Laura knew it would need to be assembled and made up before sleeping in it that night. 'I've got to go,' she said quietly.

Jenny nodded. 'Laura, I can't thank you enough for coming. I feel so much better,' Jenny said standing up and walking with her to the door. 'And, I just wanted to say, well, I can't start to forgive myself until you try to forgive me.'

Laura paused in the doorway. 'It's going to take a lot of thinking about,' she said looking into Jenny's sad eyes. 'But, I'll text you later to make sure you're OK.'

Jenny's eyes lit up at the caring gesture, which for now, Laura thought, was the most she could commit to.

Chapter Twelve

Laura put her key in the front door, closed it shut behind her and stood with her back against it as though she was barring anyone or anything from following her inside. It was her place of sanctuary now and she dropped her handbag to the floor then wearily pulled off her jacket – she felt emotionally drained.

Remembering the delivery of her new bed Laura plodded upstairs and entered her bedroom. The bed was still wrapped in polythene and stood proudly in the centre of the room with her new oak wardrobe and tall-boy placed in either corner. She plonked down on the end of the bed and sighed. This was a day she'd looked forward to since she'd ordered them in B&Q and had expected to feel exhilarated, but after the last hour with Jenny, all she felt was totally spent. Bending forward she picked up a piece of bubble wrap from the carpet, and began popping the air out of each pocket while everything Jenny had told her buzzed around her mind.

Laura had always thought she knew her husband and best friend inside out, but apparently not – they seemed like two strangers. She couldn't decide which was the most shocking revelation, Phil having sex with a Swedish girl, or Jenny being a secret drinker. She shook her head in disbelief. How could she have been so blind not to notice any of this was going on around her?

Laura thought back over the last few months, and remembered how tired Jenny had begun to look especially, in the mornings. And when Laura recalled nights in her company, she nodded her head in agreement – Jenny always had to have one more glass of wine. But, did that make a person an alcoholic? Jenny had been totally incoherent with drink on that party night and Laura remembered her hanging onto the banister as if she couldn't stand upright without assistance. Now that was, Laura decided, the look of a person with a drink problem, but, on the other hand, that was probably the first time she had ever seen her in such a state. Jenny had called herself a binge drinker, and Laura had to agree – she'd certainly done a very good job of hiding the problem.

Laura popped a few more air pockets on the bubble wrap and tried hard not to imagine Phil cavorting with a Swedish girl into different sexual positions on a bed. Jeez, she breathed heavily, how could he behave like that? She couldn't quite grasp it, and hoped for his sake that he'd been using protection while he was having all this casual sex. Suddenly, it dawned upon her that if he had been having sex with other women before he'd found his way into Jenny's bed, she prayed her friend had taken some precautions.

Laura thought of the her gran's old saying, 'God moves in mysterious ways', and decided it was probably a blessing that Phil hadn't been anywhere near her in months, or she too might have to be checked out. Maybe she should have the conversation with Jenny – in her depressed state of mind it might not occur to her. And, she thought, at least now she knew that it was Phil who had started the relationship and Jenny had no real feelings for him. In fact, what

Phil had told her about being crazy for Jenny was certainly not reciprocated, and apparently Jenny had as little, if not less, respect for Phil than she had. Hmm, she muttered under her breath, his careless infidelity had certainly backfired on him.

Laura got up and in a more positive frame of mind she began to tear the plastic packing from the bed. Jenny had done this when she wasn't in her right mind; therefore, none of the hurt inflicted had been intentional. Bundling the plastic into a ball Laura stood on the top of the landing and threw it down the stairs, then collected her new bed linen from the cupboard.

She tutted with irritation as she shook out the fresh sheet over the bed – I should have had more faith in our friendship, she thought, and that there had been a deep-rooted reason for her behaviour. Laura sincerely believed that Jenny didn't associate the drunken sex with their friendship. Laura had seen the sincere remorse and guilt in Jenny's eyes over what she'd done to her, and she also knew Jenny was missing her just as much as Laura had missed Jenny.

Pushing pillows into pillowcases she concentrated her thoughts on Jenny's appearance and the shock she'd got when she'd first opened the door. Thankfully, she'd never suffered from any type of depression or mental health problems other than after Peter was born. Laura had had a few weeks of emotional crying and had felt very low in mood which the midwife called baby blues. Her father had explained there was a huge difference between this and true post-natal depression and kept a very close eye on her, but within a few weeks she'd bounced back to her normal self and spent hours in rapture with her new baby.

Therefore, Laura decided now, as I've no idea what it feels like to be depressed I shouldn't be the one to judge Jenny's state of mind and whether this was justification to go with Phil.

With the new dove-grey cover on the quilt Laura shook and fluffed it up on the bed. The linen smelt fresh and clean, and she longed to roll into it later that night. Laura placed the finishing touches to the room with a simple framed print on the wall, cushions propped up on the bed, and new bedside lamps, then stood back and smiled with satisfaction. She took her mobile out of her trouser pocket and took a photograph to send to Peter – he'll be so proud of me, she thought, heading back downstairs with a grumbling stomach.

Laura took out a block of cheese from the fridge. She could hear her dad saying that it was time to be the bigger person, Laura, and decided, although she couldn't help Jenny wade through the quagmire in her mind, she could help with her physical well-being.

As Laura made cheese on toast, she decided that helping Jenny might also help her to put the whole sorry mess into some type of perspective. She sighed, it had certainly tested their friendship to the full, but if she didn't make an effort, then the alternative would be losing Jenny from her life – which was the last thing she wanted.

Last week, her mam had half suggested that Phil might come to his senses and want to return home to her and Peter. Laura paused as she grated cheese and considered this idea. No, she decided, apart from the fact that Jenny hadn't been the only other woman he'd been with, she thought too much of herself now to have him back. She knew there was no way, or, no amount of marriage guidance that would get her through a reconciliation. Phil was lost to her now, and if she was really truthful with herself, she quite liked this totally independent woman she was becoming.

For the last six months all she'd done was worry if he was having an affair. What she had dreaded had actually happened, but it was over now. She could relax at home because he didn't live there any more so the constant worrying was over – it was a massive relief. Maybe, in time, she thought, she would feel lonely at night, but for the moment she didn't and loved the evenings where she could simply please herself.

As she'd stepped forward alone, Laura thought, she'd already proved so much to herself lately, that going back to Phil would feel like a step backwards that she didn't want to take. It felt good for a change, to think of herself first, after Peter of course, which went without saying.

Thinking about her son reminded Laura about the photograph and as she crunched into the hot toasted cheese she sent it to him with a yellow smiley face icon.

Laura grinned as she read his reply. 'Way to go, Mam. It looks awesome.'

Her next text to Jenny she composed more carefully. 'Hi, Jenny. Although it wasn't easy coming to see you earlier, I'm pleased I did. I thought I'd call again tomorrow afternoon and bring you some chilli? X'

Saturday morning dawned with heavy rainfall. Laura stared out of the kitchen window and watched the rain run down the glass. They'd had a few weeks of unseasonably warm weather, and as it was only May, this rain was to be expected. After a blissful night's sleep in her new bed she felt energised and set about shopping to buy the ingredients to make a chilli con carne. As she browsed in the chilled cabinet in the supermarket she recalled the earlier telephone conversation with her mam who was already making preparations for lunch the next day for their Italian guest. Margaret had bought a side of beef big enough to feed an army, and Laura had offered to bring dessert. Tempting as it was to buy a dessert from the supermarket, she knew that would disappoint her dad as he wanted to give Luigi a true northern welcome, which in her home meant roast beef and Yorkshire pudding, followed by apple crumble and custard. She shivered in anticipation at the thought of seeing Luigi, and although it was only a casual Sunday lunch, it would be another occasion where she could enjoy his company outside of work.

Laura spent the afternoon in her kitchen cooking then shortly after three, armed with a large plastic container, she wandered along the cul de sac to Jenny's house.

Jenny had woken earlier than previous days and for the first time since the night of the party when she thought of Laura she had a different image in her mind. Laura's tortured, ravaged face had been replaced with the look of concern and care that she'd worn last night. The thought of Laura returning later in the day made Jenny make more of an effort as she showered and tried to condition her hair into some resemblance of what it had been prior to the breakdown. It was strange, Jenny thought brushing her teeth, how events and happenings in her life were now compartmentalised into boxes which consisted of pre- and post-breakdown. She sighed heavily – when she had these moments of rational thinking, she could feel and act normally, but the horrid memories of her depression were never far away. 'It's going to take time,' the counsellor had advised. 'You know the saying, Rome wasn't built in a day; well, that is how your recovery will be.'

And Jenny understood this, but then when she swung from hours of normality to hours of panic and insecurity about the future, it wasn't easy to cope with, and it still worried her. What if she didn't get any better than this and the depression didn't lift? Would she lose her home if she didn't feel confident enough to return to work?

At the moment, apart from taking a taxi to the hospital outpatients for her appointments each week, she hadn't been outside her door. Kate still called when John was at home to look after the boys and she usually brought staple foods of bread and milk. But, Jenny thought, as she had no appetite nor energy to cook it wasn't really a problem. The real problem, Jenny sighed, would be if she was out and saw someone she knew. How would she tell them what had happened, and of course, what was still happening to her? Her neighbour had caught up with Kate one day getting out of her car to ask if Jenny was OK, and Kate had told her it was a virus and that her sister was resting. This explanation had worked and if Jenny was outside in the garden, her neighbour would give a friendly wave.

This, however, couldn't go on forever, and Jenny began to worry about what would happen in the months ahead.

Jenny looked into her wardrobe, assessing which clothes would fit her now and which trousers or jeans she could tighten with a belt. She chose her white jeans and T-shirt and then smiled, imagining Laura cooking a chilli to bring along for her – it was her favourite.

Jenny hurried downstairs as she heard Laura ring the doorbell. 'Hey there,' she said feeling pleased to see her friend under more normal circumstances.

Laura swept into the lounge without hanging around, which, Jenny thought happily, was how she would have entered her house pre-breakdown. Jenny determined to keep those thoughts out of her mind and smiling she followed Laura through into the kitchen.

Laura took off her rain-mac and shook the rain from it then placed a container onto the work surface. 'Now, all you need to do is heat it up gently, either in the oven or the microwave, and cook your rice to go with it,' she said opening an overhead cupboard. 'No rice, OK then we'll go with plan B.'

Laura lifted out a packet of pitta breads from her handbag. 'Stick a couple of these under the grill to have with it instead.'

Jenny grinned with sheer joy at the few moments of their normal friendship returning. 'Thanks, Laura,' she uttered. 'I'll have some later.'

Laura opened the fridge door and shook her head. 'There's nothing in here – just exactly what are you eating?'

'Well,' Jenny hedged. 'Toast, and I have had some Weetabix this morning,'

Laura raised an eyebrow. 'I suppose that's a start,' she said switching on the kettle. 'But you really need to start eating properly again, Jenny.'

Jenny explained how Kate was bringing a few things,

but also how the thoughts of going out were nerve wracking at the moment. 'I know it must seem silly,' she said. 'And when I listen to myself I know I'm being ridiculous, but I can't help it. What if I see someone I know?'

Laura bit her lip. 'Okay,' she nodded. 'What about ordering online and having your groceries delivered to the house? I know plenty of people who do that and then you'll only have to open the door to the delivery man.'

Now why hadn't I thought of that, Jenny thought and smiled gratefully. Maybe along with her rationality, her problem-solving skills that she'd always prided herself upon had deserted her too.

The women moved through into the lounge with their coffee, chatting about the weather and how busy the supermarket had been, and Jenny noticed that Laura was deliberately avoiding the issue and the happenings of last night. She wanted to keep thanking Laura for giving her what appeared to be a chance at patching up their friendship, but then dithered, wondering whether to raise the matter again.

As Laura suggested light meals she could make to build up her strength and how fresh fruit and vegetables would help to clear her skin, Jenny listened with only one ear. She loved the sound of Laura's quiet steady voice and the reassurance it gave her. Finally, Jenny sighed, apart from the counsellor and Kate, she had someone else fighting in her corner – the relief brought tears to her eyes.

Jenny felt Laura grip her hand which broke her out of her reverie. 'Maybe you should ask the counsellor next week about going out? Tell him your fears and ask if he can suggest ways to talk yourself through it?'

Jenny dabbed at her eyes with the back of her hand. 'Oh, thank you, La … Laura,' she stuttered. 'I know I don't deserve this, and …' she looked past her towards the window. 'I never thought for a second that you'd be the one who'd come to help me.'

Laura bristled. 'Well, I'm trying to understand. I can't do much to help your state of mind and that's best left to the professionals. But I can look after you until you feel up to getting out and about again.'

Laura stood up to leave. 'I've got more cooking to do for tomorrow,' she said. 'But I'll text you later and try to call in from work on Monday night.'

Jenny followed Laura to the door wanting to ask her to stay longer, but settled herself that Laura would be coming back and they were at least making a start to rebuild their friendship. Whether it would work, she wasn't sure, because she knew the enormity of what she was asking from Laura, but they had at last begun.

Laura was in a total flap. She stood in front of the mirror on the inside of the new wardrobe door, discarding clothes onto the bed in frustration. She hadn't a clue what to wear for lunch with Luigi and her parents She wanted to appear casual yet attractive, and at the same time comfortable with enough room in her waistband to enjoy their Sunday lunch. Knowing her mam there would be mountains of food on the table and although it would be rude not to eat, she didn't want to gorge herself in front of Luigi.

Thankfully, Laura now realised that she had lost a little weight over the last few weeks with all the extra exercise decorating, and finally, just as she was about to give up and throw herself onto the bed in desperation, she tried on her cream wide-legged trousers. The waist actually felt slack and when she teamed them with her white shirt, she nodded in satisfaction. Opening the cupboard she looked along the shelves at her collection of shoes. She needed a little height, she mused, assessing the length of the trousers, and finally chose a pair of cream slingbacks. Pushing her feet into the shoes she twirled around in front of the mirror – they were perfect.

Just after midday as she was leaving the house with the apple crumble placed securely on the passenger seat she received a text from Luigi who wanted to check the postcode for his sat nav. Bubbles of excitement fluttered around her stomach as she drove to her parents – she couldn't wait to see him again. At the same time, she warned herself to stay calm. After all, she reasoned, it wasn't a date; it was simply a lunch invitation that had been given to a work colleague by her dad.

As she drove down Ancroft Way, she remembered the good lunch they'd had at the hospital, and frowned. She knew her dad had taken an instant liking to Luigi, but he'd met her friends from work before and never invited them home – so why had he invited Luigi? Maybe he felt sorry for him as he was in a foreign place away from home.

Laura stood in the doorway of her parents' house as Luigi pulled up outside in his grey Audi. As Laura waved and walked towards him the sun broke through a sky full of clouds and she smiled – it was going to be a happy afternoon. Luigi was dressed casually in blue jeans with a chocolate brown shirt and beige leather jacket, but as he swung his legs out of the car it was the shoes Laura noticed and she whistled softly in approval. Italian, two-tone leather shoes with pointed toes and a strap across the front – she sighed in pleasure – they were beautiful.

As Laura reached Luigi she stepped up onto her toes and kissed him on both cheeks. He reciprocated and murmured in her ear. 'At last, you have joined the European community!'

Laura giggled and wagged a finger at him feeling such pleasure at being next to him again. There was also the added bonus that she could relax in his company instead of continually looking over her shoulder as she did at work.

Luigi grinned and felt a bolt of happiness curse through him – Laura looked stunning. Her curly hair shone around her small face and the light make-up gave her face a healthy glow. But the biggest change he could see was the light and mischief dancing in her eyes as she looked at him. The haunted sadness that he'd seen in her eyes over the last few weeks seemed to have disappeared and she looked carefree: as though a weight had been lifted from her body.

'Do I look okay?' he asked, looking over her shoulder to where her dad stood at the front door smiling. Luigi made a hand gesture over his clothes. 'This is how I'd dress at home if I was going for a family lunch.'

Laura grinned. 'You look great,' she said and slotted her arm through his as they walked up to greet her parents.

'Come in, and welcome,' David cried, shaking Luigi firmly by the hand.

Margaret hovered in the hallway and Laura introduced her to Luigi. Laura noticed that her mam had made a special effort with her hair and outfit.

Luigi took Margaret's hand and bent over, planting a kiss on the back of it.

Margaret chuckled and Laura could see her mam was flustered at the show of affection that she wasn't used to, and usually shied away from.

'Ah!' Luigi cried, 'I forget.' And quickly he turned, ran back to his car and opened the boot. Laura followed him back outside while her parents went through into the lounge. He brought a bouquet of flowers and a large basket of fruit out of the boot and then hurried back to her in the hallway.

'These are for your mother,' he said as Laura ushered him through into the lounge. If Margaret had been flustered earlier then she was totally gobsmacked now as he presented her with the flowers and laid the basket on the coffee table.

Her mam's face was bright red as she gabbled her thanks over and over again. 'I usually get flowers when

I'm ill, or, on my birthday, or …' she paused then nodded towards her husband, 'when he's been up to something he shouldn't have!'

Everyone laughed and David poured drinks while Laura sat next to Luigi at the dining table in the bay window. They chatted freely and naturally as though she'd known him for years. Margaret had disappeared into the kitchen to find a vase for her flowers and her dad began a conversation about the holiday they'd taken two years previously to Venice. Laura had forgotten about their trip and was amazed at how much her dad knew about Italy and how he longed to return one day to visit Rome.

Laura could see Luigi was animated and delighted to be talking about Italian art and culture and a lengthy discussion began about the old and new Venetians who wanted to protect the island from horrendous flooding and global warming issues.

Margaret re-appeared with her two vases of flowers and placed them on the old bureau, expressing her delight at the white lilies and roses.

Margaret looked towards Luigi. 'When we were in Venice David took me on a gondola trip around the island and the Italian gondolier gave me a red rose,' she said blushing again.

'How romantic!' Luigi cried.

David shuffled in his chair. 'Well, there's life in the old dog, yet,' he said waiting until Margaret had scuttled back into the kitchen then whispered, 'That bloody rose cost me fifteen euros.'

Everyone laughed loudly and Laura went into the kitchen to help with lunch.

Laura's earlier prediction was proven right – her mam did indeed have enough food to feed everyone who lived in the street. Big china tureens were full of steaming vegetables and an enormous piece of beef sat proudly in the centre of a serving plate surrounded with Yorkshire puddings.

'Thanks for doing this, Mam.' Laura said. 'I'm still not exactly sure why Dad invited Luigi, but it's a lovely gesture.'

Margaret poured gravy from a large pan into two gravy boats. 'You don't know why?' she said smiling. 'Well, I do – he can see the same thing I can. Any man that can put a smile back on my daughter's face will always be welcome in my house.'

Laura gaped. She couldn't believe it and hadn't realised the way she was beginning to feel about Luigi was so obvious.

Margaret chided, 'Close your mouth, Laura, it's not attractive. And carry those tureens through, please.'

Laura did as her mam asked automatically, as her dad appeared to carry the beef and start carving the meat at the table.

When he'd laid three thick slices onto Laura's plate she put her hand up. 'Enough, Dad. I won't be able to move after all this,' she joked, then began to pile her plate with vegetables.

Margaret joined them and Laura poured wine into all their glasses. 'Tuck in, Luigi,' she said. 'We don't stand on ceremony here.'

Luigi raised an eyebrow and she explained further and he gratefully filled his plate.

As Laura ate she explained the recipe and reasoning behind eating a sweet Yorkshire pudding with savoury meat and vegetables, which to an Italian, she laughed, wasn't easy. But as Luigi crunched into the pudding's crispy outer and discovered the soft fluffy inside, he licked his lips declaring it was delicious. Laura saw her mam swell with pride as David also told their guest that his wife made the best Yorkshire puddings in the North-east.

After dessert and with the lingering sweet apple flavour around her lips, Laura settled herself in between her dad and Luigi on the old, worn-out sofa. Both men had their legs outstretched towards the fireplace and Margaret sat in her fireside chair sipping coffee.

'I hate this old three piece, and in particular that decrepit sofa,' Margaret pouted then nodded towards her husband. 'But your lordship won't let me buy a new one.'

David nodded in response and shuffled down further into the soft upholstered material. 'Nope, I won't. It's the most comfortable seat in the house and I'm not parting with it,' he stated emphatically.

Luigi relaxed his shoulders, folded his hands behind his head, and stretched out further crossing his feet. 'Sorry, Margaret,' he said smiling. 'But I'm with your husband on this matter. It is lovely and very squashy.'

Laura saw the corners of her dad's mouth twitch at the way Luigi had said squashy..

Luigi looked at Laura and raised an eyebrow, 'I have the wrong word again?'

Laura melted under his gaze. She shook her head slightly. 'It's fine,' she muttered. 'We all know what you mean.'

As her dad began to tell Luigi much of the local history and how their family traditions had formed over the years, Laura totally relaxed. After weeks of mental stress and upset, and the strain upon her limbs with decorating, it wasn't until her whole body had completely unwound that she realised how uptight she'd been. With a full stomach and the quiet melodic tone in her dad's voice, the warm cosy atmosphere in the lounge made her eyelids feel heavy. All her muscles were slack and droopy and she could feel Luigi next to her languishing in comfort too. His slackened body spread further towards her and the warmth of him felt so inviting she longed to cuddle up to him and lay her head on his broad chest.

Luigi sighed with absolute contentment. His belly was full of good food, he was surrounded by a nice family who had worked hard to make him feel welcome, and the lovely Laura, as he now thought of her, sitting close to him. A gentle waft of her perfume filled his nostrils as she laughed or shook her curls and he wanted so badly to put his arm around her and crush her into him that it ached. Her family atmosphere reminded him of his home years ago when he was a teenager and before his father had died. He began to tell them all how his home in Florence may look different to theirs from the outside because it was attached to the shop, but inside their living area was much the same.

At the shrill tone of a text arriving on Laura's mobile she bent forward and picked it up out of her bag.

'Oh, it's from Peter,' she groaned. 'He's popping over tonight with three bags full of washing.'

'Well, that's your night planned,' David grimaced. And, as discussions were held about the limited facilities in the student accommodation Luigi knew it was time to make a move and thank them for their hospitality.

Chapter Thirteen

Jenny flopped down onto a chair in the kitchen after putting all her groceries away into cupboards and the fridge freezer. She felt extraordinarily proud of herself after the Tesco delivery man had left and she had a plan of what she would cook for Laura's supper. The day before Laura had sent a text to say she was stopping by from work that night and Jenny planned to surprise her with chicken salad and the first new potatoes of the season.

She'd had an exceptionally good session with the counsellor that morning and for the first time she'd felt relieved to talk about her past memories instead of shrinking away from them or pushing them out of her mind. He'd listened patiently as she'd explained about the foster couple whom she'd lived with and how she'd had everything she could possibly need.

There'd always been plenty of food to eat, Jenny had told him and for the first few years she'd stuffed and gorged herself at meal times just in case there was no more – going to bed with an empty stomach was something she'd never forget. Her foster mother had always made sure she'd had enough clothes, to be warm in the winter and fashionably kitted out with summer clothes for their holidays abroad to Turkey and Barcelona. The only things that had been missing from their home were affection and love. It was only once a week when she met Kate that she'd had bodily contact with another human being, as they'd sit with their arms around each other, hugging tightly.

Jenny stood at the kitchen sink and destalked the strawberries she'd bought, then washed them under the cold tap. She would never be the great cook that Laura was, but she had bought plenty of fruit and intended to make a fruit salad that she could eat over the next few days. Hopefully it would please Laura when she saw that she was following her advice, and Jenny thought, she had to admit that doing these simple daily activities was making her feel slightly better. Or, at least, she thought, the black cloud that still hung over her didn't feet pitch black now but more of a dark-grey colour.

Jenny sprinkled a spoonful of sugar over the chopped fruit and poured cream into a small jug then stood back, smiling with a modicum of satisfaction.

Laura arrived at six and Jenny ushered her through into the dining area where she had their meal ready on the table. 'I only have to bring the potatoes through,' she gushed as Laura sat down at the table.

'There was no need for this, Jenny,' Laura said as she laid the white napkin over her lap. 'But at the same time it's very welcome. I've never stopped all afternoon and I'm starving now.'

Laura sniffed appreciatively at the aroma wafting from the large pieces of butter melting over the potatoes. 'Hmm, Jersey Royals – my favourite,' she said as Jenny joined her at the table.

As they ate Laura began to tell her about the big Irish contract they were hoping to secure and all the products she was developing. But Jenny sighed, although it was good to hear news from the outside world again, she tensed a little and laid her fork down on the side of the plate.

Laura raised an eyebrow, 'What? I'm sorry, do you not want to hear about work?'

Jenny squirmed and wondered whether to make a blasé comment to cover up for the anxiety she felt. However, Jenny thought, Laura would probably see through it anyway, and she was determined now to open up more as the counsellor had suggested. There was no point in hiding her fears away any longer. The old Jenny was in the pre-breakdown box and she had to find a way of bringing herself into the post breakdown box. 'No,' she said and took a deep breath. 'It's not that I don't want to hear about it all. I'm just so grateful that you're here and talking to me again. But, it's just that I'm a bit scared about the idea of work.'

'What?' Laura asked. 'Are you worried about the actual work or what people will say about your sick leave?'

Jenny hedged, 'Well, a bit of both actually. I don't know when, or, if I'll ever feel confident enough to go back again. At the moment I'm struggling to get past the front gate on my own, never mind the hustle and bustle of the office and the factory.'

Laura paused with a chunk of chicken on her fork. 'OK, it's bound to be intimidating now, but once you've built yourself up again and you're feeling better I'm sure you'll be itching to get back,' she said. 'Everyone keeps asking after you and you do have loads of friends. In fact, I can't think of one person who would bitch about you.'

Jenny nodded and pushed the fringe from her eyes. Laura's kindness and consideration made her feel tearful, but she pulled her shoulders back determined to make her visit as pleasant as possible. 'That's good to hear,' she uttered. 'All the same, I just feel a little anxious about the future at the moment …'

After eating a little more of the chicken Jenny felt it dry in her mouth and struggled to swallow the meat – she gulped at the water that she'd poured for them both then laid her knife and fork together in the centre of the plate. 'I'll maybe have some more later,' she mumbled.

Jenny brought the fruit salad and cream to the table and Laura exclaimed, 'Oh, great. You are trying the fruit,' she said. 'I'm sure it'll help.'

A silence settled between them until Laura laid her spoon down. 'Jenny why don't you go and get your hair cut – that's the fourth time since I've been here that you've pushed your fringe off your forehead. It's obviously irritating you and it must be a while since you've had your highlights done?'

Jenny got up and Laura followed her into the kitchen with the empty dish.

'I will do but the problem at the moment is getting there. I could get a taxi I suppose,' Jenny offered.

'Why? Is there a problem with your car?'

Jenny shook her head and hunched her shoulders. 'Oh no. It's just that I don't feel up to driving at the moment.'

'OK,' Laura said and picked up the car keys from a hook above the bread bin where Jenny usually kept them. Laura then took hold of Jenny's arm and gently but firmly walked her friend out to the garden gate, opened it, and stepped out onto the pavement.

Laura could feel Jenny shiver slightly when she was outside and beeped off the alarm on the car. 'Climb in, Jenny,' Laura said. 'And I'll sit next to you.'

Jenny slid onto the driver's seat and grabbed hold of the steering wheel feeling a mixture of fear and pleasure. She was delighted that Laura was helping her and felt relieved that someone was taking charge of her situation, but at the same time she felt anxious. Her hands started to sweat on the steering wheel. 'What if I can't drive any more? I haven't driven since before the breakdown – what if I've forgotten how to do it? I might run somebody over or crash the car!'

Laura sat next to her and laid her hand over one of Jenny's. She squeezed it reassuringly. 'I know you can drive, Jenny. In fact you're a better driver than I am,' she said. 'I think it's simply that you've lost your confidence in everything you used to do. But people suffering from depression do drive. They go to the hairdressers, they go shopping, and they try to live their lives to the best of their ability.'

Jenny's heart was thumping in her chest. 'But my hands are all sweaty,' she whispered.

Laura said, 'Turn the key, Jenny. I'll stay with you and we'll drive around the cul de sac until you get the feel of the car again. I know you can do this.'

As Jenny slid the handbrake off and moved away from the kerb Laura began to regale the memory of a road trip they'd taken three years ago to Aberdeen and how Jenny had driven all the way back home. By the time Jenny realised what she was doing, the fear had left her mind and she'd driven down to the town centre, which by early evening was quiet with very little traffic on the roads, and returned the same way.

Jenny felt pleased, no, she thought, more than that – she felt exhilarated as she pulled up outside her front door and parked behind Laura's Mini. She had always loved driving, and as Laura had earlier mentioned, been a good driver. She breathed out deeply and turned to face Laura. 'Thank you. Oh thank you for this, Laura. I'm not sure I'd have had the courage on my own,' she said.

'Well,' Laura observed. 'I think you would have done. I'm by no means an expert, Jenny. But I think if you let these fears build up and linger then it'll be worse in the long run. Now, get the appointment for the hairdressers made. And, if you get one for Saturday morning I'll come with you and get some chopped off this unruly mop of mine.'

Laura clicked onto Google and entered Newcastle Quayside flats into the search box. Alex had left the office early for the day and Laura had finally managed to get some quiet time to think about her housing situation. Her dad had suggested that putting the house up for sale earlier rather than later in the year would be a good move as spring was traditionally known as the best time of year to sell a house. Laura agreed with his statement, but she did want to have some idea of where she'd like to live before contacting an estate agent.

For some reason, Laura had the image of a trendy upmarket flat in her mind which would be the total opposite to their sixties traditional semi-detached house. So, she mused, if she was having a complete new start in life on her own then maybe her surroundings should be a total change too. However, when she looked at the price of a two-bedroomed flat and exactly how little space there was for the money, she took a deep breath and sighed heavily.

At the knock on the office door she looked up quickly to see Luigi lounging against the doorframe. Her heart skipped and she felt a rush of pleasure surge through her. She hadn't seen him since Sunday as the sales and commercial teams, had been away for three days at a conference in London.

'Hey there,' she said smiling. 'Come in – it's good to see you back.'

Luigi sauntered into the office crossed to her desk and she stood up to kiss him on both cheeks. She smiled to herself realising how common a practise this was now as opposed to a few weeks ago when she had hung back from him.

Briefly he told her about the time spent in London and how glad he was to be back. 'It is so very hot and noisy down there,' he said grinning. 'It's nice to be back to the quiet north of the country.'

Laura giggled and realised just how much she had missed talking to him. They'd exchanged a few texts but she'd longed to hear his voice and now she gazed into his eyes, reminding herself how sexy they were.

Luigi stared back at her feeling fit to burst. On the train home he'd thought of nothing else but seeing her again, and once he'd got into the taxi he'd made a snap decision to come back to work instead of going home as all the others had done. He felt his shoulders relax in her company and knew he'd made the right decision to come back. Laura was good for him.

Peering over her shoulder, he looked at the search on her computer screen and raised an eyebrow. 'Flats on Newcastle Quayside?'

She followed his eyes to the screen and nodded. Since their time together on Sunday Laura had decided that the next possible chance there was she would tell Luigi all about Phil and her circumstances. Up until now she'd held back, feeling work wasn't the right place to have such conversations, and of course, she hadn't really known what was going to happen in her marriage. However, she knew now that her marriage was over because she had been the one to make that decision and felt ready to talk about it. She wasn't going to wait around for other people to have an impact on her life any more, not Phil, nor Jenny, nor her parents, only her.

Laura smiled at him and gently touched his arm. 'If you're not too tired after the journey would you like to come and have a drink with me?'

'Mamma Mia!' he cried excitedly. 'I'd love to. You don't know how long I've waited for this, my lovely, Laura.'

Laura chuckled at the endearment as she closed down her computer and Luigi took the stairs two at a time back to his office to collect his bag.

His mind whirled with joy at the fact that she actually wanted to spend time with him. When he'd been in London at the conference he'd overheard some encouraging news in the men's toilets one night. Luigi hadn't been eavesdropping, but he'd heard Phil telling the commercial director that he'd left Laura and was living in a flat in Jesmond. His thoughts had been two-fold as he'd got into bed that night.

His heart ached for Laura because she'd gone through a major upset in her life, but the news also gave him reason to hope.

Luigi picked up his leather holdall and draped the strap for his lap top onto his shoulder. Maybe this was why she looked more settled and happier at her parents' house on Sunday, he mused, hurrying back out to the main doors. Whatever the reason, he thought delightedly, being close to her for a while made him happy.

Laura was waiting for him and he hurried behind her across the car park.

He stopped abruptly when she reached her old red Mini Cooper and pulled a comical face. 'Do the company not pay you enough to buy a new car?'

She took his lap top from him and helped him stow his bags in the boot. 'I love it,' she cried defensively. 'It was my very first car and I'm sentimentally attached to it.'

Luigi shook his head and grinned. He would have ridden on the back of a moped, he thought, as long as he was next to her. 'OK, so where are you going to chauffer me to?'

She laughed at the sight of Luigi as he climbed into the passenger seat and sat with his knees hunched up nearly under his chin. 'Sorry,' she said. 'You haven't got much room but the pub isn't too far away.'

'I'm fine,' he said and they began to discuss the flats she'd been looking at on Newcastle Quayside. 'Is there a particular reason that you want to be down by the river?'

Laura smiled. 'Not really. But I thought I'd tell you what's been happening over a glass of wine and then you could give me your opinion about flats in the area.' It suddenly dawned upon her that she didn't know where he lived and asked him.

'Actually, I had the same dilemma when I arrived here,' he babbled in a light voice. 'I found the modern apartments had lovely new décor and they were bang on trend, but there's not much interior space and of course, there's no outside space at all. Whereas my older ground floor flat has a lovely garden and the rooms have much more space which suits a big guy like me!'

Laura stopped at the junction at the end of the drive and looked at him. She shook her head and tutted. 'Just because you're not slim doesn't mean you're fat. Now, if you've got a bottle of wine at home we could talk there?

Or, if not I'll drive us to a pub?'

Luigi swallowed hard at her compliment, and with the thought of her coming to his home – his heart began to race. 'I have a beautiful bottle of Chianti that was produced in central Tuscany very near to Florence. It has been patiently waiting for a special guest to walk through my door,' he said.

Laura giggled. 'That sounds great,' she said. 'But where is it? Right or left?'

'Aaah, turn right,' he said. 'I live at Moor Court, in Gosforth.'

Laura wandered around Luigi's lounge looking at
the prints on the wall of the Ponte Vecchio Bridge,
Signoria Square, and the Dome of Brunelleschi in
Florence. He stood behind her, pulling the cork out of
the bottle of Chianti telling her about each place.

She wore a blouse with a small opening at the back
of her neck and he stared at a curl of hair that was
caught around the button. Placing the bottle of wine
down onto the small table he reached out and slotted a
finger through the curl. 'It's tangled on the button,' he
said then left his hand resting on the nape of her neck.
A current of desire flooded through him and he ran
his tongue over his dry lips. He moved his face nearer
to the back of her ear and inhaled her smell – he
needed to touch her so much his trousers tightened
and he groaned in her ear.

Laura swooned inside and felt her knees quiver with
the touch of his hand on her skin. She'd always been
ultrasensitive around her neck and ears, and she could
feel the months of pent-up sexual frustration gnawing
at her body begging for release. She turned around to
face him. 'Come and sit down,' she whispered taking
his hand. 'I have to tell you about things first.'

They sipped the Chianti from large glasses and
Laura gazed around the big Art Deco living area. Two
wide curved windows threw light onto the lemon-
painted walls and two pale grey settees. An
occasional standard lamp and two table lamps with
cream shades and chrome bases stood next to an
enormous palm tree. Luigi, she decided, had
exceptionally good taste.

'It's such a coincidence,' she said. 'I've just chosen
these exact colours for my bedroom.'

Luigi grinned. 'I know. I saw the tins of paint in the wagon at B&Q. But I haven't decorated this room – it was already done when I arrived.

The only thing I am doing are the Italian tiles in the bathroom which I will show to you later.'

Laura nodded and smiled at the word wagon instead of trolley. She took a mouthful of rich red wine, felt her shoulders relax, and taking a deep breath she turned her face towards him. With her brown pencil skirt stretched just above her knees and her small feet delicately crossed at the ankles, Laura started her story from the beginning. She cradled the glass as she talked and took small sips when she felt her lip quiver and fought back tears. When she told Luigi how she had found Phil naked in Jenny's house, she saw him clench his fist around the glass and curse softly in Italian.

'Cara,' he muttered. 'You don't need to say any more.'

But Laura shook her head. 'I do,' she said firmly. 'I need to tell you everything because it is important to me.'

Laura pushed on and finished by telling Luigi how Jenny seemed to be getting better, but that her marriage to Phil was well and truly over.

'I am very impressed,' Luigi said lightly touching the side of her cheek with his finger. 'I don't know if I could forgive a friend that had done this to me.'

Laura tilted her head and paused. 'I haven't forgiven her, Luigi. Well, not yet, and there's a large part of me is not sure that I ever will entirely. But I do still care what happens to her and I figure if I walk away from her now while she's ill then I'll feel bad about myself. Can you understand that?'

Luigi looked at her and felt an enormous wave of pride and adoration for this small but strong-minded woman. He laid his hand over his chest. 'You have a heart as big as an lion,' he said shaking his head and feeling his throat grow thick. She needs space, Luigi thought. This isn't the right time for us to be together, but knew no matter how long it took her to get over this; he would be waiting. His heart felt heavy with disappointment and he frowned as gently he removed her hand and held it in between his. 'You need time to work your way through this, Laura,' he said.

Laura bit her lip. The thought of losing him was scary because she wanted to be with him so much, but how did she say that without sounding desperate? She looked into his eyes and raised an eyebrow hoping he would know what she was thinking – whatever this was between them she didn't want to miss out.

Luigi squeezed her hand. 'I am a very patient man,' he said. 'And, when you are ready, Laura, I'll be here.'

Chapter Fourteen

Laura found Jenny in her small back garden as she pulled up outside her house on Friday night shortly after six. She was surrounded by a collection of large and medium sized blue ceramic pots and a watering can. A large sack of compost and trays of bedding plants with other exotic looking plants sat on the small side wall.

'Hey, there, what's this? Have you been watching Alan Titchmarsh on TV?'

Jenny looked up from where she was kneeling in her old jeans and smiled. 'Noooo,' she said. 'After I'd managed to do the online ordering for my groceries I figured the garden centre might do the same. And my garden always looks such a mess compared to the neighbours' so I thought I'd have a go at planting some things.'

Laura slipped her jacket off, sat down on the wall next to Jenny and held her face up to the late evening sun. 'Oh, that fresh air and sun feels nice after being cooped up all day in the office,' she breathed. 'It's good to see you outside pottering. Are you feeling a little brighter?'

Jenny nodded. 'I can't face going to the gym so I figured this would be a way of getting some gentle exercise while I'm at home,' she said then pushed her fringe from her forehead wearing a pair of flowery gardening gloves. 'And before you nag about my hair I've got us appointments in the salon tomorrow morning at eleven.'

Laura nodded in satisfaction and pleasure at Jenny's uplifted spirits – she looked so much better in just a short week. The red spots on her forehead were fading and although her eyes were not shinning or bright, there was a definite glimmer of positivity in them now. Laura decided some praise and congratulations were overdue and she did just that.

While Jenny finished potting the plants Laura went into the kitchen and brought out two long glasses of lemonade. Jenny looked at Laura as she held her face up to the sun with her eyes closed – she looked different somehow and not like her usual quiet self. Jenny wondered what it was that had changed. Laura's jaw seemed set now when she talked, and her posture was strong as she walked with her shoulders pulled back. And there was a certain confidence in her remarks and suggestions that Laura hadn't possessed before.

Jenny gulped at the refreshing drink and frowned. Shamefacedly, she admitted to herself that she'd been so wrapped up in herself she hadn't given any thought as to how Laura was coping at home without Phil. Since her first visit last week they'd both purposely skated around the issue, and selfishly she hadn't wanted to spoil Laura's visits with more upset. Did Laura want to talk about Phil now, she wondered, and tried to think of a way of finding out what was going on around the cul-de-sac.

'Has Peter been at home this week?' Jenny asked suddenly.

Laura snapped her eyes open then sat forward. 'No, why do you ask?'

Jenny shrugged. 'Well, I just wanted to find out how you're managing at home without Phil, but I didn't know how to ask without upsetting either of us again.'

Laura sighed knowing Jenny was right. They'd have to talk about it sometime but she too had skirted around things not wanting to open old wounds. 'Well, at first it seemed strange being on my own, but to be honest I've got used to it now and don't mind it at all. I haven't heard any more from Phil, which is fine because I'd rather have it that way than constant reminders.'

Jenny took off the gloves and sat up on her hunkers staring at Laura. 'Right,' she nodded taking in the information. 'Maybe, I mean, well he might want to come home at some stage?'

'Well, he isn't,' Laura said resolutely shaking her head. 'And the reason I know that is because *I* don't want him back, Jenny.'

Jenny gulped the rest of the juice from the glass. 'Good, well, that's fine.' Jenny floundered. She didn't know what to say to this different Laura. In the past her friend would have burst into floods of tears and punished herself with recriminations, but she could tell that the woman sitting in front of her would never do that.

'I've started decorating the house,' Laura told her. 'I've painted and wallpapered the lounge and bedroom, and have a new bed and furniture to match. It looks lovely.'

Laura stopped after this admission not wanting to tell Jenny that she intended to move to a smaller place. It might make Jenny feel even more guilty if she thought that her decision to move was because Phil had left. Which, in a way it was, but it was more her own choice than anything else – she really didn't have to move out of the house, but she wanted to. There was, Laura knew, a great difference in these two statements.

Laura took a deep breath. 'And, I'm going to start on the bathroom next. The tiles and old shower are awful. So, it's out with the old and in with the new,' she breezed.

Jenny gaped at her friend. 'Gr … great, well, I've got the number for that interior designer if you want it?'

'No thanks,' Laura said. 'I don't need it. I've designed it all myself. And when you're feeling up to it you can pop round and see what I've done. I've really enjoyed it, actually.'

Laura looked at the surprise on Jenny's face and decided that she still looked too fragile to cope with any more changes. She smiled reassuringly, 'So, are we going to have supper – how about a curry?'

Jenny got up from her knees and smiled at Laura. Well, Jenny thought, there'll always be some things that a person can't change and Laura's love of food was one of them. Laura stood up, grabbed her jacket, and linked Jenny's arm as they went inside to search for the number of the Indian takeaway.

The next morning Jenny had driven them to Gosforth High Street and found a parking slot for two hours. Laura had happily chatted all the way down to the hair salon then suggested a shopping spree afterwards. But, Laura could feel the anxiety coming off Jenny in spades as she linked her and they entered the salon. The young girl at Reception commented that it had been a while since Jenny had been and Laura had intervened explaining that she'd had a nasty virus and had been laid up for weeks.

As the hairstylist finished Jenny's hair and showed off her handiwork in the mirror Jenny jumped up out of the chair and hurried to the desk with her purse. Laura joined her and once they were outside on the pavement Jenny set off at a fast pace walking quickly to the car park.

Laura hurried alongside to keep up with her. 'Your hair looks gorgeous,' she prattled as they reached Jenny's Micra. 'The highlights are fab!'

Jenny nodded and brought the keys out of her denim jacket pocket. Laura noticed her hands trembling as she held them out to her.

'Laura would you drive us back? I can't face it.'

Laura took the keys and opened the driver's door while Jenny slid onto the passenger seat.

Jenny sat forward and covered her face with her hands taking huge sighs of relief. She knew that Laura was staring at her and must think that she was crazy, but she'd found the whole experience traumatic. The noise in the salon of women talking and laughing and hair dryers whirling had seemed deafening. And, when the young girl who washed her hair began asking her inane questions about holidays she'd wanted to scream and run from the room.

Jenny began to breathe slowly and deeply as the counsellor had taught her to do if she felt panicky and perspiration began to form on her lip – she longed to be at home where she felt safe.

Laura drove out of the car park heading home and kept up a steady stream of general chat about their hair styles and colour while Jenny took comfort from her friend's presence. She knew she would never have been able to do this on her own.

As soon as Laura turned off the engine Jenny opened the car door and was practically running down her garden path. She hurried through to her lounge and flung herself down onto the settee with waves of relief flooding through her body.

'Are you OK?' Laura asked sitting down next to her and rubbing her back.

Jenny took a few deep breaths. 'I think so. It was awful,' she said, then began to tell Laura how she'd felt inside the salon.

Laura said, 'Well that's probably because you've got used to the peace and quiet of being at home for weeks – and anywhere will appear loud and noisy at first.'

Jenny nodded and felt her heart rate slow back to normal. She wiped the back of her hand across her mouth. 'Oh, Laura, will I ever be myself again? How will I ever get back to work if I can't find the confidence to go out on my own?'

Laura smiled and rubbed Jenny's shoulder. 'You will eventually. Remember how the counsellor told you to space things out and do activities in reasonably-sized chunks.'

They talked about Jenny's confident old self and both agreed that there were aspects of her bolshie personality that were best left behind in the past, but there was also some traits that she could change and adapt.

'Stop being so hard on yourself and try to look on it in a positive way,' Laura said. 'You can be a whole new woman and keep all the good bits about yourself, of which I might add there are many. And in time, you'll learn to cope and find your strength in different ways by talking with us and using your new hobbies. And ...' she added drawing her eyebrows together, 'by staying off the booze.'

Jenny nodded. 'I know, and it's daft worrying about the future and my career, but I suppose as a working woman it's what I'm used to doing.'

'True, but you've always been more ambitious than I ever was,' Laura said.

Jenny thought about this comment and knew it was the impression she'd always given people. Time to put things straight, she thought. 'I wasn't really, Laura. Getting my job as QA manager came about simply by throwing myself back into my work after each of the miscarriages. I found that work helped to keep the pain and misery from my mind. And, the harder I worked the higher up the ladder I climbed,' she said staring down at her hands. 'But, I realise now that I should have dealt with it and grieved properly like the counsellor has told me.'

Laura looked down at Jenny's hands which were trembling and she noticed that Jenny had stopped biting her nails and picking at the skin. She had come a long way in a few weeks, Laura thought, and could tell how hard her friend was trying. Laura supposed that this was a good sign and the time to worry would be when Jenny stopped trying altogether. Laura laid her hands over Jenny's. 'Don't talk about it now if it's too painful.'

But Jenny looked up at Laura and pulled her shoulders back. 'No, I'm going to,' she determined. 'This new woman can talk about painful issues and try to deal with them. I'm not going to bury my grief away in my mind any longer. It has to come out in the open.'

Jenny began to talk about when she'd first met Steve and how she'd fallen for him very quickly. 'But I still wasn't too sure how he felt about children until he took me to his family home for the first time. We were surrounded by his nieces and nephews shouting and playing and jumping on top of him in the garden,' she said grinning at the memories. 'As Steve was the youngest of five, his older brothers and sisters had produced nine children between them and he told me it was his turn to add to the brood. And our kids will always have loads of cousins to play with he'd said, to which I'd laughed and agreed with him. The next day when we'd ended up in bed together and lay talking about our future he'd stated that he wanted at least four children. And I'd happily gone along with him. From that day forward I never even thought about using contraception, and knew that if and when it happened we'd both be over the moon – married or not – it wouldn't matter.'

Laura could feel Jenny's hands calm under hers now and she confidently removed her own thinking about Jenny's words.

Laura thought how different it had been with her and Phil. They'd never even discussed having children or getting married and being pregnant had suddenly landed upon them when really, they were far too young to cope. As she dragged her mind back from the late nineties, she sighed, maybe in one way; she could begin to understand why Phil's dad gave him the money to escape.

Chapter Fifteen

By the end of the week Laura didn't know how much longer she could last without touching Luigi. Every time she saw him at work her heart would race and thump along as though she'd just completed a marathon. An ache would begin in her chest and she literally couldn't stop thinking about him caressing her body – it was hard to keep her eyes off him. She longed to be with him and her feelings were actually coming between them when they talked about the products they'd developed. The products were now ready to present to the Irish contingent and the meeting had been arranged for the following Friday. Laura worried she wouldn't be at her best if she couldn't focus her mind on something other than Luigi's body.

'You seem a little distracted.' Luigi asked as he perched on the end of her desk.

Laura swallowed hard, trying not to stare at his large thighs that were clad in navy blue trousers. She could smell his aftershave and when she raised her eyes she noticed the black hairs on his chest peeking out from his open shirt collar. Laura appreciated the fact that he wanted to wait, but how much longer would that be? Maybe she was supposed to wait for him to say when the time was right, or, was he waiting for her to say that? She decided to take the plunge and croaked, 'I ... I wondered if you'd like to come to mine for supper tonight?'

Startled by the question Luigi knocked Laura's container of pens and pencils from the side of the desk and cursed under his breath.

'Well, yes. That would be very good,' he said and then bent over to pick up the pens that had scattered across the floor.

Laura looked at the blue material stretched tight across his firm bottom and bit her lip. Dear, God, she thought, how much more was a woman supposed to take?

Running through the door from work at six Laura hurriedly put a chicken in the oven to roast and stood under the shower longer than usual as her mind whirled with the thoughts of what she was about to do. Maybe she was overreacting to the feelings she had for Luigi as she'd been on such an emotional rollercoaster lately, and she thought, a counsellor would probably advise her to wait until these feelings settled. But, she didn't want to be sensible Laura any longer – she wanted to be carefree and enjoy herself.

The bright chestnut colour the hairdresser had used on her curls was vibrant and shiny and she applied just a little make-up very carefully. She pulled on a cream sleeveless dress over her head which settled with a jaunty frill just above her knees and then slipped her feet into cream slingbacks. At the sound of the doorbell, and with a churning stomach, Laura ran down the stairs and opened the front door.

Luigi too had been in a bit of a flap as he drove over to her house. He'd been totally surprised when Laura had asked him outright if he'd like to come for supper and although he'd agreed he did have certain reservations. He'd found it hard enough this week keeping his distance from her at work, and although he knew it was his suggestion to wait until she was ready, he hadn't envisaged what a struggle this was going to be. If all she had in mind was food and drink then it was going to be excruciating for him to keep his emotions in check, but at the same time he couldn't refuse her anything – it was beyond him.

Laura showed Luigi around the downstairs explaining the new decoration and how it had been before as they sipped a glass of wine. At the mention of the bathroom she led him upstairs and showed him the tired old tiles and shower. Luigi made suggestions about rearranging the position of the bath which would leave room for a modern walk-in shower and glass screen, and what colours she could use to distract from the fact that although it wasn't a small room, it did have a tiny window.

Luigi followed her into the main bedroom at the front of the house and grinned at the colours of grey and lemon. 'Ah,' he said. 'But you've done such a marvellous job, Laura. And, they are the same colours as mine – I will feel quite at home.'

Realising what he'd meant to say hadn't sounded quite right as they were standing in her bedroom. He flushed and rubbed along the neck of his T-shirt. 'Sorry, I …'

Laura took a deep breath. It suddenly dawned upon her that she had no experience of how to date, or how to entice a man; her last effort with Phil had been a disaster. But, she concluded, she felt like a different woman now and knew if Luigi did knock her back she wouldn't fall in a heap.

Laura wasn't sure if this was the wrong thing to do or not, but she didn't want him to feel uncomfortable in her home. She walked towards him and wound her arms around his neck. 'Luigi, please kiss me,' she whispered.

Luigi gasped and stared into her eyes that were now wide with passion for him. He put his hand onto her throat and gently tilted her head back slightly then covered her lips with his. She met his passion as he kissed her and encircled her tongue with his own. Desire and passion flooded through him.

Laura was lost in his kiss, his lips, and the feel of him pushing hard against her belly. She pulled him further towards the bed and then broke away from his mouth to take a big gulp of air. 'I need you, Luigi,' she said urgently. 'I've wanted to be with you for so long now I can't bear to wait another minute.' She ran both her hands inside his T-shirt and up his chest, working her fingers between his hairs and moaning with desire.

Luigi shook his head. He couldn't believe that a woman like Laura would want him as much as he wanted her. 'Are you sure?' he croaked. His mouth was dry with lust, but knew deep down that she had to be certain. Quickly he looked around the room. 'I am in another man's bedroom.' Laura pulled back from him. He was worrying about Phil, she thought, which although was endearing to know that he cared about her, it also made the hairs bristle on the back of her neck. 'You're not!' she shouted. 'This isn't another man's bedroom. This is my bedroom and I know my own mind. I have no feelings left whatsoever for Phil. And I don't want to be with anyone else but you!'

Luigi's heart soared. He put his arms around her and pushed her gently back onto the bed. 'Oh, cara,' he whispered, and lay next to her, running his hands up the side of her silky dress.

Confident now that she'd made him understand how she felt, Laura began to push his T-shirt up his chest until he removed it and threw it to the floor. She wriggled up to a sitting position and pulled the dress over her head. Desire surged through her body and she scrunched handfuls of his hair. 'Please, Luigi,' she moaned. 'Make love to me now.'

Luigi groaned in ecstasy at this beautiful little woman underneath him. He quickly pulled off his jeans and shorts then heard her gasp in surprise. 'I'll be careful, my darling,' he whispered into her ear.

She'd only ever known Phil before, but she matched his rhythm and movement.

Afterwards, Laura's curls were plastered to her forehead as she lay with her face on his chest, listening to the steady beat of his heart. She curled her toes and sighed happily with the relief that oozed through her body – she'd spent months longing for this release and told him exactly that.

'Ah, my lovely Laura,' he muttered. 'I'm so glad to be of service to you.'

She giggled and then sat up in alarm at the smell wafting up the staircase. 'The chicken!' she cried then grabbed her robe and fled downstairs. Rescuing the well-done chicken from the oven, Laura set it onto a tray with some crusty bread rolls, and the bottle of wine. She turned the lock on the front door and switched out all the lights then headed back up to the bedroom. They were going nowhere tonight, she decided happily – she had a lot of making up to do.

They did in fact, stay in bed most of the weekend – Laura felt insatiable and couldn't get enough of him. On Saturday night they lay together in front of the electric fire on her new white sheepskin rug. She told Luigi about the night she'd tried to seduce Phil and how dreadfully it had knocked her confidence. 'I thought it was me and that I was no longer any good at sex,' she said.

Luigi clicked his tongue in annoyance. 'Laura, sex is just an act that a man and a woman do together. When it is not good it is because the couples are not right for each other, or there is no special feeling between them. You were fantastic last night, and this morning,' he soothed then grinned mischievously. 'And then again this afternoon. We are just getting to know each other's bodies, and for me, well, I couldn't ask for anything more – you are *bellissimo*!'

Luigi failed to understand how any man could turn down such a beautiful woman as Laura. She was loving and gentle, yet could be passionate and sensual in every sense of the word – she oozed sex appeal from every inch of her body. It was his job now to build up her confidence and make her believe in herself again. He wanted to make her feel like a million dollars, or euros, he thought grinning.

'And, have you still got the outfit?' he asked raising an eyebrow. When she'd nodded he whispered, 'Go and put it on for me.'

A few minutes later, Laura sauntered back into the lounge wearing the black cami, stockings, and high heels. Bolstered up by two glasses of brandy they'd had earlier, she began to parade around the lounge, swinging the bottle of brandy casually in her hand.

Luigi sat on the rug watching her and caught his breath. He wanted her over and over again and felt greedy yet powerless all at the same time. The black cami was just short enough to show off her neat bottom as she sashayed backwards and forwards in front of him, and her small breasts peeked out of the cami as though they were saying come get me – she looked amazing.

'You're already fantastic, Laura,' he said with pride shinning in his eyes. 'Are you sure you're not Italian?'

She giggled as he pulled her down on top of him into his lap revelling in the sight and feel of her. 'You look like a model in a magazine,' he coaxed. 'Just let yourself go, Laura, and do what comes naturally. Your legs look great in those stockings, and the high heels are so sexy they're driving me crazy!'

He felt her release and marvelled again at how quickly and easily their bodies had become one. He'd struggled as a young man to discover how to pleasure a girl and it hadn't been until he was married that he swiftly learned that pleasing his woman was every bit as important, if not more, than the pleasure he took from her. Yet, this feels so different to my marriage, he thought, and this beautiful woman sitting in my lap is so very special. He'd once read that there was a big difference between having sex and making love and he had to admit that being with Laura was the first time he'd felt it. Laura made him feel special in his heart and although he wanted to protect and look after her, at the same time he respected her for the independent woman she was.

On Sunday morning, Laura woke early and felt Luigi wrapped around her back snoring lightly – she couldn't believe that this gorgeous man was sleeping next to her and sighed at the security of his broad chest behind her. She knew by previous comments Luigi had made that he thought of himself as overweight, but she didn't care what shape or size he was – in her eyes Luigi was the perfect lover.

She grinned to herself and squeezed her thighs together with the memories of the night before and how she had made love to him. As she'd stood outside the lounge door in the sexy lingerie she'd been hesitant, but when she saw the obvious delight on his face, she'd decided she had nothing to lose and even surprised herself.

He was so much more passionate than what Phil had ever been and he encouraged her to take the lead, which was a new experience for her. In the past she'd always had to wait for Phil to make the decision as to whether they would make love or not. But now Luigi asked her to rouse his body whenever she wanted him. He shouted her name loudly and told her over and over again how beautiful she was. He called her cara, which she knew was an Italian expression of endearment, and she returned his compliments in her own way. Maybe this was the Italian way to make love, she mused, but whichever way it was she wasn't complaining – she loved every minute they were together.

'Good morning, my lovely Laura,' he whispered into her ear and she laughed.

She wriggled around to face him and he kissed the tip of nose.

'Did you sleep well?' she asked staring into his half open eyes.

'I did, this new bed of yours is *perfetto*,' he said. 'Which, is just as well because we've hardly been out of it since Friday night. Shall we go out for brunch somewhere and call at my flat?'

Laura wondered if there was a reason why he wanted to go back to his place and raised an eyebrow. 'Yes, of course, if you want to,' she said.

'Good,' he said throwing the quilt aside. 'I'll go into your shower and then we'll call at mine first so I can change my clothes.'

As Laura heard the shower running she went into the bathroom and laid two fresh towels on the rail.

'Thank you, cara,' he said through a face of shampoo.

Grabbing her arm he expertly removed her robe and pulled her into the shower with him.

She gasped as the hot water splashed down around them and then hooted with laughter as he rinsed the shampoo off. The drops of water glistened on his black hair and his green shinning eyes danced with happiness. Laura sighed with pleasure – he looked absolutely gorgeous.

OK, she thought, he doesn't want me to hold back, so I'm not going to. She squirted a handful of body wash into the palm of her hand and began to lather, him watching and smiling in delight as he groaned at the touch of her hands.

Laura giggled. 'You really are the Italian stallion,' she murmured and then explained what his nickname was when he'd first joined the company.

Luigi roared with laughter and then turned her around to face the tiles washing her back. 'Now you can tell people what the stallion is really like!' he cried and she laughed until longing overtook her again and she clung onto the shower curtain.

Chapter Sixteen

Four weeks later, Laura was wandering around grinning at anyone and everyone. She knew she must look like some type of half-wit, but simply couldn't help it – she'd never felt so happy. Luigi was everything she could ask for in a man. Honest, considerate, a strong, passionate lover, and above all else, Laura knew he was now her best friend. He'd slipped into the role and she relied upon Luigi trusting him with her secrets and innermost feelings. As she'd lain in his arms the night before, he'd cupped her face with his hands and she'd thought for a moment that he was going to say the three magic words, I love you.

But, she thought, pulling up outside Jenny's house, she was glad he hadn't because she wasn't sure she could say those words to any man yet and actually mean them. She loved many things about him, and he made her very happy, so much so, she could honestly say that she wasn't interested in any other men – but did that actually mean she was in love with him? She shook her head at that question, and began to think about another decision she'd been mulling over all week – should she tell Jenny about Luigi?

She did want to tell her friend all about him, but had held back the last few times she'd been to see her because as awful as it may seem, she still didn't know if she could trust her again. After all, Laura thought, remembering their conversation in Debenhams, Jenny had liked Luigi first, and although Luigi had told her Jenny wasn't his type of woman, would her friend be jealous? Laura bit her lip, feeling the old resentment and bitterness towards Jenny sweep over her. She sighed with the knowledge that these feelings weren't going to disappear overnight, and it could be months or even years before she could forgive her completely.

Laura was still calling on Jenny twice a week, and although her progress was slow she looked and said she felt much better. Jenny was going out and about again on her own now, still having her counselling sessions, and taking her medication. Last week Jenny had asked the counsellor's opinion about returning to work soon. And Muriel had asked their HR department to ring Jenny who suggested a phase-back-in scheme they could put together for her return.

Laura climbed out of her Mini and frowned. If Jenny did go back to work soon then she'd certainly have to tell her, because as hard as she'd tried to keep her relationship with Luigi a secret at work, she knew everyone was talking about them.

'Hiya,' Laura called as she opened Jenny's front door. There was no sight of Jenny and suddenly Laura froze in the hallway. She could hear footsteps above on the landing and broke out into a cold sweat. Memories of the night of the party overpowered Laura and she felt her knees quiver. Who was upstairs? Was it Jenny with another man?

Suddenly, Jenny appeared at the lounge door. 'Laura?' she asked. 'What's wrong?'

Jenny followed Laura's eyes that were staring upwards and saw the terror on her face. She took Laura's arm and pulled her through into the lounge. 'It's Steve,' she said quietly. 'He's in the loo …'

Laura took a deep breath and chastised herself for being silly then sat down on the settee slipping off her jacket. The lounge seemed full of yellow roses which were in three separate vases and she inhaled the fragrance. Jenny had told her how Steve had rang when he heard she'd been ill and had offered to go with her to the counselling sessions and sit in the waiting room. Apparently, today had been one of those days.

Jenny stood in front of Laura and fiddled with a silver bracelet. She felt incredibly hurt that Laura could even think she would sleep with Phil again. She raised her eyes and nodded through the open doorway towards the stairs. 'I would never do that again, Laura,' Jenny said.

Laura could feel her cheeks flush and she bit her lip. She'd overreacted and made a fool of herself. 'Sorry,' Laura said. 'I know you wouldn't. I don't know what came over me.'

Thinking of that night made Jenny shudder. It seemed so far in the past that she struggled to believe herself capable of doing it – but, she had, and she'd betrayed her closest friend. She looked at Laura, knowing it was going to take a long time to build up the trust again between them. Jenny didn't say this out loud, but could tell Laura knew it was what she was thinking.

'Hi there,' Steve boomed, making a noisy entrance through the lounge door.

Laura stood up and he pecked her on the cheek. 'Hey Steve, how's life treating you?'

Steve Campbell was what Laura's mam had once called a long red streak. He was six foot three, thin as a rod, with a full head of ginger hair. Even in his thirties, Laura noted, the colour was just as bright and hadn't faded one iota. He was also one of the friendliest and kindest men Laura had ever met.

'Fine,' he said. 'Well, shocked and upset last week when I heard about my little Jenny …'

Jenny comically raised an eyebrow, 'Me, little? I didn't shrink when I had the breakdown, Steve,' she pouted good-humouredly. 'I'm still six foot!'

Steve grinned. 'Ah, but you'll always be my little one,' he said taking hold of her hand.

Steve sat down at the opposite end of the settee to Laura, and Jenny moved to sit in the armchair, but he pulled her down in the middle of them.

Laura said, 'Ah, that's nice, Steve. It's good to see you again and nice to see you're being such a good friend to Jenny.'

Still holding onto Jenny's hand he squeezed it tightly. 'Well, I don't do much I just sit in the waiting room and then make us a cup of tea when we get back, he said. 'And, I would have been here sooner if I'd known, but I didn't find out until last week when I bumped into Phil.'

Both women looked at each other and Laura raised an eyebrow then sighed.

'Yeah,' Steve continued, 'I hadn't seen him for weeks to play golf then I saw him coming out of a pub in Newcastle. Apparently, he's going out with a physiotherapist who works up at Freeman Hospital, and is also messing around with a young widow in Manchester!'

This time both the women looked at each other and screwed up their noses in disgust.

'Jesus, I'm sorry, Laura,' he mumbled. 'I never thought ...' and then looked beseechingly at Jenny for help.

Jenny tutted but smiled. 'You see, Laura, Steve still has as much tact as he's always had!'

All three of them burst into laughter, and Laura reassured him. 'It's OK, Steve,' she said. 'I'm over the worst of it all now. Phil has hardly been at work because he's doing a special project which means a lot of

travelling. But he has his own life to live, as I have mine.'

Steve puffed out his chest. 'Well, all I can say he is an idiot and after I heard what he did to Jenny when she was ill, well, let's put it this way, he's no friend of mine any more. In fact, I've even taken his number out of my mobile!'

Jenny nodded. She knew Steve was defending her and didn't really deserve his support. 'No, Steve,' she said. 'We have to be honest here. It was my fault as much as Phil's for letting it happen. And at the time, although I didn't realise I was ill, neither did he.'

Steve grimaced and clenched his fists. 'Even if he didn't know, he still should have had the decency not to mess about with his wife's best friend,' he stated firmly. 'Oh, and by the way I heard about Peter punching him a bloody nose, Laura?'

Laura blushed. 'I know and Peter shouldn't have, but he was just so shocked and upset. I'm hoping in time though, he'll try to patch things up with Phil. After all, no matter what type of idiot Phil is being at the moment, he's still Peter's dad ...'

Jenny sighed. 'Yeah, and kids need both their parents,' she whispered. Childhood memories fleeted through her mind. 'And at least Peter knows who his father is.'

Jenny remembered the steady stream of her mother's boyfriends. 'Me and Kate had to call Mum's boyfriends 'uncle',' she said. 'I think there was an Uncle Geoff, and an Uncle Rob, from all the ones I remember. Oh, and an Uncle Howard, now he was a nice guy. He used to give me money so that I didn't have to rob it out of Mum's purse when she was unconscious.'

Laura looked at Jenny with tearful eyes and Steve squeezed her hand tighter.

Jenny continued, 'You see, I had to buy food and clothes for me and Kate because the teachers at school had begun to comment upon our shabby uniforms. I used to give all my clothes to Kate when they were too small for me. And that's why she won't entertain hand-me-downs now. When she's worn something for a year or so, it goes to charity shops and then she buys new stuff – it drives John crazy!'

Laura rubbed the side of Jenny's arm. 'You don't have to do this now, love,' she said.

Jenny took a deep breath. There was a large part of her agreed with Laura because she didn't want to talk about it and the pre-breakdown Jenny would have brushed the thoughts from her mind and changed the subject, but she remembered her morning counselling session and pushed on. 'I need to,' Jenny said. 'I have to get used to talking about it because the counsellor reckons it's a good thing to do especially when I'm with my friends. And …' she looked between them both, 'you two *are* my oldest friends.'

Laura nodded, and Steve let go of Jenny's hand then wrapped an arm along her shoulder hugging her tightly.

'This week in the sessions we've been talking about my tough personality and how embittered I can appear at times,' she muttered looking down at her hands. 'I think it first started in my early teens when we were at school and Kate's classmates taunted her about our clothes and the cheap trainers we wore. I was always sticking up for her against the bullies, but now I've realised that by the time I was fifteen I'd become a bully myself, and had developed this angry and resentful attitude towards everyone.'

Steve cried out aloud, 'But that's not bullying, Jenny. It's simply self-defence!'

'Nevertheless, Steve, it is a form of bullying. I used to think that if I got in first the kids would know I was a force to be reckoned with and would leave little Kate alone.'

Laura cringed listening to Jenny's school memories. She remembered how her own mam used to have her uniform ready every morning hanging on the wardrobe door, washed and pressed to an inch of its life. And how both her parents were at every parent's evening, proudly glowing at all her achievements, however small they were. She recalled the birthday parties they'd thrown for all her school friends and how days before her mam would stand in the kitchen baking for hours.

Laura couldn't for one moment fathom what Jenny's life had been like, let alone understand it. Laura looked at her friend now, sapped of all her strength and confidence. It was, she thought, as though we've switched places and personalities. I've gained strength and confidence from being left alone, whereas Jenny has lost all of hers and is struggling to find herself again.

Unable to stop herself a big tear ran down Laura's face. 'Oh, Jenny,' she muttered. 'It must have been a living hell for you. No wonder you've made yourself ill trying to deal with all of this.'

Jenny shook herself and patted Laura's hand. 'Now look what I've done! I've unloaded myself onto you two and depressed us all,' she said. 'But I do thank you for listening.'

Steve removed his arm from Jenny. 'I'll make us some coffee,' he said brightly. 'Hey Laura, I must say you look fantastic at the minute – you're positively blooming! If I didn't know any better, I'd think you were in lurve …'

Jenny kicked him lightly on the ankle. 'Go make the coffee, Steve, and please try to put your brain into gear before you open your mouth.'

Laura giggled and watched him head into the kitchen. In one way she was pleased that Steve had been there because it had solved her dilemma – there was no way she could tell Jenny about Luigi tonight – it would have to wait for another time.

Chapter Seventeen

By the end of July Laura was spending most weekends with Luigi. He'd accompanied her to view some properties in the area, but Laura had made the decision that when, or if, she got a buyer for the house, she would first rent somewhere for six months. Phil wasn't putting any pressure on her to sell, but he had said it would be better sorted out sooner rather than later, then, financially, they could both move forward. Where Phil would be moving Laura didn't much care – he was hardly ever in her thoughts nowadays.

It was amazing, she thought, as she left work early on Friday, how quickly her life had changed. She climbed into her car and threw her laptop onto the back seat to head over to Luigi's flat. If someone had told her last Christmas that within seven months her marriage would be over, she'd be selling the house, and having an amazing relationship with a hot-blooded Italian, she'd have laughed in their face. But here she was doing just that, and loving every minute.

She sighed with pleasure thinking of Luigi and how he certainly lived up to the Italian reputation. It wasn't so much the sex, she mused, turning the key in the ignition, although that was incredible; it was his passionate personality and verve for life in general. Every weekend he planned an activity for them to do together, whether it was a visit to the cinema, a walk in the countryside, ten pin bowling, or swimming at the local pool. In the past her free time had consisted of shopping at weekends and hanging out with Jenny while Phil enjoyed his solo activities, but now she agreed with Luigi that it was nicer to do things together as a couple.

The weather forecast for the weekend was good and she'd decided to take Luigi up to Northumberland to walk on the beaches, and he had tickets to see a play that night at the Theatre Royal in Newcastle.

The next morning, they stepped out of Luigi's flat into the car park and Laura rummaged in her bag for her car keys.

'Oh no,' Luigi stated shaking his head firmly. 'I know this is your plan for the day out, but there's no way we are going any amount of distance in that car! My legs won't survive.'

He pulled his car keys out of his knee-length denim shorts and opened the door of the Audi as she giggled and slid onto the seat. On the drive north Laura gave directions as the sun shone brightly and she peered at him from behind her sunglasses. He looks gorgeous today, she thought, smiling. Because of his olive skin he seemed tanned all year round. She glanced down at her own white legs that were partially covered by a flowery short skirt. She'd lost a few pounds lately and with Jenny's help on Thursday night they'd shopped together for new summer clothes. 'Mamma Mia!' Luigi had said in the bedroom earlier that morning when she'd dressed in the skirt and a white off-the-shoulder top. Laura wasn't certain whether the outfit was too young for her. Luigi, however, loved it, 'In those white leather sandals, cara, you look like a Spanish lady stepping out of her hacienda.'

There was nothing, Laura thought, that she could do or say that ever seemed to trouble him.

He supported and encouraged her with all her decisions, and if he had a different viewpoint he would give it is such a way that she never felt browbeaten as she had done in her marriage.

They crossed the road and reached the wide expanse of white sand.

Luigi was amazed and took off his sandals to wriggle his toes in the sand as they began to walk. The sea at that time of day was way back on the beach but he still wanted to wade through it.

Laura was pleased he was enjoying himself. 'We have some of the best beaches in the country,' she told him. 'Unfortunately, we don't often get warm sunny days like this to enjoy them.'

They stopped for lunch at a beach-side café and then returned to the car and drove back down towards Embleton beach. With the radio playing they both sang, out of tune, to a Beatles song and Luigi explained how listening to English pop songs had helped him learn the language at school. Laura wiped her glasses on the rib of the gypsy top, and decided she'd never felt so happy.

By four in the afternoon Embleton beach was practically deserted. Although the sun had disappeared and the sky was mainly full of cloud, it was still warm and they chose a spot near the dunes to sit side by side on Luigi's jacket.

Laura sighed. 'I just couldn't believe it when Steve told us that Phil is seeing two different women at the same time,' she said, and drew circles in the sand with her fingers.

Luigi draped an arm along her shoulders. He shook his head and wondered whether to tell Laura about the lap dancer in Leeds. He'd noticed lately that whenever Phil's name was mentioned at work her eyes seemed to fill with sadness and he couldn't bear to see her upset. He wanted all of their time spent together to be happy and carefree, but when he saw her lift her head up towards him he realised she wanted to talk about her husband. 'I hate to even think of you with such a despicable man like Phil,' he said shaking his head and tutting with annoyance. 'The one thing I cannot understand is why you were married to a man like that for such a long time.'

Laura sighed heavily and wondered if Luigi thought of her as a doormat type of woman who would put up with anything just to keep her husband. 'But he wasn't always like that,' she exclaimed. 'You don't think for one moment that I would have stayed with a man if I'd known about him cheating behind my back, do you?'

Luigi squeezed her shoulders. 'Oh, cara,' he murmured. 'Of course I didn't mean that. But I do know how kind hearted you are and I thought maybe you had put up with many things for the sake of your son. I think in some marriages this is a common situation.'

Laura frowned and then explained how Phil used to be when they were first married, how he'd been a great dad to Peter, and how everyone knew Phil as Mr Nice Guy.

'Hmm,' he muttered darkly. 'Well, he certainly has changed now, because I can think of many words to describe Phil, but nice is not one of them.'

Luigi looked out to sea rather than stare at the pained look in Laura's eyes. When he saw her upset he raged between feeling actual hurt in his belly which made him want to howl like a child, or such anger that he could cheerfully punch Phil until he squealed like the cowardly pig he was.

Laura looked at the same view of the shore and cursed herself for talking about Phil in the first place. She knew how Luigi hated him and it had put a dampener on the afternoon. Laura craned her neck back and looked up at the seagulls screaming above them and remembered how Peter had been frightened of the noise when he was a toddler and how Phil had scooped him up into his arms. She had enjoyed memories like this before Phil's infidelity had been exposed, she thought, but with now with Michael's words buzzing around in her mind she felt that they were all ruined. Did Phil wish he'd taken the money and run off to avoid marrying her because she was pregnant? And had all of those years been a lie?

She looked back down and saw Luigi's face close to hers. He whispered, 'I'll give you a penny for them?'

She shook her head and determined to cheer up. 'They aren't worth a euro,' she said. 'Let's forget it and talk about something else.'

'No,' he said. '. I can't bear to see you upset, but if you need to tell me what is on your mind then tell me.'

Laura smiled and nodded. 'OK,' she said, grinning, and then told him what she'd learnt from Michael.

'And Phil's dad is …' he asked circling a finger next to his temple, 'Not in his normal mind?'

Laura explained about the Alzheimer's and watched Luigi translating the information in his head. He raised an eyebrow. 'This is a cruel blow to an intelligent man, but you cannot be sure he was talking about Phil. Plus, if you insist that Phil tells you the truth he will lie his way out of it to save hurting your feelings, yes?'

Laura realised Luigi was right. 'Probably,' she said. 'I know there's nothing to be gained from asking Phil, but all the same it gnaws away at me to think I've spent years loving a man that might have only married me because I was pregnant!'

'Well, I don't think it is a clear-cut situation where children are involved,' he said and took her hands in between his. 'Shortly after me and Adrina were married she was late with her period and was very angry. She stormed around the house telling me that if she was pregnant she would get rid of the baby as she didn't want to be burdened with children when we were only twenty-two. I was distraught to think she'd even consider an abortion and had been delighted at the thought of becoming a father. The next day she told me that the period had just been late and she was so relieved she danced around the kitchen clapping her hands with happiness.'

Laura could feel the sadness in his slumped body and she squeezed his hands. 'Oh, Luigi,' she uttered. 'Were you very disappointed?'

He nodded. 'I went and sat outside in the evening sun with a glass of wine, and although I knew she was right because we were very young, I wanted to weep,' he said.

Laura ached for him and wondered if still dreamt of having his own family. Thirty-one wasn't old these days to be a parent, she thought, and then smiled realising they were on the same wavelength as he asked to meet Peter one day.

She smiled and he traced her cheek with his finger.

'Actually,' she said, 'I haven't seen too much of him during the last few weeks. He has a job in a bar working for the summer to save money for another hiking holiday. And, only last night I was wondering when you two should meet each other …' she paused and looked directly into his eyes. 'I didn't want to tell Peter about you earlier just in case, well, I wasn't sure if our relationship was going to last …'

This is it, Luigi thought; it's now or never, and decided to take the plunge. He'd been bursting all week to tell her how he felt, but had held it in check because he didn't know if it was too soon after the horrid few months she'd been through. But now he couldn't hold back any longer. 'Well, I'm in this for the long haul, cara,' he said and took a deep breath. 'I … I've fallen in love with you and can't bear the thought of ever being without you.'

Laura gasped. Oh my God, she thought, trying desperately to remain calm. This, she knew, was a defining moment between them and she could feel her knees trembling. Whereas, a few weeks ago she hadn't been certain if she could ever love again, now she knew for certain that what she felt for this man was indeed love, and she too never wanted to be parted from him.

'I love you too, Luigi,' she said shyly. She cupped his face with her small hands and took a deep breath. 'From the minute I leave you I can't stop thinking about you until I see you again.'

Her hands were warm on his face and his insides felt light – he wanted to whoop with joy. Knowing she felt the same was more than he could have ever dreamt possible and he kissed the inside of her palm as she ran her other hand through his thick hair.

'But what will happen to us?' Laura asked, 'I mean, will you go back to Italy eventually?'

He raised an eyebrow and grinned. 'I'm not sure, Laura,' he said. 'But wherever I go you're coming with me and, if you don't want to move abroad then this is where I'll stay right beside you.'

Laura felt as though she was flying with pure joy – she looked into his eyes and kissed him long and hard.

When Luigi pulled away from her mouth he sucked in lungful's of breath, and then grinned playfully. 'What a kisser!' he declared, pulling her back down into the sand. He lay behind her, with one arm wrapped securely around her middle, nibbling the top of her ear.

'I love you, I love you,' he kept whispering between kisses and Laura moaned softly. Luigi took this as a sign that she wanted more. They'd only made love that morning, but even if it had just been an hour ago it wouldn't have mattered – he lost all sense of time when he was with her and couldn't get enough of her body. Now that he knew she loved him it gave him the confidence to be himself, and he grinned mischievously. Let's see how brave she is, he thought, and whether she has more confidence after all the weeks we've spent together. He pushed his hand up her skirt.

'Luigi,' she giggled. 'Someone might see us!'

When she felt his fingers trail up to the top of her thigh and the softness of his hand on her skin she knew she was lost. The desire raged through her and she longed for him as if she hadn't seen him for a month. With a dry mouth she croaked, 'Shall we go home?'

Luigi pulled the white frill on her top further down her arm and began to kiss along the back of her shoulder. She groaned in delight and he saw her dig her nails into the sand. He started kissing the nape of her neck which he knew drove her wild. 'Ah my lovely Laura. But I can't wait that long,' he murmured.

She gasped and wildly looked around the beach. 'But we can't do it here.'

'Why not?' he soothed. 'There isn't anyone within miles of us – we are completely alone.'

Laura bit her lip as she felt him fiddling with the zip on his shorts. She'd only ever read about this in books or seen it happen on films. Did people actually have sex on a beach? As the feelings of lust burned inside her body she knew even if she wanted to she couldn't stop him now. She remembered a phrase she'd read in a teenage magazine the day before at the dentist surgery, and cried aloud, 'YOLO!'

'Is my sexy lady ready?' he whispered. She moved with him and forgot where she was as she climbed to the most intense place she'd ever known. As she felt the ecstasy flood through her in waves she heard the lap of the sea, and opened her eyes screaming his name as loudly as the seagulls above them.

Later, as they sat in the car at Seahouses with a fish and chip supper wrapped in newspaper Laura ate hungrily. 'There's nothing like a romp on the beach to give you an appetite,' she giggled.

He nodded, 'But I have to ask you one thing, Cara. What does YOLO mean?'

She laughed aloud, 'You only live once!'

On Monday morning Laura swooned around the office with vivid memories of her lovely weekend fleeting in and out of her mind. On their drive back from the beach, Luigi had said, 'Ah, cara, this song is for us.' He'd turned up the radio full blast with a recent song and they'd both sang along to the chorus, 'we can learn to love again'.

Alex has asked her the same question twice before she realised and then apologised to him making a ditzy blonde excuse for her absentmindedness. At his suggestion she wandered along to the canteen for a strong coffee and an early lunch.

Muriel was sitting alone at a table with a small container of salad in front of her and Laura joined her.

'I must say you look fantastic at the moment, Laura,' she said. 'And as there's just the two of us here I thought I'd say, good luck with your new man.'

Laura sighed. Everyone must know about her and Luigi for sure even though they had tried to keep it quiet. She decided there was no point in trying to bluff her way out of this with Muriel and apart from anything else, the older lady deserved her honesty and respect. 'Thank you, Muriel, I hadn't realised it was common knowledge.'

Muriel daintily put her fork into a cherry tomato and nodded. 'Well, I'd heard the rumours a few weeks ago, but then one of the girls from Finance saw you both up at Bamburgh beach on Saturday.'

Laura's heart nearly stopped, but when she reassured herself that their coupling had been later in the afternoon on Embleton beach, she sighed with relief. Muriel had raised an eyebrow and Laura knew she was waiting for her to say something.

'Well, there's no point in denying it,' Laura said and bit her lip. 'Yes, I'm seeing Luigi and …' she said pausing to look towards the door to make sure no one else was around, 'I'm loving every minute of it.'

Laura had thought Muriel would be wary and warn her about doing things on the rebound from Phil, and that her behaviour was not befitting a married woman, but Laura smiled in response when Muriel took her hand across the table and squeezed it tight.

'Good for you,' she stated. 'Just get out there with Luigi and have a great time. I know you've been through an awful few months lately and some people may advise to take your time, but not me. I believe in taking the bull by the horns and running with it while you have the chance.'

Laura relaxed her shoulders and grinned. 'Thanks, Muriel. It means a lot to have your support,' she giggled. 'They're some horn to hang onto, believe you me …' Muriel threw her head back and howled with laughter. They chatted briefly and then Muriel explained that she was having an early lunch before the board meeting. The older lady took Laura into her confidence and explained how the company was being bought out by a large PLC conglomerate in Manchester. 'But you're not to worry because we've been promised that all our jobs will be safe.'

Hmm, Laura thought, so that's why Phil has been spending so much time in Manchester with his merry widow, and then Muriel confirmed that Phil had secured himself a promotion to direct the new marketing team.

As Laura drove around the cul-de-sac shortly after six that evening the news about the takeover loomed large in her mind. Muriel had reassured her that her job would be safe, but she sighed at how differently her thoughts were now. If she'd heard news like this last year she would have instantly worried about being made redundant and losing the job she loved. Panic and worry would have filled her at the mere thought of them all having to look for work elsewhere, or even worse, having to move away from the area. But now, she thought, pulling up outside her house, if that did happen it really wouldn't be the end of the world, and confidently decided she'd be able to cope with the challenge. That was it, she thought, making big changes in her life didn't scare her any longer, and to be truthful, the thoughts of moving away to a new job and location with Luigi filled her full of excitement.

Laura let herself into the house making plans to take a long hot soak in the bath, but stopped suddenly in the hall as she heard noises from the kitchen. She hurried through into the kitchen shouting hello and then gasped at the sight of Peter buttering a slice of bread with jam.

'What are you doing here?' She exclaimed. 'Why didn't you tell me you were coming? I would have cooked something for us.'

Peter nodded towards the two piles of washing lying on the floor in front of the washing machine. 'Well, I didn't know if you would be around. I thought you might be staying over at your Italian lover's place.'

Laura gasped. Her hand flew to her neck and she felt her cheeks flush. How in God's name did he know about Luigi? Her stomach twisted with guilt, knowing that however he had found out, she should have been the one to tell him. Her mouth felt dry and she croaked, 'H ... how do you know?'

Peter sneered. 'Oh, I met up with Dad yesterday. He'd rung me last week and I went to talk to him yesterday in his flat.'

The thought that Peter had been to see Phil and she didn't know anything about it brought her up sharply – why hadn't either of them rung her?

'OK,' she nodded. 'Well, that was good. I mean, for you and Dad to talk.'

'Yeah,' Peter said screwing the lid back onto the jar. 'Dad's pleased that you're getting on with your own life, but he does think it's unfair to be cast as the baddie in all of this.'

Laura took a deep breath and felt a sinking feeling in the pit of her stomach – she stared at her son.

Peter put the jar back into the fridge and slammed the door shut. 'Because he reckons you were probably shagging the Italian behind his back months before he'd been with Jenny!'

Laura grabbed hold of the work surface behind her and felt as though she'd been physically punched. The bloody liar, she raged silently. How could Phil tell their son lies like that? Obviously, she thought, Phil would say anything to talk Peter around, and she knew the creep would be begging for Peter's forgiveness, which she could understand, but spreading vicious lies about her was beyond the pale. She folded her arms across her chest and stepped back. 'Now, just a minute,' she stated. 'That's utter rubbish. I didn't even know Luigi back then.'

Peter straightened up and pulled his shoulders back. Laura looked at the tall young man in front of her with anger and hurt blazing in his eyes. It was so very hard, she thought, to see her little boy in him now, and she had to fight the urge to wrap her arms around him and hold him tight – as ever, she wanted to make all the pain go away so he would feel better. Laura slowly shook her head and blew out a long breath as he stood facing her with his feet apart and his hands on the waistband of his jeans ready to do battle.

She stepped towards him with the palms of her hands turned upwards as if begging him to believe her. 'Please, Peter, you have to trust me on this one. Your dad is making all this up in an effort to get around you.'

Peter continued to stare at her and then shrugged his shoulders. He pulled himself up to sit on the top of the bench and tapped the toes of his trainers together. Laura could see the doubt flicker through his eyes now and prayed he was weakening. She pushed on. 'OK, Peter, name one occasion when I have ever lied to you. You saw first-hand the mess I was in when we found out what your dad had been up to. Would I really have been like that if I'd been with another man at the time?'

Laura watched him distractedly run a hand through his hair. She sighed and felt her stomach twist –

hadn't he been through enough during the last few months without suffering more upset? Indecision fleeted through her mind as she stared down at her son's trainers. In the past she'd often seen adults use children as weapons in their separation and divorce battles and had hated it. She frowned, wondering whether this was exactly what she was doing now.

'I don't know!' Peter yelled suddenly and jumped down from the bench. 'You could have been keeping this from me all the time because you always treat me like a child!'

Laura's heart began to race. She could feel her temper rising and she willed herself to stay calm. 'OK,' she said. 'If you want to be treated like an adult I'll tell you all about Luigi.'

But Peter shook his head and strode towards the kitchen door. 'I don't want to know anything about him,' he snarled.

Laura walked behind him staring at his ramrod back in a thin denim shirt. 'Look,' she cajoled, 'I didn't tell you at the beginning because I was worried it might upset you all over again. And …' she paused. 'Well, I wasn't too sure how long it was going to last with Luigi.'

'Oh right,' he scathed then swung around glaring at her. 'So, you didn't tell me just in case he turned out to be just a quick shag?'

Laura had reached the open doorway and grabbed hold of the stencil with one hand then clenched her other fist. 'Don't you dare speak to me like that! If you want to be treated like an adult then behave like one!'

Peter turned and stormed through the lounge as she hurried after him.

'So, Peter. It's OK for your dad to screw around with other woman, but when it's my turn to have a relationship then I'm automatically branded a slapper?' 'But you're my mother!' he yelled.

This struck a chord with Laura and she slumped down onto the arm of the settee as she heard Peter slam the front door. Tears filled her eyes and she banged her fist on the cushion at the back of the settee in frustration. This was so unfair. It was always one rule for men and another rule for women.

What was she supposed to have done – wait for the divorce before it was her turn to find some happiness in life? Perhaps she had let Peter down by not being there for him, and had she spent so much time with Luigi that she had neglected her son. She swallowed down a ball of misery that gathered in the back of her throat, and then sobbed.

As she soaked in the bath she received a text from her dad telling her not to worry about her wayward son because he was with them and having a stopover. Laura sighed, feeling the warm water relax her shoulders – if there was anyone Peter would listen to and that could make him see reason it was his gramps. But, Laura thought, pushing her big toe up into the tap, maybe it would be best to cool things for a while with Luigi and try to spend more time with Peter. They'd never had such a ferocious argument before and this slanging match, she thought, had unsettled her. Maybe, her son wasn't coping as well as she'd thought he was and he needed more support.

Later that night she talked to Luigi on his mobile from a hotel in Edinburgh. It was the beginning of a sales and commercial seminar which would last five days. After they'd talked about the company takeover and the new opportunities that might be ahead for them both, Laura told him about the argument with Peter and what Phil had said.

'That bastard!' Luigi fumed and shouted, 'I could quite easily rip his testicles from his body!'

Laura could imagine Luigi's eyebrows drawn together and his cold hard eyes as he swore in Italian. She took a deep breath – the last thing she needed now was more confrontation with Phil. 'Look, he's not important any more,' she soothed. 'It's Peter that is my priority now. And ...' she paused then bit her lip. 'I think we should take a breather for a while until I try to get things sorted out with Peter.'

Laura heard Luigi sigh heavily down the phone with disappointment and she felt her insides slump, feeling exactly the same. She smiled, loving the sound of his deep voice.

How was it possible to miss someone so much in less than twenty-four hours, she thought, shaking her head in disbelief. To be separated from him for even one night now was going to be unbearable because she loved him so much, but she remembered her son's hurt and troubled face and felt torn. Laura apologised to Luigi, telling him how much she would miss him and how already she felt much better for talking the problem through with him.

Reluctantly, Luigi agreed. 'As much as I will miss you I totally understood that the needs of your son must come first.'

Luigi sighed with disappointment as he turned off his mobile, poured himself another glass of wine, and recalled Laura's words. She'd said for a while, but how long did that mean? He frowned and dreaded the thought of only seeing her from a distance at work and not being able to touch her. He lay back on top of the huge bed, staring at the ceiling remembering the last few months he'd spent with Laura. From the very first time he'd made love to her, right up to the day on the beach when she'd told him she loved him and had screamed his name as loudly as the gulls above them. It was just beginning to dawn upon him how special this feeling of love was, and as it was a totally new experience for him, he sighed in confusion at how much it actually hurt. Maybe if he talked to Peter and told the boy just how much he loved his mother it might help. But what if that didn't work? If Laura's son wouldn't accept him in his mother's life, Laura might decide to reject him too.

His mouth dried and he swallowed hard, thinking of the pain this would cause when the tinkle of an email popped up onto his mobile and he grabbed the handset. Shaking his head in disbelief, he looked twice at the email address realising it was from his wife, Adrina. Maybe there'd been a problem with the divorce papers he'd signed last month or they hadn't reached her solicitor's office. But, as he read through her email he gasped in shock at her news.

Dearest Luigi,

I have separated from Antonio and have returned to Florence. I'd like to talk to you about our marriage before signing the divorce papers. Your mother has told me that you are due home for two weeks at the end of August. I am staying with them for the moment and hope we can spend some time together when you get here?

Love as ever, Adrina. XX

Luigi was flabbergasted. He sat up on the bed and shook his head. Adrina really was priceless, he thought grimacing. Obviously, now she was alone again she thought she could pick him back up again like a broken doll she'd cast aside. He punched the pillow and sighed with unhappy memories of the day he'd flown from the airport, heading towards England. Although he hadn't been completely devastated when she'd gone off with another man and he'd known his marriage was over, it hadn't been until he met Laura that he'd realised how much his confidence had been dented by his marriage. Well, no more, he determined, it had been his lovely Laura that had put him back together again and the way he felt about her outdid his feelings for Adrina ten-fold. He replied:

Adrina, thank you for the email, but I cannot see that we have anything to talk about. Our marriage is over and I have no intentions of rekindling anything between us. I would be grateful if you would sign the papers as soon as possible. It is true that I have two weeks' holiday in August but may not spend all of this time at home, Luigi.

What a night, he thought, wondering whether she would reply before he went to bed. This would certainly scupper his plans for August, he decided gloomily, because he had intended to ask Laura to go to Florence with him for the break and to meet the family. But, if Adrina was there this plan would need to be changed as no matter how many times he rebuked his wife she wouldn't give up if it was something she really wanted. And this would make things very awkward for Laura. Maybe he could take Laura to Rome or Venice instead, he thought, and then heard the incoming tinkle of Adrina's reply.

But, caro, I have money now which would make our lives together so much better than when we were younger. And I would like to invest in the family business with your sister, so that when you come home to live we can all work together again and be very happy. I can take us and the business up to another level with my fabulous new connections. Your mother and sister think it is a great idea. XX

Luigi sighed at the calculating business tone in the email and he imagined her loud, domineering voice – it set his teeth on edge. As they'd grown up together he'd thought her tall swagger was glamorous and that her natural beauty was enough to outweigh her spoilt and selfish personality. Now he knew different – the swagger was haughty and arrogant, and her beauty by no means made up for her cold nature.
He replied:

No, Adrina. This will never happen. There isn't enough money in the world that could fix our problems. England is my home now and for the present I don't intend to leave it. Whatever my family want to do with the business is entirely up to them. I wish you all success in the venture but it will never include me. I hope I have made myself clear, Luigi.

Luigi switched off his mobile and climbed under the sheets knowing his mother and sisters would hound him for days now with calls and texts to try to change his mind. He spread his legs out wide in the empty expanse and wished with all his heart that Laura was with him.

Chapter Eighteen

Just as Laura was rinsing her coffee mug in the kitchen the following morning Peter and her dad came through the front door, laughing. She hurried through to the lounge and looked at her dad who was wearing blue Ray-Ban sunglasses.

'Aren't they hideous, Mam?' Peter said grinning and she too burst into laughter.

Standing behind Peter, David removed the glasses and winked at Laura. She sighed with relief, knowing that everything was going to be OK and could sense that he had managed to help Peter is someway.

David pouted, 'Well, I thought they were on-trend?'

Laura giggled and Peter raised an eyebrow in mock exasperation at his gramps.

Peter stood in front of her and looked down at his feet. A sheepish half-cocked smile spread across his face. 'I'm sorry, Mam. I said some stupid stuff yesterday and well, I didn't mean any of it.'

Laura's heart soared with relief. She went to him and wrapped her arms around his waist hugging him tightly. 'Of course, you didn't,' she said. 'We never do. We're family, so it doesn't count, right?'

David wandered into the kitchen and switched on the kettle while Laura removed her arms and they both sat down on the dining room chairs listening to David making tea.

'I need a strong cuppa,' David said. 'Because we had a few pints last night and it takes me longer these days to shift a hangover.'

Peter grinned and Laura sighed. This was the man-toman session that Phil should be having with his son and not her dad. Mmm, she mused, maybe that's just the way families work sometimes and was only glad that Peter had some male influence at hand to support him. With mugs of hot tea and chocolate biscuits to dunk they sat around the table talking about what had happened.

Laura looked from her dad to Peter. 'I suppose your grandma spoilt you rotten last night?'

'Not really, but she did make me my favourite chicken dinner with Yorkshire puddings,' he said grinning. 'But it wasn't all high times. Gramps has read me the riot act and told me that it's high time I grew up and began to act my age. And he's right. I'm sorry, Mam.'

'It's over and behind us now,' Laura said waving her hand in the air. 'Forgiven and forgotten, but we do need to talk about where we go from here.'

David said, 'I've told Peter that I'm delighted to see my daughter happy again after what she's been through and that he should be too. And that I've met Luigi who has my seal of approval because he is a nice guy.'

Laura smiled and blushed slightly. 'He certainly is. And none of this was planned,' she said taking Peter's hand. 'I should have tried to explain that last night instead of being defensive and losing my temper. Luigi was just a friend at work first and then we grew close while working together on a project, and then I fell for him. Hook, line, and sinker.'

Peter nodded. 'OK,' he said and sipped the hot tea. 'You can tell me all about him later.'

Laura beamed at her dad. 'Luigi is up in Scotland for the week at training and business seminars but maybe when he gets back, and in your own time of course, you can meet him.'

Peter agreed and dunked another biscuit licking the melted chocolate from his long fingers.

'And just for the record, Peter,' David said. 'Your dad is talking a load of rot! Your mam was devoted to him all their married life, and still would be if he hadn't changed. I know my own daughter and she hasn't got it in her to deceive anyone – she couldn't tell a lie to save her life. So the suggestion that she was with Luigi before your dad left is complete and utter nonsense!'

Peter sighed. 'I get that now. But why did my dad have to say that? It's weird …'

Laura broke in. 'Don't be too hard on him, love,' she said. 'He's floundering at the moment. It sounds to me as though he's desperate to make amends with you whatever the cost.'

David shook his head and smiled at Laura. 'Where on earth did I get you from?' he said shaking his head in bewilderment. He smiled at her with fondness and love shining in his twinkly eyes. 'This lovely daughter of mine has always had an immense capacity to forgive people and understand their wrongdoings. And …' he paused, looking directly at Peter. 'What she's done to help drag your aunt Jenny from the depths of despair is nothing short of a miracle.'

'Well, it's what you taught me when I was growing up,' she said, smiling back at him. 'There's always a reason behind people's actions and there are usually two sides to every story. You used to drum that into me when I was little.'

It was a lovely moment between them all, and not for the first time, Laura knew exactly how lucky she was to have such a close and loving family.

David patted the back of her hand. 'Well, I'm not sure that even I would have had the courage to do what you've done. Me and your mam are very proud of you.'

Laura's face flushed bright red and she placed her cool hands against her cheeks. 'That's enough, Dad,' she said. 'I'm not blooming Mother Teresa!'

They all laughed out loud and Laura told Peter about her plans to spend more time with him. 'We can go out for lunch when you're not working, or, in the evenings we can go to the cinema. I've got holiday at work banked up and can always take some odd days,' she said draining the tea from her mug. 'I suppose in a way I want to make up for not being around over the last month. It won't happen again, Peter.'

Peter groaned. 'Whoa, hold up,' he said. 'You don't need to do that, I'm absolutely fine, so stop worrying.'

Peter told Laura about a new girlfriend he had and they began to talk seriously to each other. Laura told him how she'd changed mainly because at the time, she'd had no other choice, and had learnt how to think for herself very quickly. She also told him how much she was enjoying her newfound independence and about her dreams for the future. Peter listened without commenting, but Laura could tell by the way he smiled that she had his support now, which made her glow with contentment.

'I'm even toying with the idea of working freelance for myself to get higher up the ladder. There are quite a few women who do the same as I do, but they work temporary contracts developing new recipes for all the big food companies up and down the country. It'll mean travelling more, which at one time would have scared me a little, but now I think it sounds quite exciting,' she said.

Peter got up and walked over to the piano. He sat on the stool and as she followed him across the lounge she heard the soft click of the back door and knew her dad had sneaked out. She sat by Peter's side on the piano stool and watched his fingers quietly flow over the keys. 'Way to go, Mam,' he said.

Laura knew this was his way of unwinding and in the past it had always soothed her frayed nerves too. She leant slightly into his thin shoulder. 'In a sad way, Peter,' she said. 'Phil leaving us has done me a favour. It's opened up a whole new world to me and so far, I love what I see.'

After spending more time with Peter, Laura felt as though she'd made headway with their relationship problems. Later that evening she told Peter that she was calling around to see Jenny. She decided to tell Peter about Jenny's upbringing and childhood. In the past, Laura would have tried to shield her son from the gory details and gruesome stories, but this, she decided, was a turning point in their adult relationship and she felt sure she was doing the right thing. 'Look, Peter, I need to explain this to you because I think it's important that you know, and I don't think your Aunty Jenny will mind.' As she told him what she'd learned in the last few months she watched his eyes fill with sympathy.

'So,' Laura said sighing. 'Although her breakdown isn't an excuse for what she did with your dad, I do firmly believe that if Jenny had been in her right mind she would never have done it.'

Peter nodded gravely. 'Aunty Jenny is to be pitied more than anything else,' he mumbled staring at the silent TV set. 'It makes me cringe to think how spoilt I've been by you and Dad.'

'I know,' she agreed. 'I felt exactly the same when she told me about the horrors at school. When I think how happy and cosseted your grandparents made me feel when I was at school compared to poor Jenny, well, it doesn't bear thinking about.'

Laura picked up her sweater from the chair and stood up. 'I'll only be a couple of hours. We're going to have pizza for supper, and then I'll be home,' she said.

'Hang on,' Peter said grabbing his denim jacket from the behind the front door. 'I'm coming with you to see her.

I'll have some pizza then head into town to meet the guys.'

As they wandered around the cul-de-sac in the late evening sun Laura warned Peter that Jenny had lost a lot of weight and hadn't looked quite herself until the last month or so, but was now picking up and looked much better. Laura wasn't too sure whether seeing Peter would be another upset for her friend, but Jenny had seemed so much better lately and, Laura wanted to abide by her decision to include Peter in all the happenings in her life.

'Hiya,' Laura called as they walked through the front door and into the hall. Laura took a deep breath and braced herself for the next few hours because she knew this was the time to tell Jenny about Luigi.

Jenny hurried through from the kitchen and stopped dead in her tracks when she saw Peter. A huge grin on her face stretched from one ear to another and she cried out in delight, 'Oh, Peter!'

He walked straight towards her and put his long skinny arms around his aunt while Jenny hugged him long and hard. Laura looked at Jenny's face over her sons shoulder and saw her eyes shining. Jenny mouthed the words 'thank you' to Laura, and she grinned back.

Fussing around Peter, Jenny gave him the pizza menu and told him to choose his favourite as she poured them cold drinks. Jenny's eyes never left him as though she was mesmerised by him and Laura could tell how much she had missed Peter.

After pizza and discussions about their trips to his favourite places when he was younger, Peter kissed them both and pulled on his jacket. He promised Jenny he would never walk past her door again without calling, and then left the two women alone.

Laura sank back into the settee, feeling completely relaxed again in Jenny's company and smiled at the look of happiness in her friend's eyes. Over the last month Laura had felt their friendship slip back into its normal pattern and she could tell by Jenny's reactions and expressions that she too felt the same.

Jenny plumped up a cushion and laid her head back against it, sighing happily. 'Well, that was certainly a tonic. Seeing Peter again has made me feel better than any pills could – thanks for bringing him, Laura.'

Laura smiled and told Jenny it had been Peter who had asked to come and that he'd really wanted to see her. They chatted about how much taller and grown up he seemed, and Laura told her about his new girlfriend whom she hoped to meet next week. Jenny nodded happily and Laura decided to start with the news about the proposed takeover at work first.

Jenny looked troubled and a fleeting haunted look filled her eyes. 'Hmm, maybe I need to come back to work asap, just in case there isn't a job for me to come back to.'

Laura soothed Jenny with Muriel's reassurances, but then agreed that if she did feel ready then maybe this was a good time to start the phase-in program that HR had suggested. They nodded to each other and Laura sipped the cool lemonade, thinking how Jenny seemed to be more like her old self as each week passed. Her skin was clear, her hair styled and cut a little shorter into a long swinging bob, and she'd had a pink manicure on her fingernails that had previously been so badly bitten. Laura caught Jenny staring at her and raised an eyebrow. 'What's the matter?' Laura asked.

Jenny narrowed her eyebrows to almost a squint. 'Steve's right. You've definitely got a certain buzz about you. Your eyes are shinning, you've lost weight, and there seems to be an aura around you. In fact, you're positively glowing,' Jenny said grinning.

'And, as I know for sure Phil is long gone I reckon you've met another man?. Come on, tell me.'

Laura smiled and took a deep breath, here goes, she thought, and started at the beginning with how she'd worked with Luigi on the Irish project and how it had progressed to a full-blown relationship. She watched Jenny's eyes widen and her jaw drop in surprise.

Laura sighed. 'I've put off telling you about it, because I know you liked Luigi when he first joined the company,' Laura said and bit her lip. 'Please don't think I'm doing this as some type of pay-back, Jenny, because I'm not. None of it was planned, it just sort of happened, really. He quickly became a good friend and someone to talk to when I went back to work after Phil left. And it grew from there ...'

Jenny sat forward and threw her arms around Laura. 'Don't be silly! I know you wouldn't do anything like that. I'm just stunned that you've gone with another man so soon after Phil, that's all,' she said.

Laura told her how she felt about Luigi. 'I know, it's completely out of character for me, but I feel like a different woman now. The old Laura would never have had the confidence to even look at such a good-looking man. I would have thought he was too far out of my league to even take a shot. But now, well, as the saying goes, YOLO!'

Jenny giggled as Laura explained the meaning and agreed with her completely. 'Well, I have some news in that department too,' she said. 'Steve stayed over this weekend after we'd been out for dinner ...' Jenny paused and then gazed past Laura's shoulder towards the window. 'He's been such a great friend lately and a total pillar of support to me throughout my sessions.

I was worried about relying upon him so much, but the counsellor tells me it's a good thing once in a while to be dependent on someone. And Steve wants us to go to marriage counselling together to talk about the past mistakes we made.'

Now it was Laura's turn to look shocked. Instantly she rose to Jenny's defence. 'Mistakes you made? But he was the one who walked out on you.'

Jenny sighed. 'I know, but Steve reckons I pushed him away after the miscarriages and was so wrapped up in my own grief that I didn't see that he was suffering too. He cried the other night and told me how much it still hurts then accused me of not recognising the fact that they were his babies too,' she said. 'And, if I'm totally honest with myself, I know he's right – I did do that, Laura.'

Laura wasn't too sure what to say. To Steve's credit he had stood by her through this breakdown where many men, as Phil had proven, would have run for the hills. And it was obvious that he still loved Jenny, but what if he let her down again? Laura didn't want to put a dampener on Jenny's good spirits, but all the same, she was concerned. 'Please take it slowly, Jenny,' she said.

Jenny's face cracked a smile and she nudged Laura in the ribs. 'Like you're doing with the Italian Stallion, eh?'

'I know, but he sure lives up to his name,' Laura whispered. 'I can't keep my hands off him!'

They looked at each other and fell back into the settee in fits of giggles.

By the time Laura finished work on Friday, her mind, as Peter would say, was in a much better place. Relieved that both Jenny and Peter were supportive of the fact that she was having a loving relationship with a new man, she hurried home to shower and change.

Luigi was on a team-building course in a hotel in the Scottish highlands where his mobile signal was practically non-existent. She hadn't heard his voice for five days as their only communication had been via text. As she stood under the shower and shampooed her hair she sighed. In Luigi's last text he'd said that he'd be back around six that night and Laura planned to surprise him by waiting at his flat. Yesterday, she'd thought, the surprise had seemed like a great idea, but now she wasn't so sure. While wrapping a towel around her hair she thought of the words of the rest of his text. He'd told her he was making plans to go to Italy in four weeks' time, and that he hoped she would be ready to see him before then. His texts had seemed somewhat stilted and not his usual easy-going self which made Laura worry. Did he mean for a holiday, she thought, shivering with apprehension, or, maybe he was going back for good? Laura's old insecurities emerged to the forefront of her mind as she imagined him leaving to go back to Italy to live, and waving a fond farewell whilst sporting a blasé, it was only a casual fling attitude. Maybe she was about to look like an old fool who had had her head turned by a handsome Italian who had wooed her into his bed with his charm and easy seduction. Her stomach lurched with anxiety. But wait a minute; she reasoned, it was me who had made the first advance to get him into my bed, and not the other way around. She smiled and pulled her shoulders back, determined to stay in a positive frame of mind. Of course Luigi won't do that, she mused, and comforted herself with his words of love spoken on the beach and how he'd told her that he would never leave her.

As she stood in front of her wardrobe deciding what to wear she glanced out of the window and saw the sun streaming through the thin voile. It had rained solidly for two days, but just as she'd left work the sun had come out and she'd taken this to be a good omen. Laura lifted the hanger out of the wardrobe containing her flowery short skirt and white gypsy blouse. The memories of the last time they spent together flooded through her and she ached in places she didn't know existed. The longing to hear his voice, feel his arms around her, and kiss his lips was overpowering. She had missed Luigi so much, and last night as she'd lain in bed she'd decided that now she didn't feel complete without him.

Just after six Laura pulled up outside Luigi's flat and turned off the ignition. His car wasn't there so she figured he must still be driving back down from Scotland. She lifted her mobile out of her handbag and searched for his number. Should she spoil the surprise and tell him that she was waiting for him, or, sit and wait. Her finger hovered above the button, but then she snapped it shut suddenly and frowned. As her mam often said, hold the faith, and bide your time, because everything will be OK in the end.

Luigi's back ached with sitting in the car and driving for hours. He'd stopped a couple of times on the motorway for food and the toilet, but wanted to push on as he was desperate to be back in his flat – it would mean he was closer to Laura. There'd been no communication from her for two days now, and although he knew she must have given up trying to ring as there was no signal she could at least have sent more texts. He dreaded the thought that something dreadful had happened. Questions raced through his mind at a rate of knots until he felt as though his head would explode. Was she avoiding telling him that it was over between them? As he drove down through Gosforth and reached the turning into her cul de sac he swung the wheel recklessly and drove around to her house.

Her car was nowhere in sight and worryingly at such an early time on a summer night all the curtains and blinds were drawn. He sighed; there was little point in getting out and ringing the doorbell because it was obvious she wasn't there. What the hell was going on, he worried, and pulled back out onto the main road.

Laura got out of her car and began to pace up and down outside the block of flats. Where was he, she puzzled. Perhaps he'd stopped off somewhere on the way down the motorway? Once again, she stared at her mobile, wondering whether to ring him. Her stomach churned, but she couldn't decide whether the churning was with nerves or excitement. She bent down checked her lipstick in the side mirror of her car then pulled her face into an exaggerated grin just as an old man walked past and glared at her.

The whole of Luigi's insides were deflated as he drove along the road towards his flat. Earlier he'd been longing to reach home, but now he wanted to turn around and escape somewhere which didn't hold any memories of Laura. He imagined walking into his lounge and knew the memory of how she had lain in his arms on the settee, or, sat on top of him in his bed would torture him and he sighed heavily. If he had lost her he wasn't sure how, or if, he was going to cope without her. Swallowing a lump in his throat Luigi turned the corner to the block of flats and saw her sitting on the top step outside the front door. He gasped in shock and rubbed his eyes. The sun was on the windscreen and for a split second he was blinded. Was she an apparition? Or, perhaps it was a case of when you wished for something so much your mind could conjure it up as a mirage?

But no, he breathed out in relief, it was definitely her and he pulled next to her Mini. She jumped up and lifted a hand in greeting, but he couldn't read the expression in her eyes.

Laura's heart was thumping so loudly she felt sure he would be able to hear it. She began to walk towards him with quivering legs and decided that he certainly didn't look very happy to see her. There was a tension in his jaw and his eyes were downcast while he kicked at a pebble on the gravel path. He must be going back to Italy to live, she thought miserably, and felt an actual physical pain cross her chest. Please, God, she prayed silently, don't do this to me.

'Hey, there,' he said as he reached her and bent down to peck both her cheeks.

Momentarily, she forgot her European greeting and the fact that she needed to stand on her tip toes to reach his height. 'Hello,' she said quietly. 'I thought

I'd surprise you. But if this is a bad time and you're tired we can meet up tomorrow …' she paused and looked down the street. 'You must have had a very long drive?'

Luigi nodded. He couldn't read the expression on her face, but she bit her lip which he knew meant she was worried. His mind filled with a sense of dread wondering how she was going to tell him it was over. He prayed that it wouldn't be drawn out; because there was only so much sympathy he could take. 'No, its fine,' he said. 'Come in and we'll get a glass of something.'

Luigi followed behind her through into the lounge remembering the day on the beach and how he'd pulled the blouse down to kiss her neck, and then later how he'd pushed his hand up this very skirt that was now sashaying in front of him.

Laura sat down on the settee with a glass of wine in her hand and sipped. She couldn't find any comfort in the richness of the flavour because she felt as though her breathing was so shallow that her whole being was suspended in the air. A heavy silence hung in the room and she heard another car parking up outside with the radio playing loudly.

She thought of this big bear of a man with his gentle loving touch and squeezed her thighs and knees together, crazily longing just to be close to him. Was he waiting for her to speak? Or should she give him time to say what had happened.

Luigi wandered around the lounge wringing his large hands together and then eventually stood in front of the fireplace facing her. 'Look,' he said. 'If it's over and you're sitting there trying to think of a way to break it to me gently then don't! I can't take much more – this is agony!'

Laura gasped. 'But, it's not me that thinks it's over. I'm good to go. Peter is right behind me now,' she said.

'He is?' Luigi whispered and took a step towards her not daring to hope that he had another chance. His heart hammered against his ribcage and the blood pounded in his ears.

Laura put her head on one side and frowned. 'But I thought you were going to tell me that you're moving back to Italy.'

'What!' he shouted. 'Why the hell would I move back to Italy when I've just got promotion in the new sales team?'

She jumped up off the settee. 'Well, on your last text you said you were going in four weeks' time?'

Luigi took another step forward and stared into her eyes. 'Yes, I'm going for two weeks' holiday, and, I was going to ask you to come with me, but when I got out of the car your face was so miserable, I thought …'

The bubble started just under her ribs and she felt it move up her body in waves of pure joy and happiness. She started to hurry across the room to him and he rushed at her crying aloud, 'Oh my lovely Laura.'

She leapt at him and threw her arms around his neck then wrapped her legs around his waist as he pulled her into him. Bouncing her in his lap he cried, 'Oh, cara. I thought I'd lost you!'

Laura threw her head back and laughed. 'So did I. We've just had our wires crossed, that's all.'

He carried her into the bedroom and threw her onto the bed and she held open her arms for him to lie on top of her. It felt so good to have the weight of him on her again, and she began to kiss him feverishly which made him writhe.

'Let's see how we can uncross these lines,' he said pulling the gypsy top right down to her waist and burying his face in her chest.

She giggled and pushed her hands up inside his T-shirt caressing his broad back. 'Dear God, but I've missed you so much. I feel like its months since we've been together.'

He kissed the side of her neck and whispered in her ear, 'You must believe in me, Laura,' he murmured. 'I meant what I said. I love you, and I'm not going anywhere without you.'

Laura ran her fingers into his thick hair, knowing he was holding back. 'What's wrong?' she whispered.

'Oh, there's nothing wrong,' he said propping himself up on one arm and gazing over her body. 'But I'm going to keep making love to you over and over again until you get it into your head exactly how much I do love you.'

She stared into his green eyes dark with passion.

'Laura,' he muttered sucking the nape of her neck. 'You must repeat after me. Luigi loves me and doesn't want to be with anyone else!'

Waves of desire were cursing through her body and she gasped in big breaths of air.

She could hardly speak but managed to babble, 'Yes … Yes, I know you do.'

He chewed on her ear lobe. 'That's not good enough. I want to hear the words.'

She repeated what he'd said. 'I love you, Luigi,' she moaned in between small cries of pleasure.

'Again, Laura!' he shouted and began to move quicker and deeper. 'Tell me again and again and again.'

Laura was lost in a sea of ecstasy. She almost screamed and choked on the words, 'I know you love me and will never leave me!'

With his big arms wrapped around her hugging her so tightly she could hardly breathe, Laura grinned and pushed her bottom into his lap as he cradled her back. 'I love you. You love me. And I do believe in us,' she whispered feeling tears of emotion run down her cheeks. She had never felt so deeply in love or as close to anyone in her life.

Laura felt his wet eyelashes on the skin of her shoulder as he murmured words in Italian. 'Cara, I couldn't live without you. And it has taken this little separation for me to realise this too,' he said. 'I have found my other half in life and I'm not letting you go!'

Laura swivelled around to face him and gently touched his wet cheek. 'I feel exactly the same, my love. You are the soul mate that I didn't know existed. Thank God I found you.'

Printed in Great Britain
by Amazon